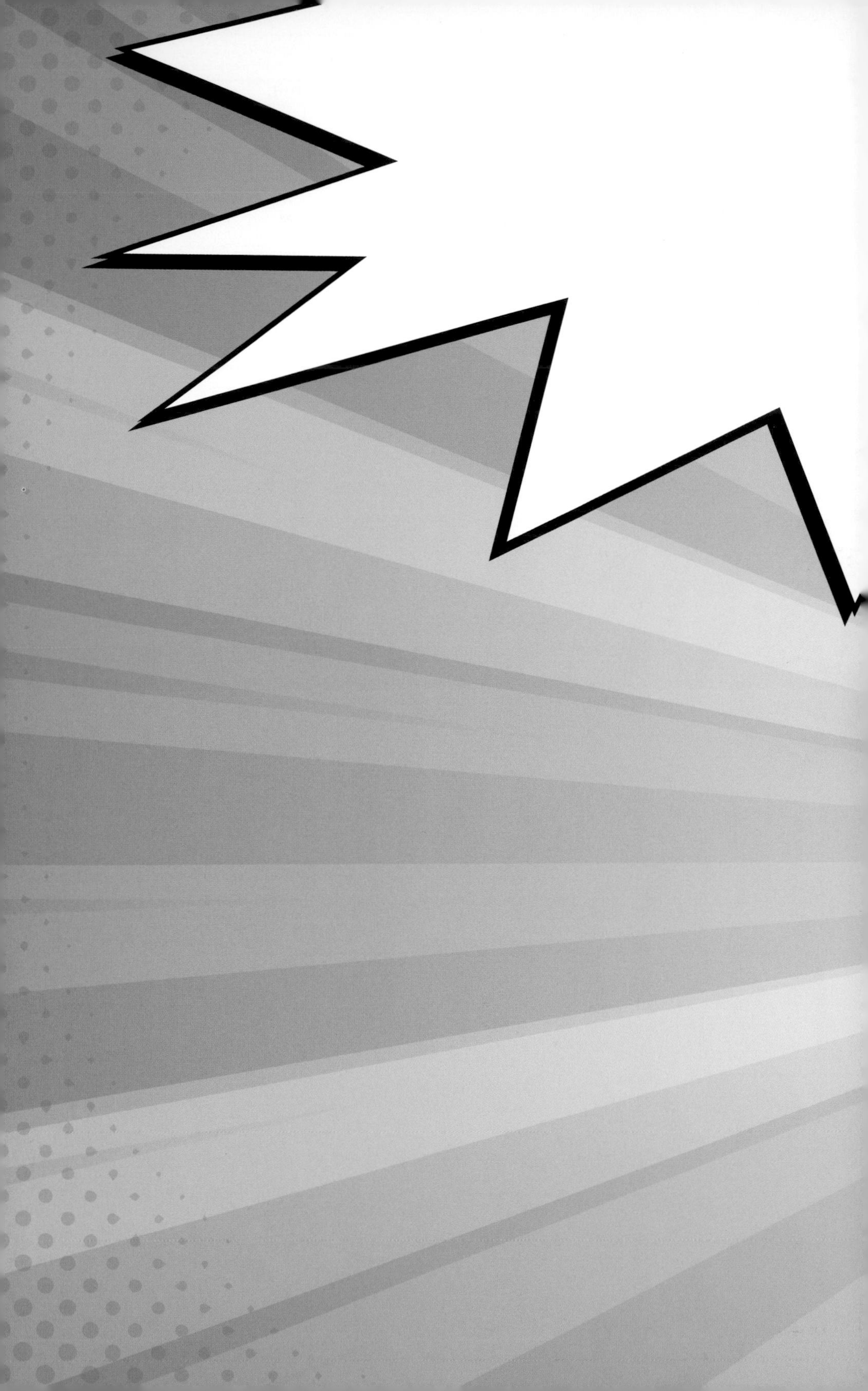

SUPER TURBO

VS. WONDER PIG

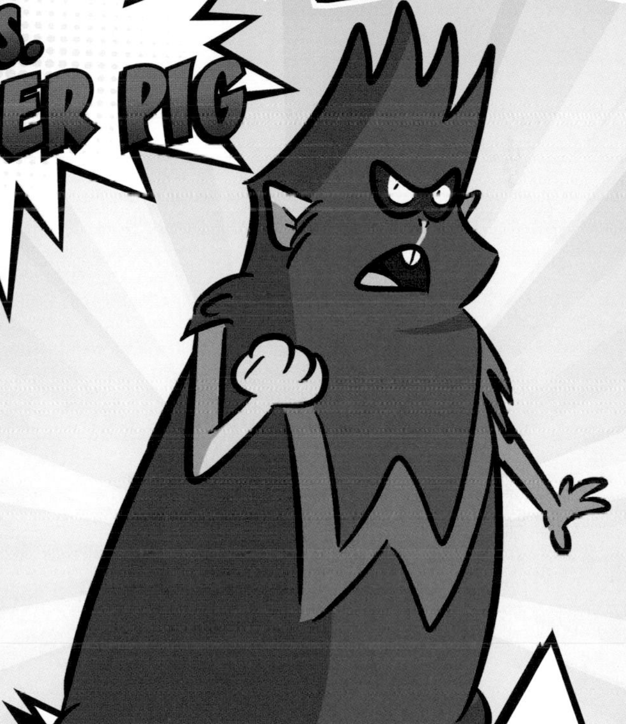

WRITTEN BY EDGAR POWERS
ILLUSTRATED BY SALVATORE COSTANZA
AT GLASS HOUSE GRAPHICS

LITTLE SIMON
NEW YORK LONDON TORONTO SYDNEY NEW DELHI

LITTLE SIMON
AN IMPRINT OF SIMON & SCHUSTER CHILDREN'S PUBLISHING DIVISION
1230 AVENUE OF THE AMERICAS, NEW YORK, NEW YORK 10020
FIRST LITTLE SIMON EDITION NOVEMBER 2021 * COPYRIGHT © 2021 BY SIMON & SCHUSTER, INC. ALL RIGHTS RESERVED, INCLUDING THE RIGHT OF REPRODUCTION IN WHOLE OR IN PART IN ANY FORM. LITTLE SIMON IS A REGISTERED TRADEMARK OF SIMON & SCHUSTER, INC., AND ASSOCIATED COLOPHON IS A TRADEMARK OF SIMON & SCHUSTER, INC. FOR INFORMATION ABOUT SPECIAL DISCOUNTS FOR BULK PURCHASES, PLEASE CONTACT SIMON & SCHUSTER SPECIAL SALES AT 1-866-506-1949 OR BUSINESS@SIMONANDSCHUSTER.COM. THE SIMON & SCHUSTER SPEAKERS BUREAU CAN BRING AUTHORS TO YOUR LIVE EVENT. FOR MORE INFORMATION OR TO BOOK AN EVENT CONTACT THE SIMON & SCHUSTER SPEAKERS BUREAU AT 1-866-248-3049 OR VISIT OUR WEBSITE AT WWW.SIMONSPEAKERS.COM. DESIGNED BY NICHOLAS SCIACCA * ART SERVICES BY GLASS HOUSE GRAPHICS * ART AND COLOR BY SALVATORE COSTANZA * LETTERING BY GIOVANNI SPATARO/GRAFIMATED CARTOON * SUPERVISION BY SALVATORE DI MARCO/GRAFIMATED CARTOON * MANUFACTURED IN CHINA 0821 SCP * 2 4 6 8 10 9 7 5 3 1 * LIBRARY OF CONGRESS CATALOGING-IN-PUBLICATION DATA NAMES: POWERS, EDGAR J., AUTHOR. | GLASS HOUSE GRAPHICS, ILLUSTRATOR. TITLE: SUPER TURBO VS. WONDER PIG / BY EDGAR J. POWERS ; ILLUSTRATED BY GLASS HOUSE GRAPHICS. DESCRIPTION: FIRST LITTLE SIMON EDITION. | NEW YORK : LITTLE SIMON, 2021. | SERIES: SUPER TURBO, THE GRAPHIC NOVEL ; 6 | AUDIENCE: AGES 5-9 | AUDIENCE: GRADES K-4 | SUMMARY: "SUPER TURBO AND HIS PALS IN THE SUPERPET SUPERHERO LEAGUE ARE USED TO FACING DOWN THE EVIL AT SUNNYVIEW ELEMENTARY TOGETHER, AS A TEAM. BUT WHEN WONDER PIG STARTS ACTING STRANGELY ON THE SAME DAY THAT TURBO'S CAPE GOES MISSING, TURBO IS SUSPICIOUS"—PROVIDED BY PUBLISHER. IDENTIFIERS: LCCN 2020049162 (PRINT) | LCCN 2020049163 (EBOOK) | ISBN 9781534485402 (PAPERBACK) | ISBN 9781534485419 (HARDCOVER) | ISBN 9781534485426 (EBOOK) SUBJECTS: LCSH: GRAPHIC NOVELS. | CYAC: GRAPHIC NOVELS. | SUPERHEROES—FICTION. | HAMSTERS—FICTION. | PETS—FICTION. | ELEMENTARY SCHOOLS—FICTION. | SCHOOLS—FICTION. CLASSIFICATION: LCC PZ7.7.P7 SW 2021 (PRINT) | LCC PZ7.7.P7 (EBOOK) | DDC 741.5/973—DC23 LC RECORD AVAILABLE AT HTTPS://LCCN.LOC.GOV/2020049162 LC EBOOK RECORD AVAILABLE AT HTTPS://LCCN.LOC.GOV/2020049163

CONTENTS

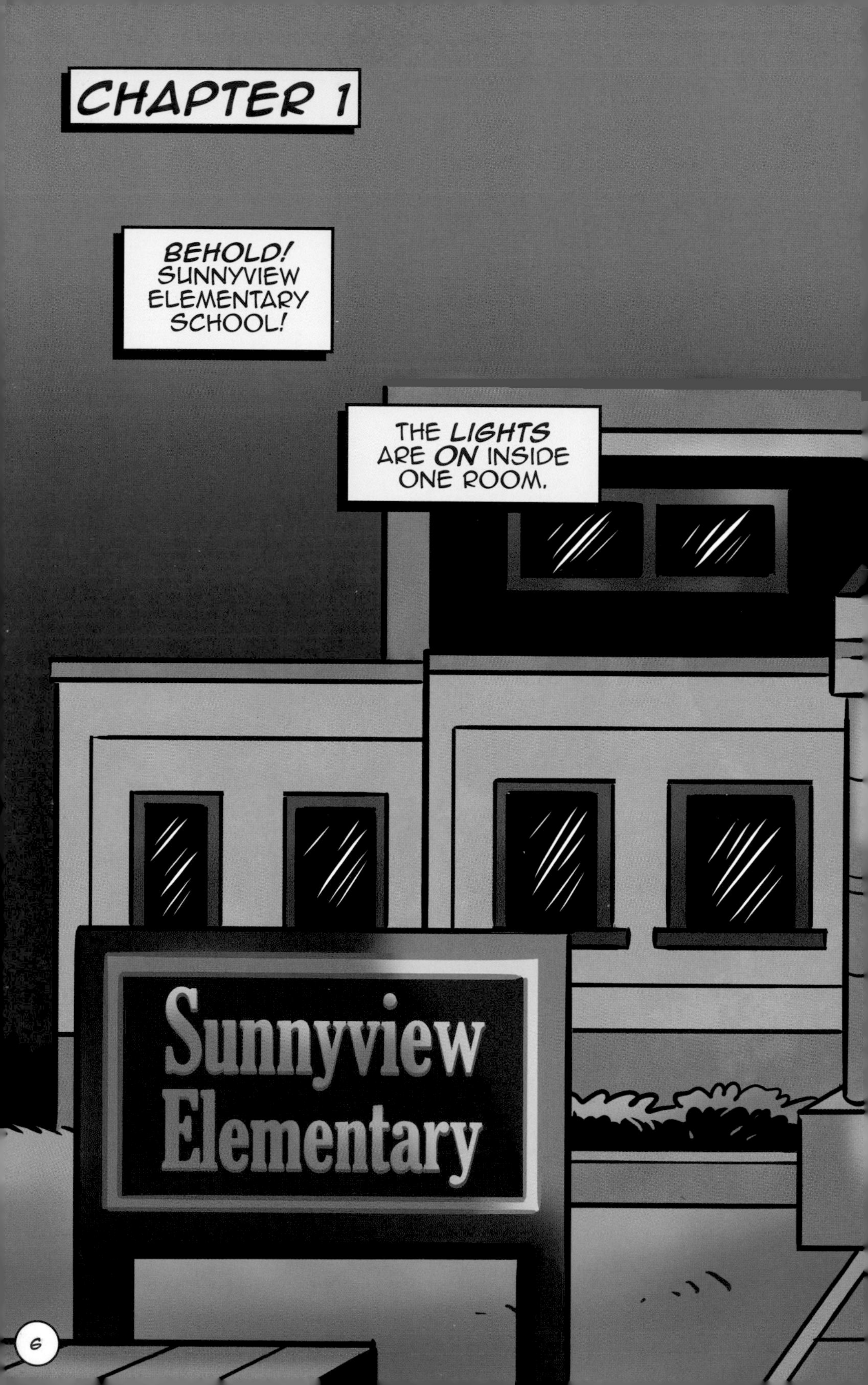
CHAPTER 1
BEHOLD! SUNNYVIEW ELEMENTARY SCHOOL!
THE LIGHTS ARE ON INSIDE ONE ROOM.
Sunnyview Elementary

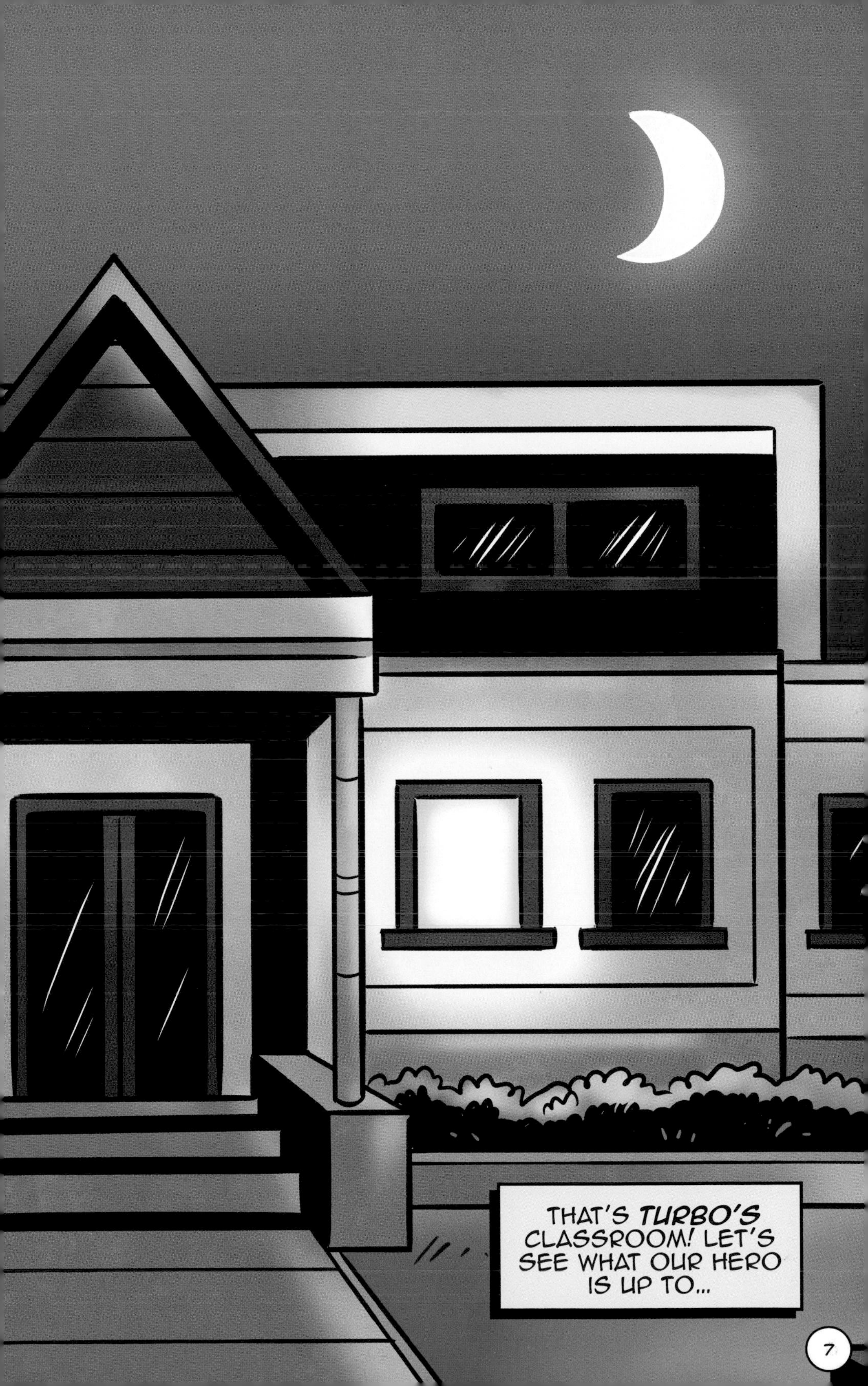
THAT'S *TURBO'S* CLASSROOM! LET'S SEE WHAT OUR HERO IS UP TO...

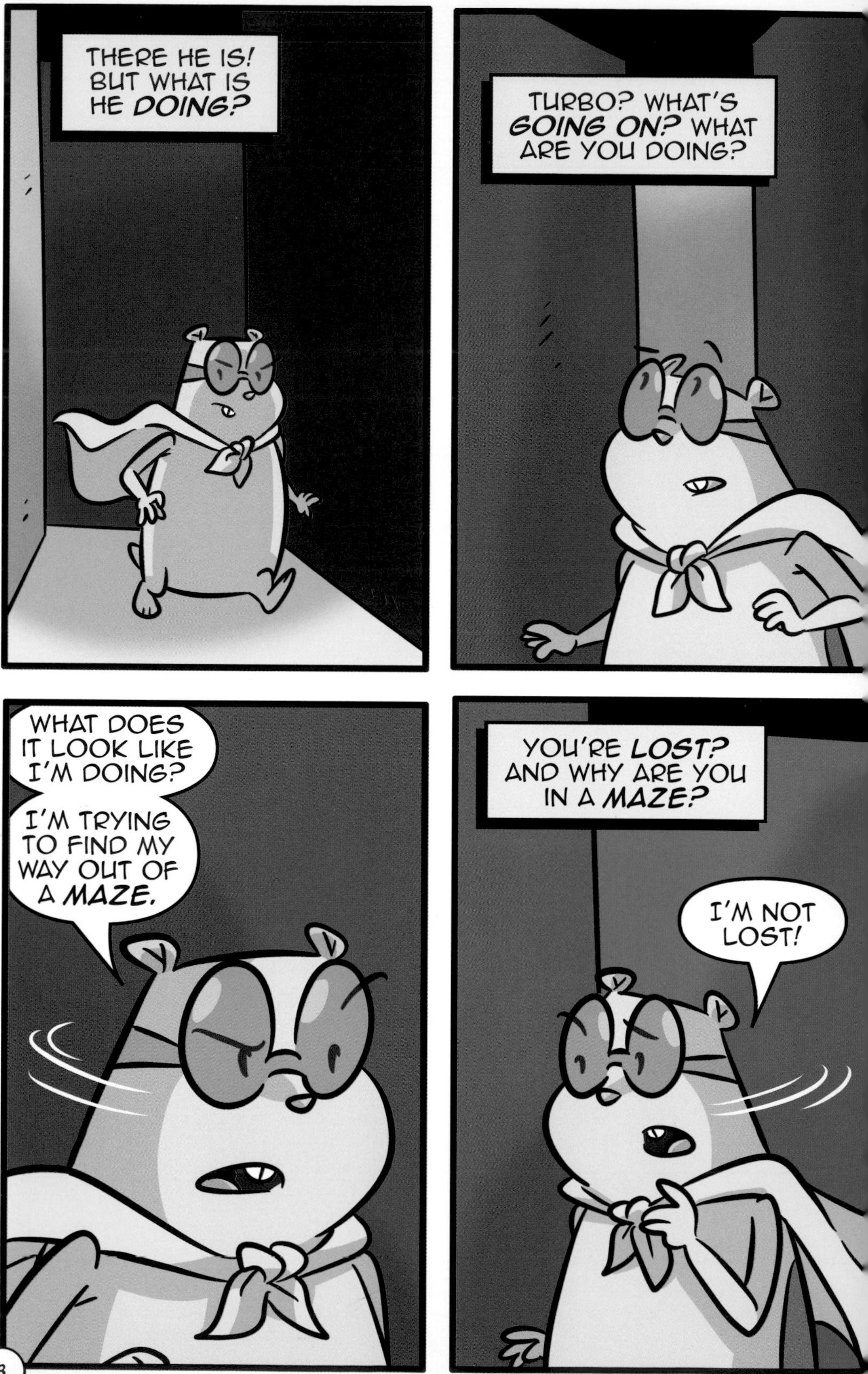
THERE HE IS! BUT WHAT IS HE DOING?
TURBO? WHAT'S GOING ON? WHAT ARE YOU DOING?
WHAT DOES IT LOOK LIKE I'M DOING?
I'M TRYING TO FIND MY WAY OUT OF A MAZE.
YOU'RE LOST? AND WHY ARE YOU IN A MAZE?
I'M NOT LOST!

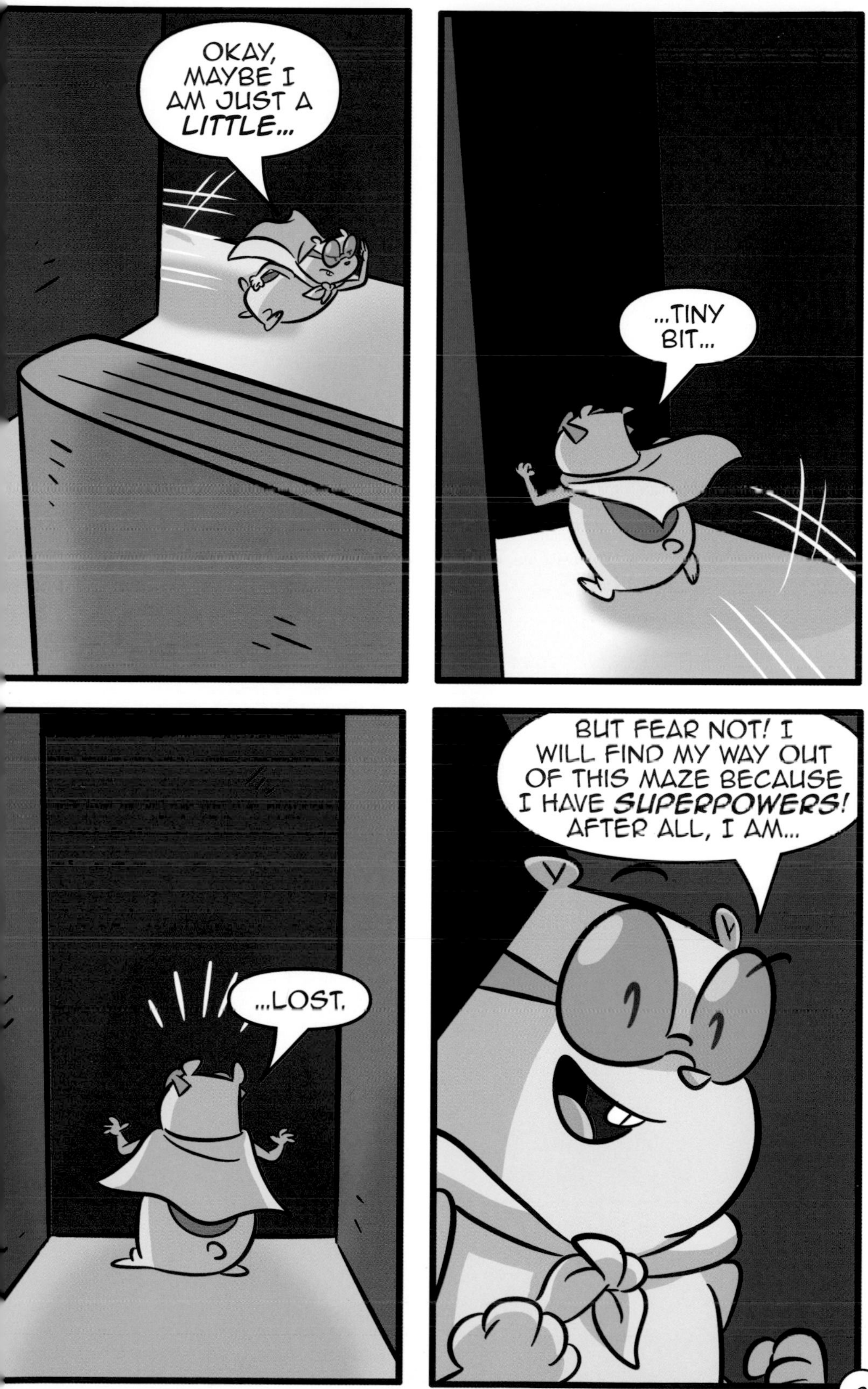
OKAY, MAYBE I AM JUST A LITTLE...
...TINY BIT...
...LOST.
BUT FEAR NOT! I WILL FIND MY WAY OUT OF THIS MAZE BECAUSE I HAVE SUPERPOWERS! AFTER ALL, I AM...

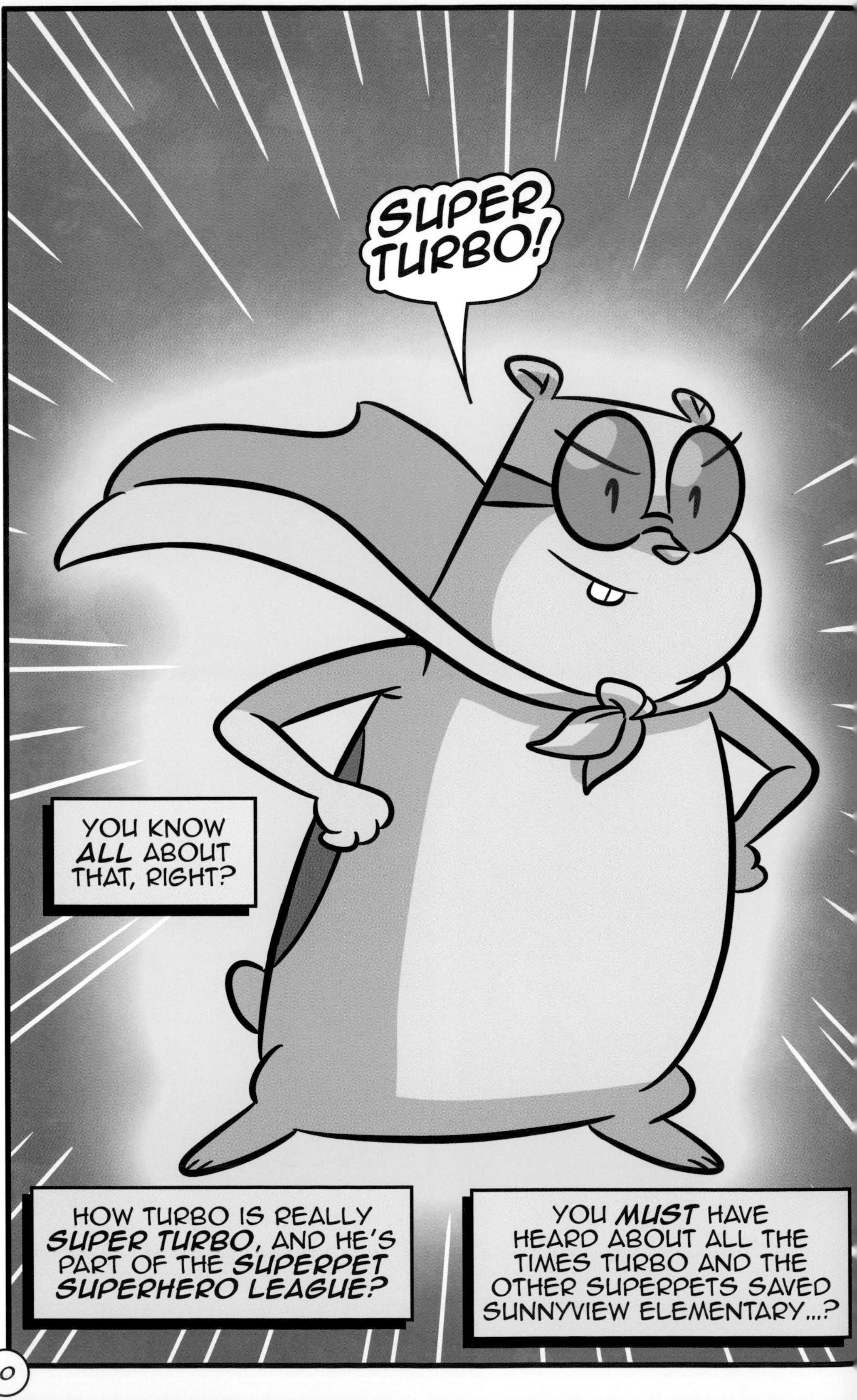
SUPER TURBO!
YOU KNOW ALL ABOUT THAT, RIGHT?
HOW TURBO IS REALLY SUPER TURBO, AND HE'S PART OF THE SUPERPET SUPERHERO LEAGUE?
YOU MUST HAVE HEARD ABOUT ALL THE TIMES TURBO AND THE OTHER SUPERPETS SAVED SUNNYVIEW ELEMENTARY...?

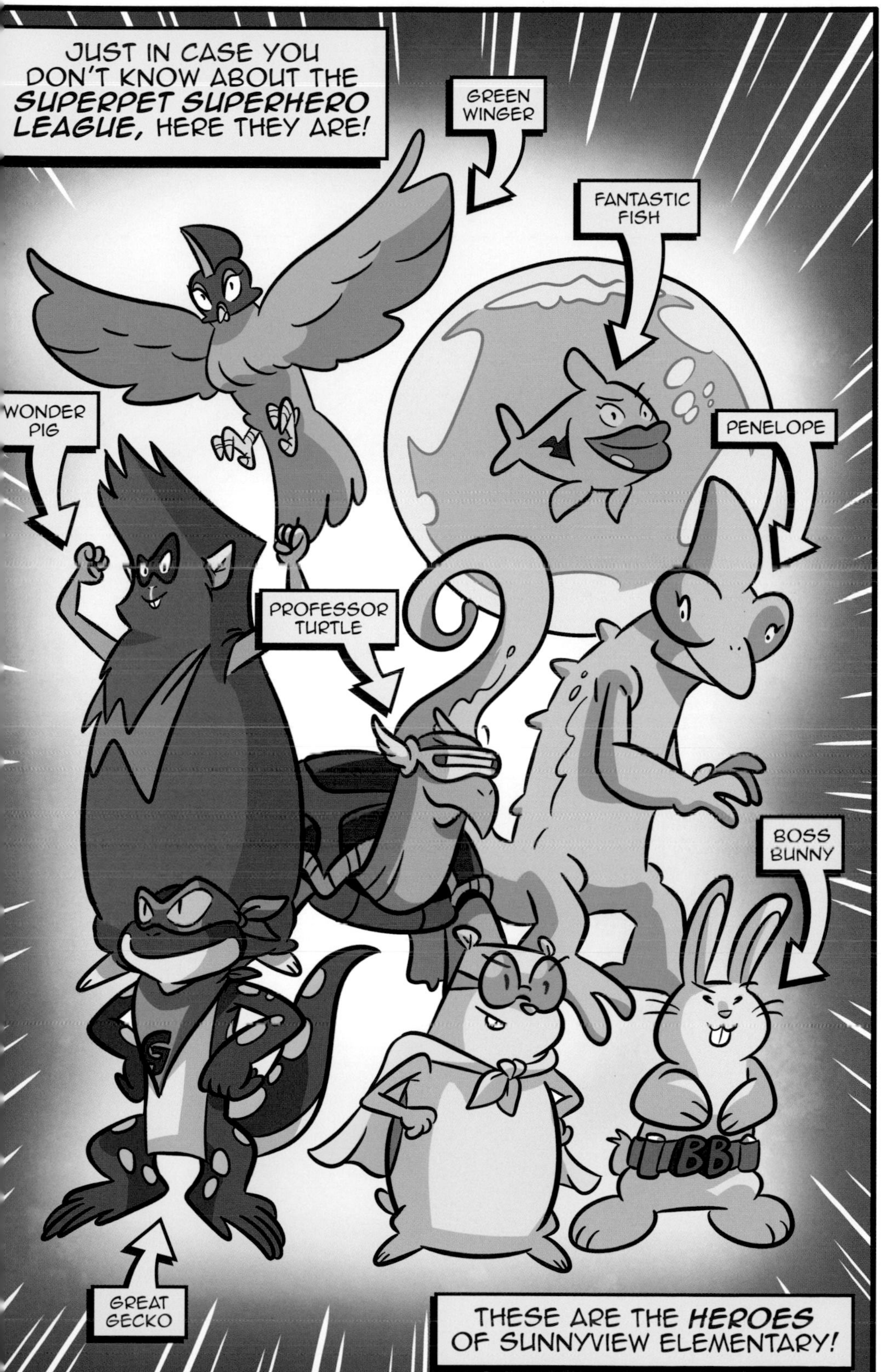

JUST IN CASE YOU DON'T KNOW ABOUT THE *SUPERPET SUPERHERO LEAGUE*, HERE THEY ARE!
GREEN WINGER
FANTASTIC FISH
WONDER PIG
PENELOPE
PROFESSOR TURTLE
BOSS BUNNY
BB
GREAT GECKO
THESE ARE THE *HEROES* OF SUNNYVIEW ELEMENTARY!

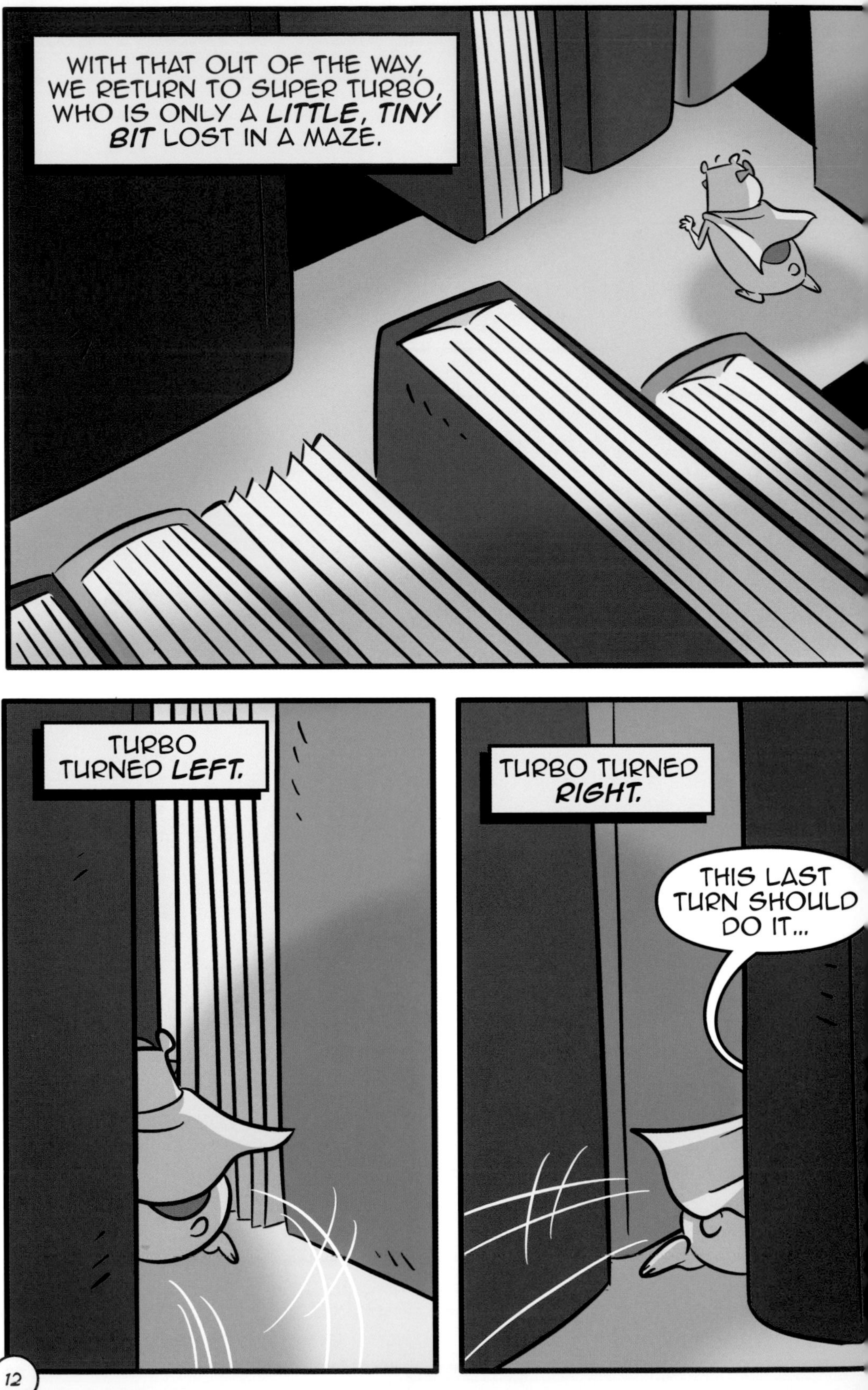
WITH THAT OUT OF THE WAY, WE RETURN TO SUPER TURBO, WHO IS ONLY A *LITTLE, TINY BIT* LOST IN A MAZE.
TURBO TURNED *LEFT.*
TURBO TURNED *RIGHT.*
THIS LAST TURN SHOULD DO IT...

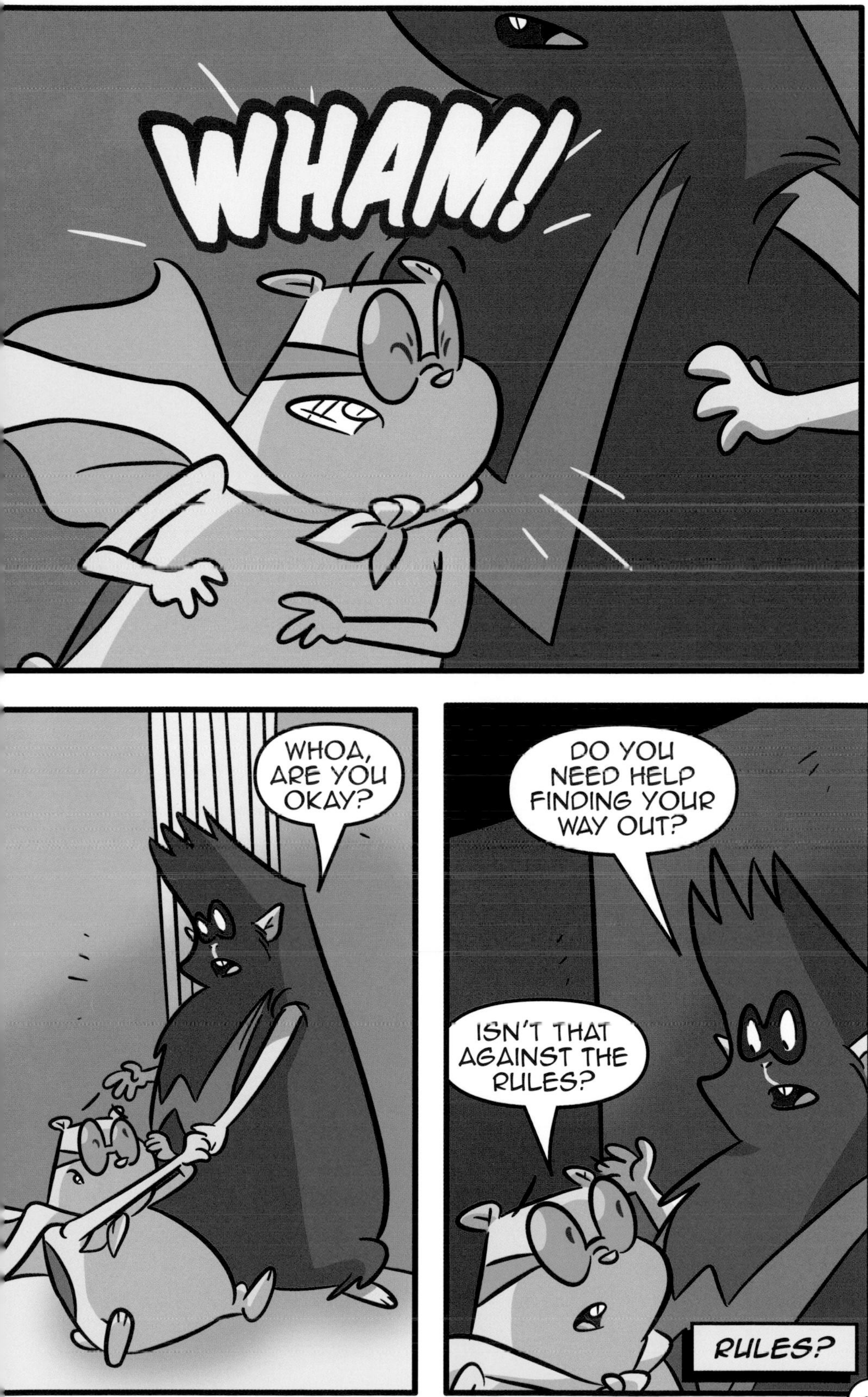
WHAM!
WHOA, ARE YOU OKAY?
DO YOU NEED HELP FINDING YOUR WAY OUT?
ISN'T THAT AGAINST THE RULES?
RULES?

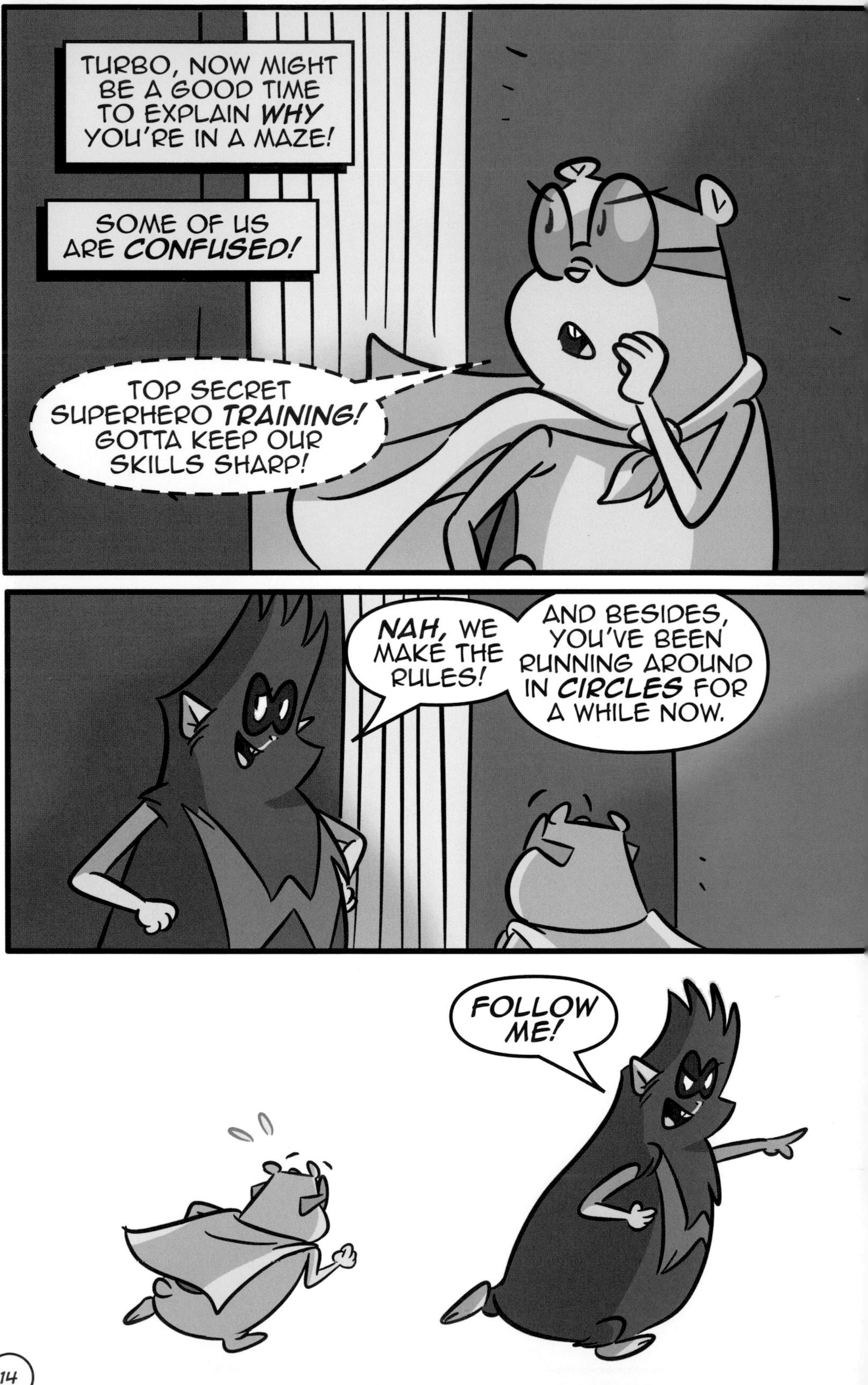
TURBO, NOW MIGHT BE A GOOD TIME TO EXPLAIN WHY YOU'RE IN A MAZE!
SOME OF US ARE CONFUSED!
TOP SECRET SUPERHERO TRAINING! GOTTA KEEP OUR SKILLS SHARP!
NAH, WE MAKE THE RULES!
AND BESIDES, YOU'VE BEEN RUNNING AROUND IN CIRCLES FOR A WHILE NOW.
FOLLOW ME!

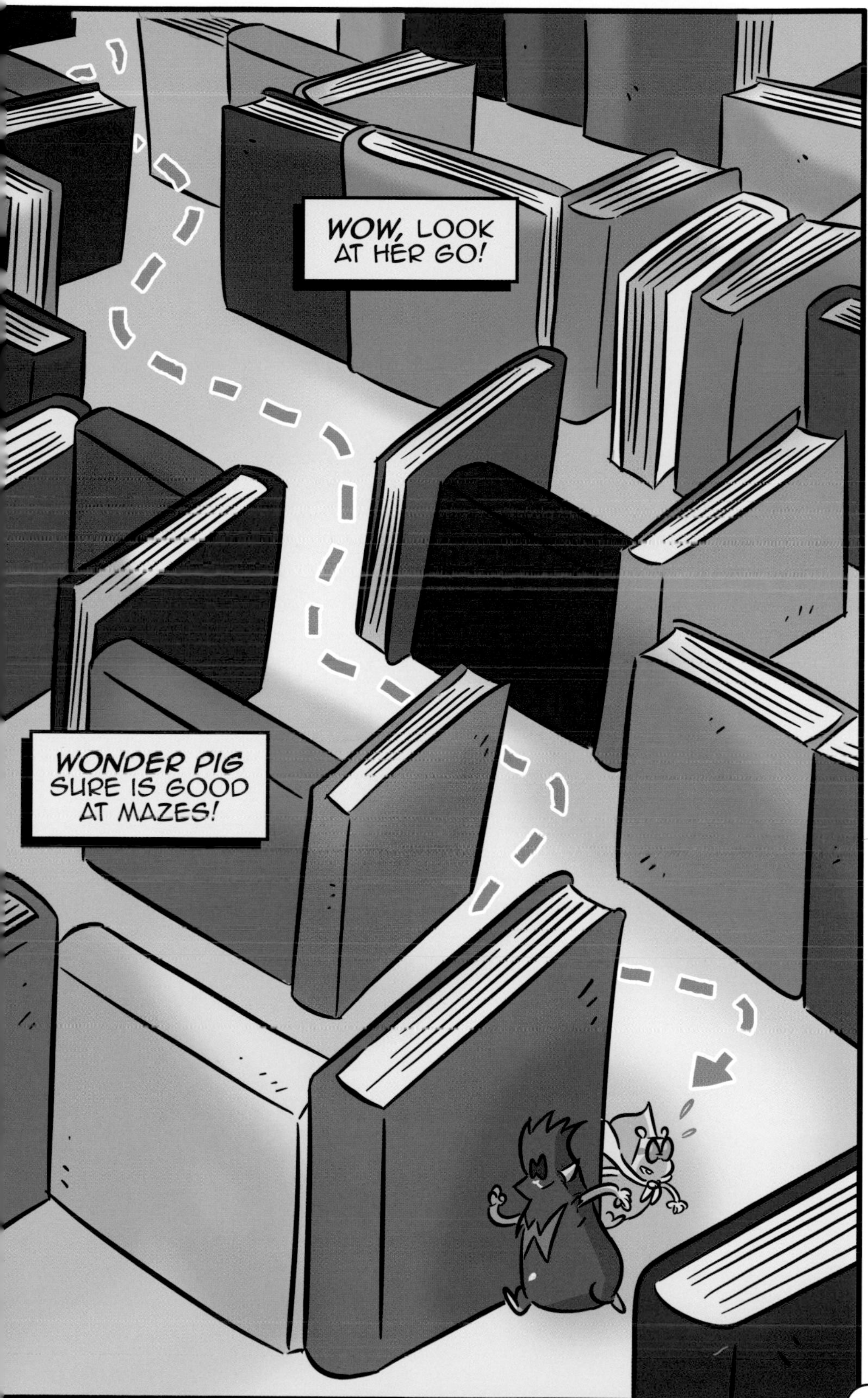
WOW, LOOK AT HER GO!
WONDER PIG SURE IS GOOD AT MAZES!

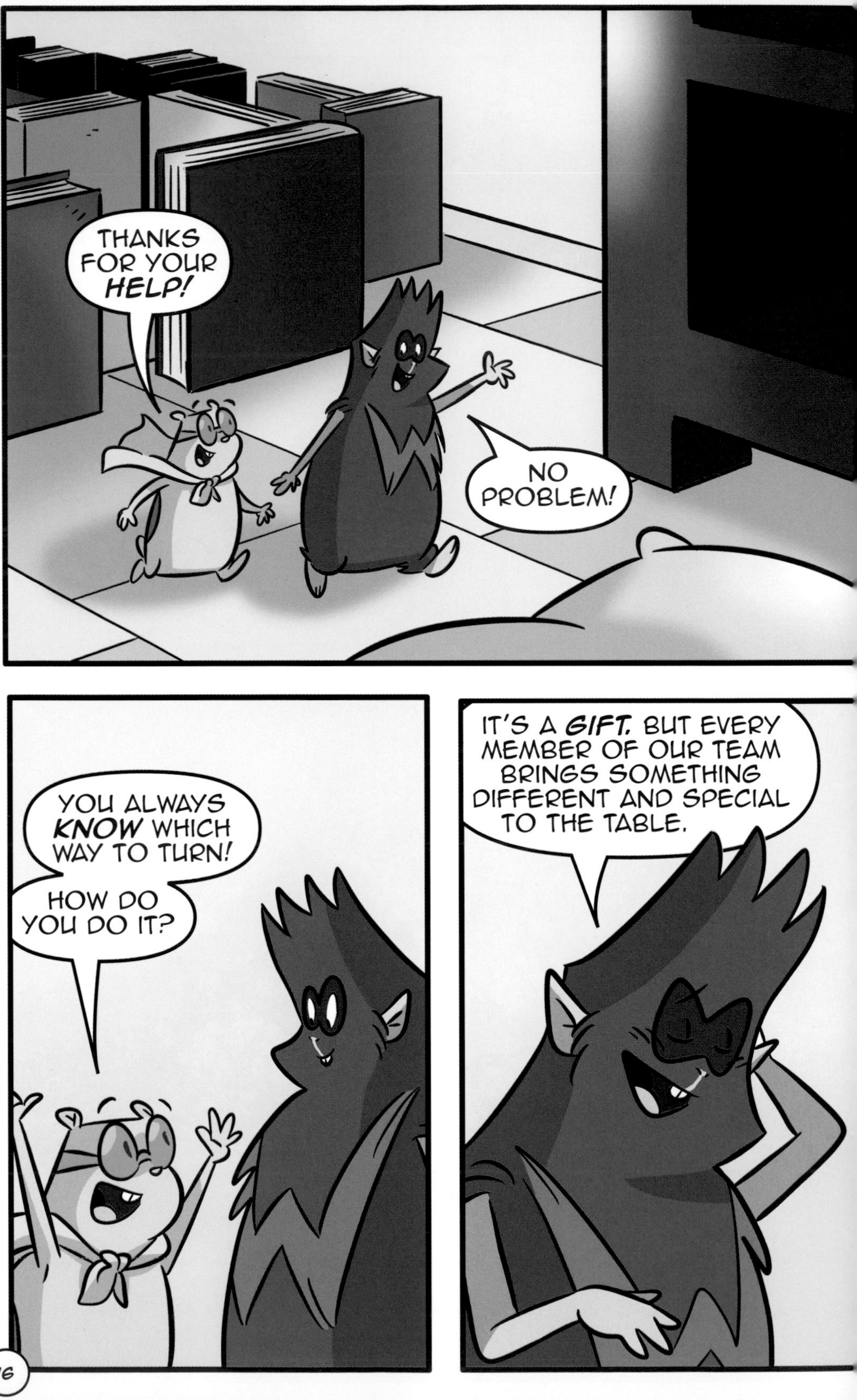

THANKS FOR YOUR *HELP!*
NO PROBLEM!
YOU ALWAYS *KNOW* WHICH WAY TO TURN!
HOW DO YOU DO IT?
IT'S A *GIFT.* BUT EVERY MEMBER OF OUR TEAM BRINGS SOMETHING DIFFERENT AND SPECIAL TO THE TABLE.

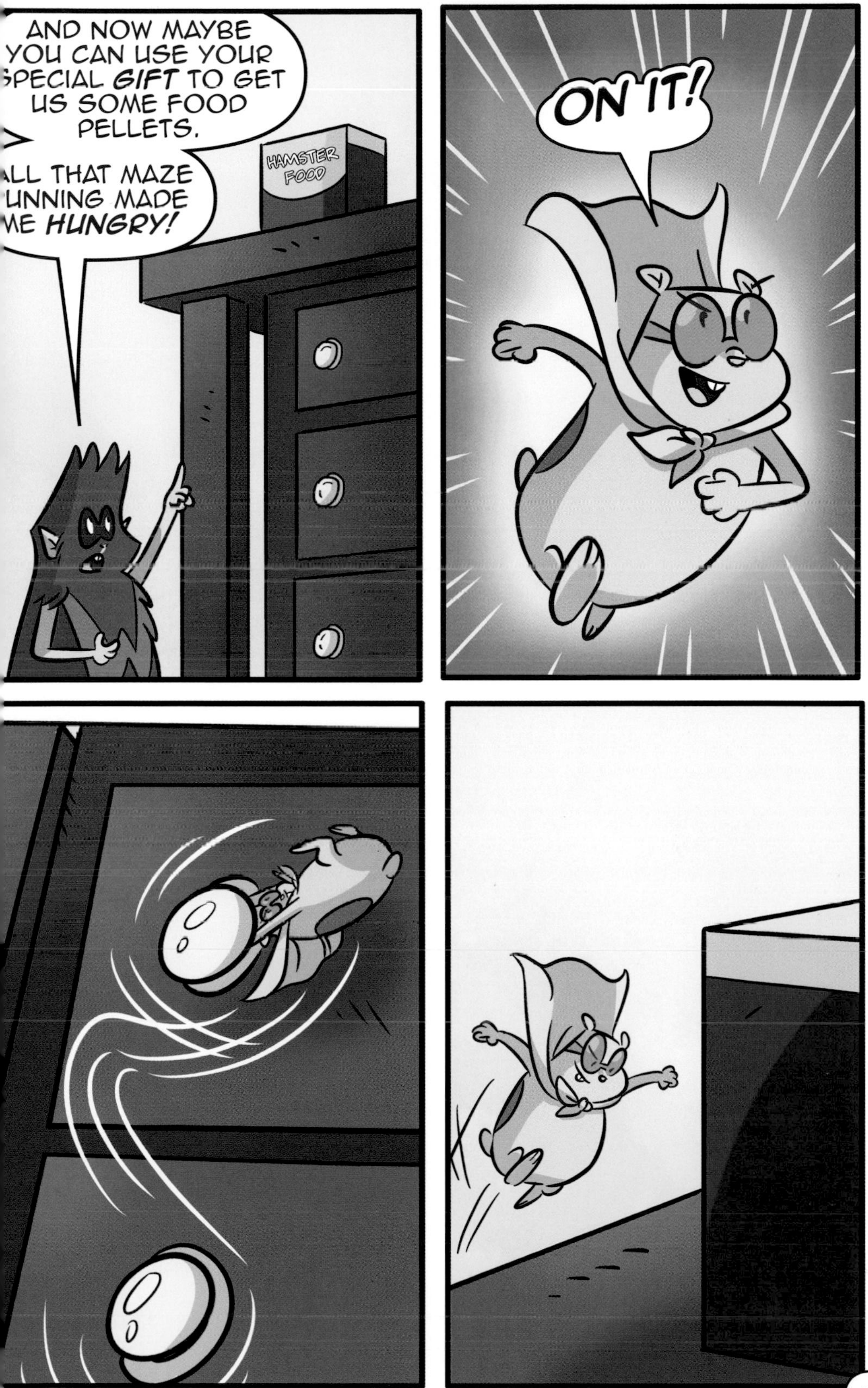
AND NOW MAYBE YOU CAN USE YOUR SPECIAL GIFT TO GET US SOME FOOD PELLETS.
ALL THAT MAZE RUNNING MADE ME HUNGRY!
HAMSTER FOOD
ON IT!

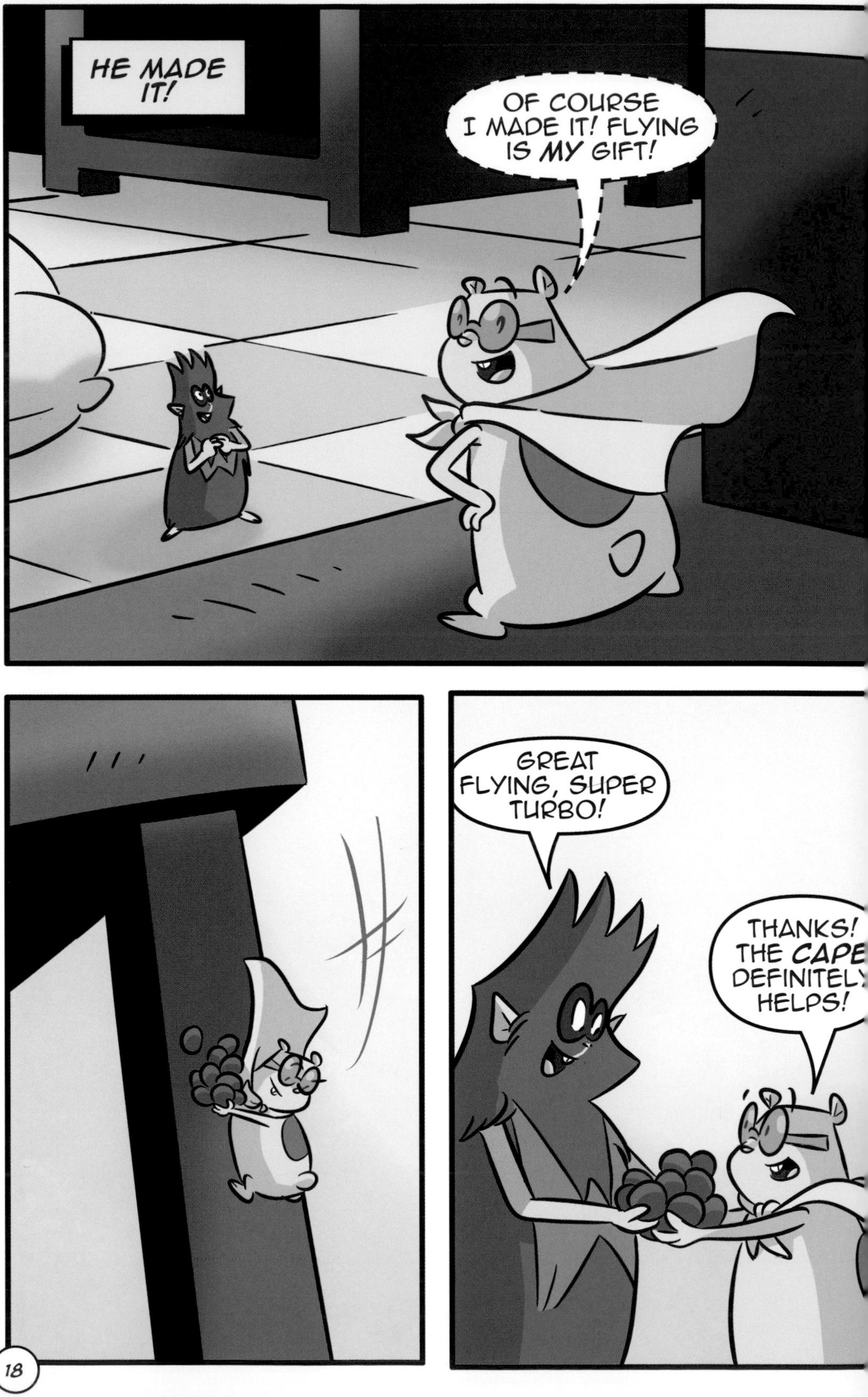
HE MADE IT!
OF COURSE I MADE IT! FLYING IS MY GIFT!
GREAT FLYING, SUPER TURBO!
THANKS! THE CAPE DEFINITEL HELPS!

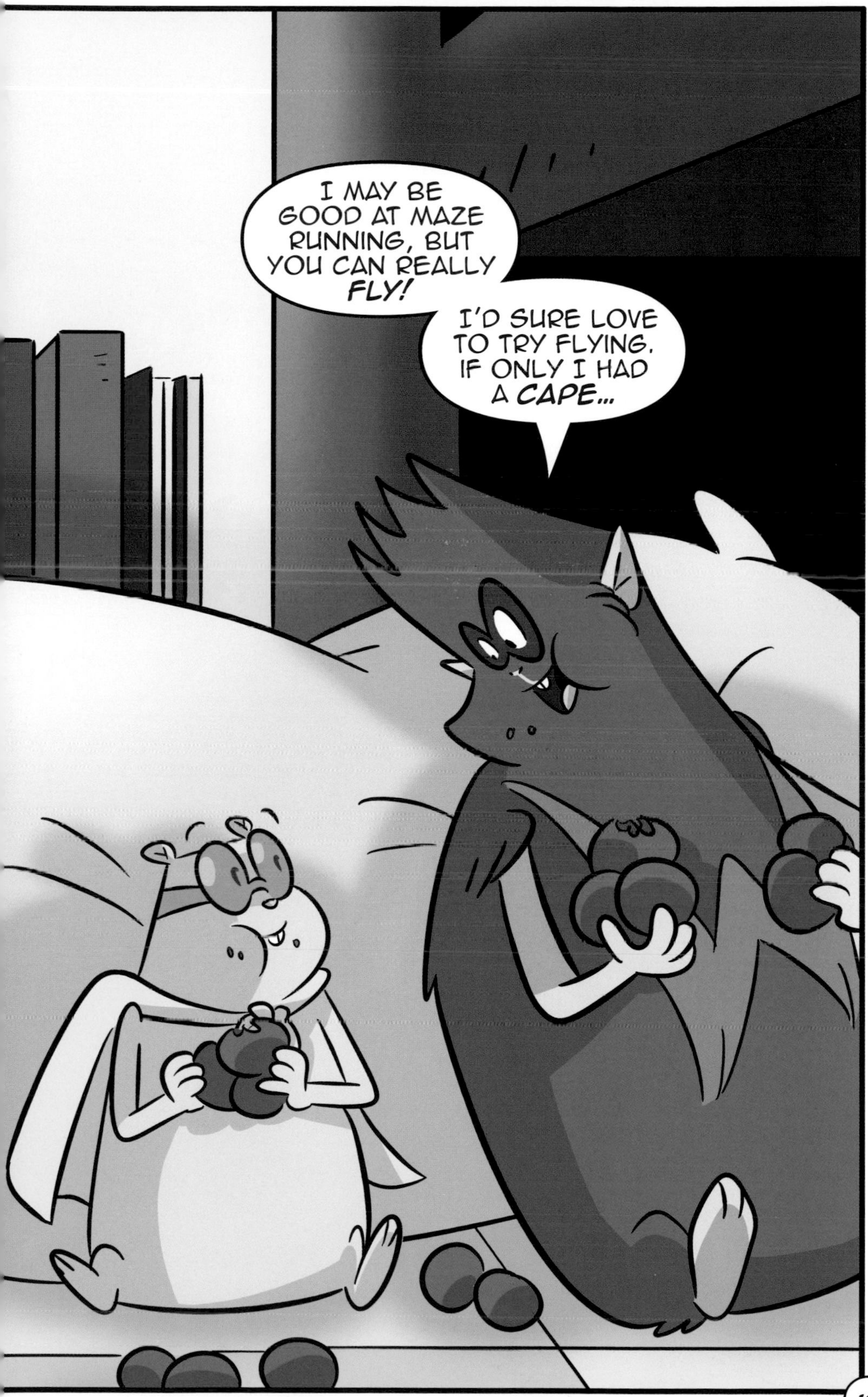
I MAY BE GOOD AT MAZE RUNNING, BUT YOU CAN REALLY FLY!
I'D SURE LOVE TO TRY FLYING. IF ONLY I HAD A CAPE...

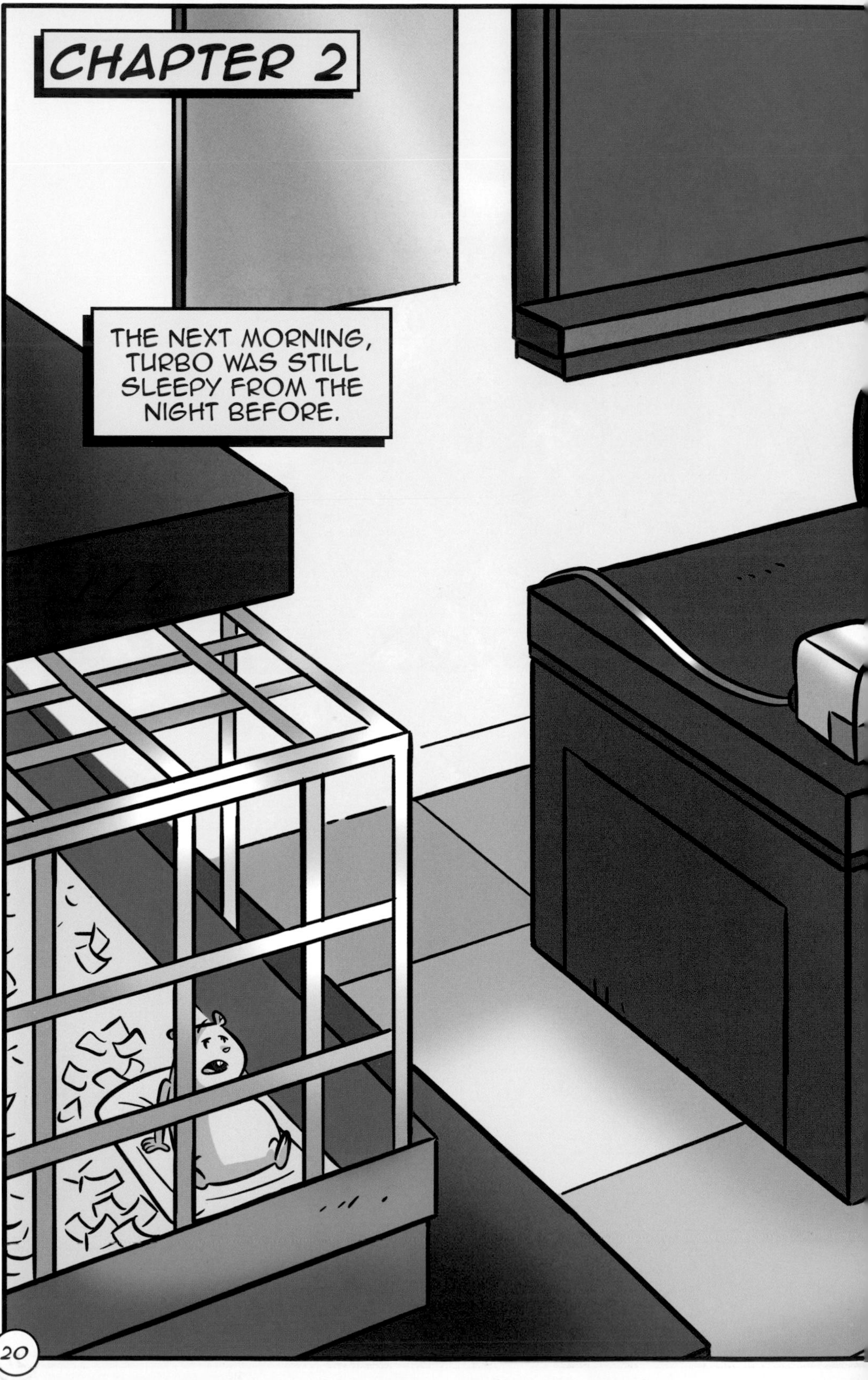
CHAPTER 2
THE NEXT MORNING, TURBO WAS STILL SLEEPY FROM THE NIGHT BEFORE.

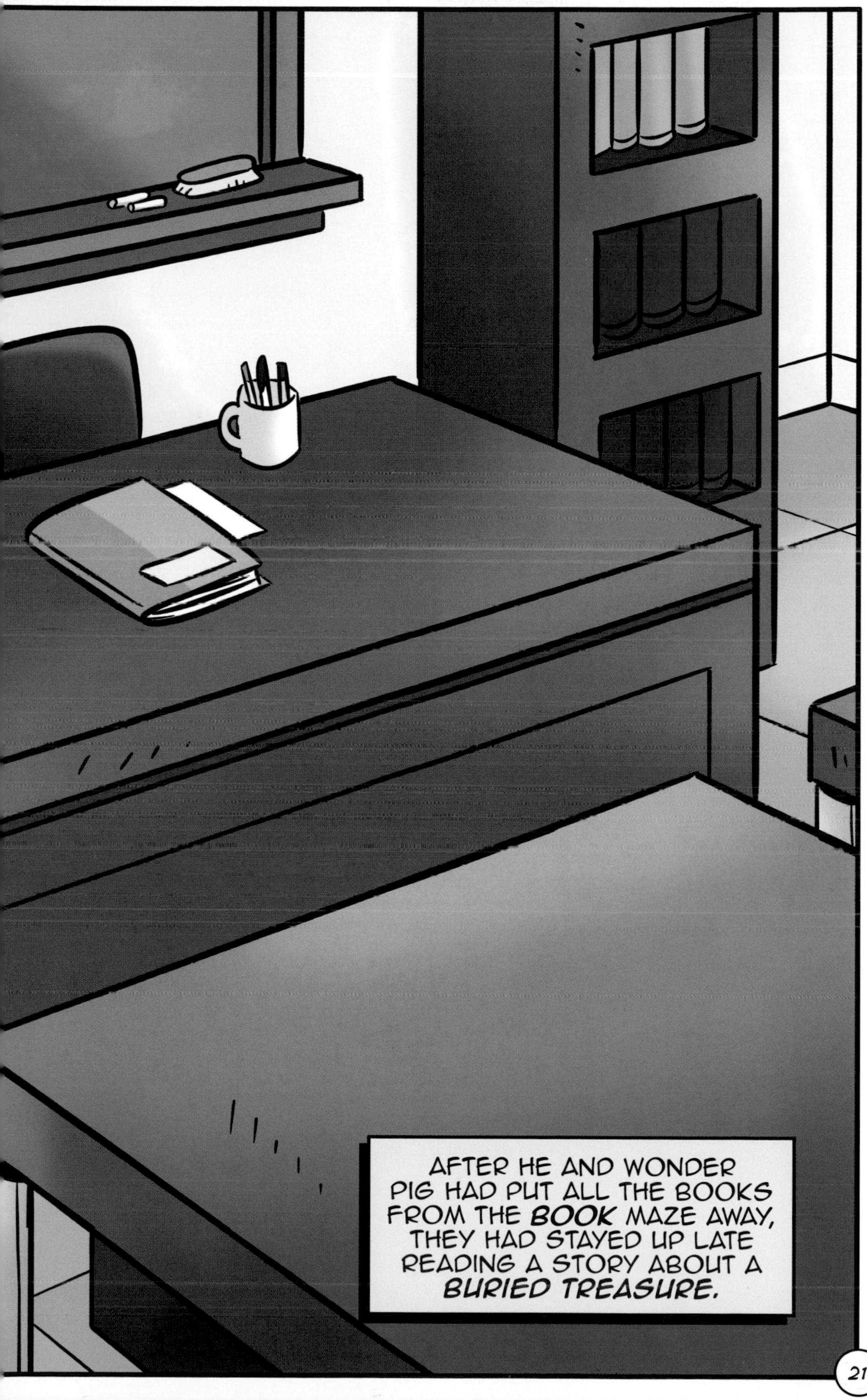
AFTER HE AND WONDER PIG HAD PUT ALL THE BOOKS FROM THE *BOOK* MAZE AWAY, THEY HAD STAYED UP LATE READING A STORY ABOUT A *BURIED TREASURE.*

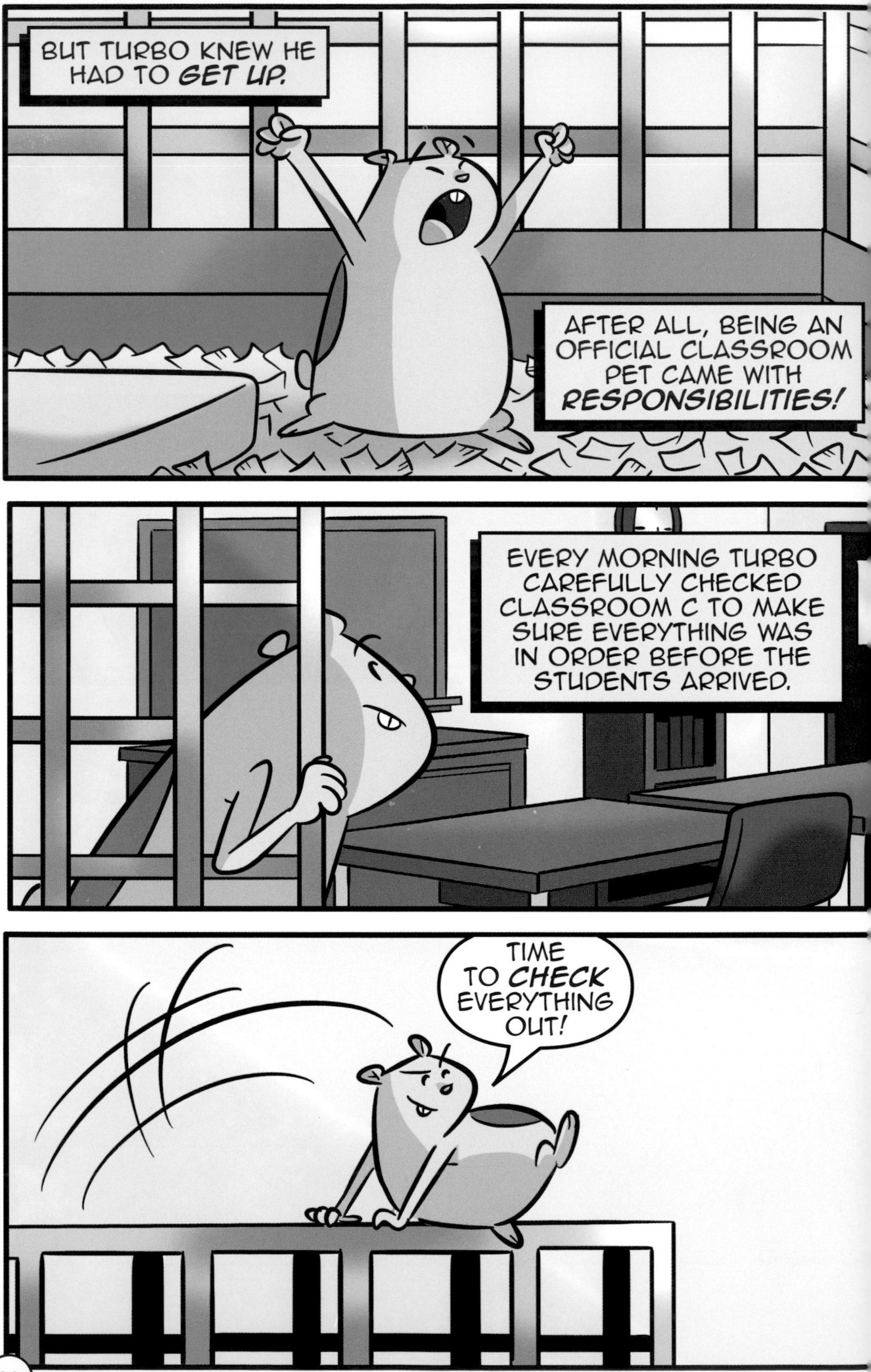
BUT TURBO KNEW HE HAD TO GET UP.
AFTER ALL, BEING AN OFFICIAL CLASSROOM PET CAME WITH RESPONSIBILITIES!
EVERY MORNING TURBO CAREFULLY CHECKED CLASSROOM C TO MAKE SURE EVERYTHING WAS IN ORDER BEFORE THE STUDENTS ARRIVED.
TIME TO CHECK EVERYTHING OUT!

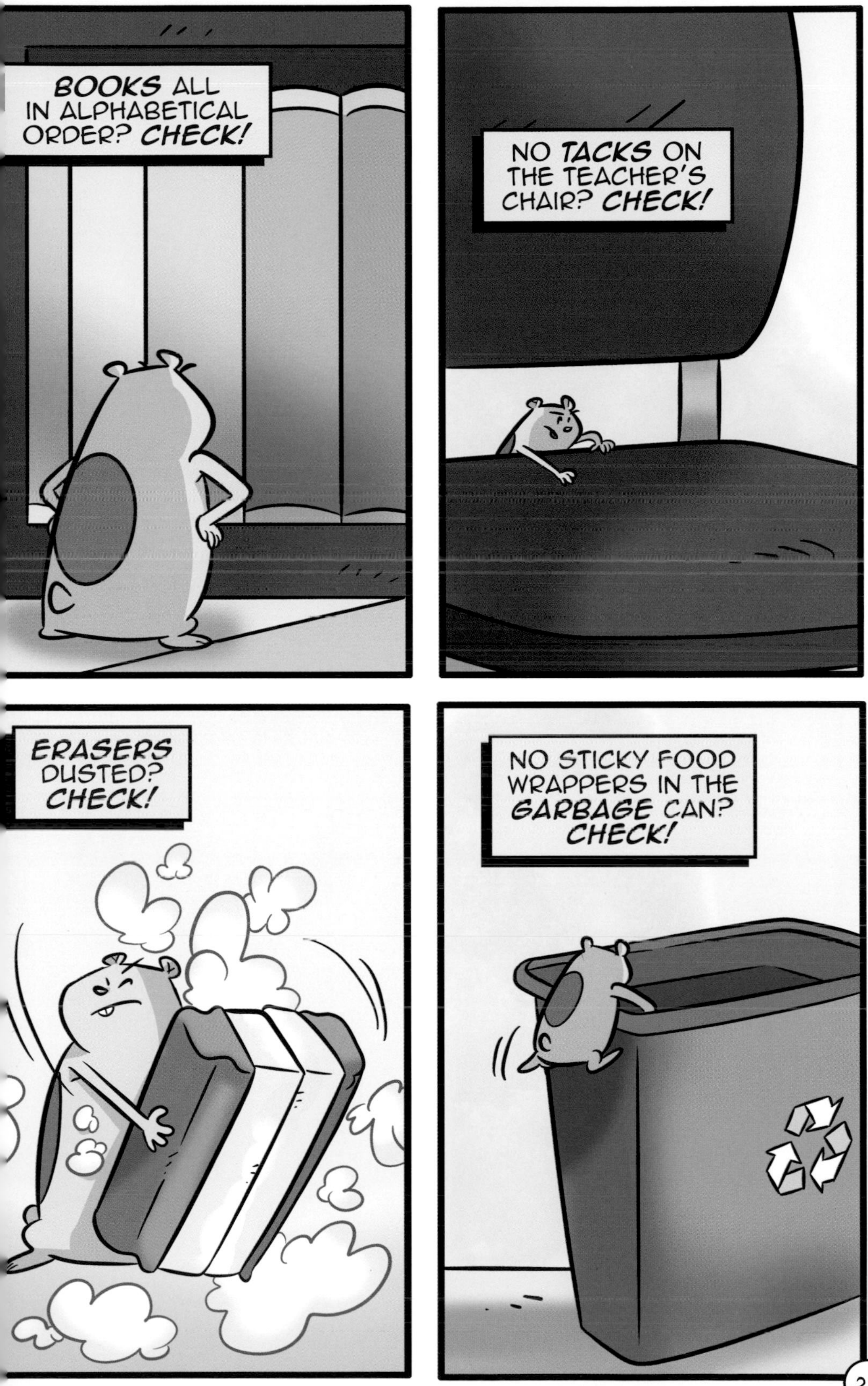
BOOKS ALL IN ALPHABETICAL ORDER? CHECK!
NO TACKS ON THE TEACHER'S CHAIR? CHECK!
ERASERS DUSTED? CHECK!
NO STICKY FOOD WRAPPERS IN THE GARBAGE CAN? CHECK!

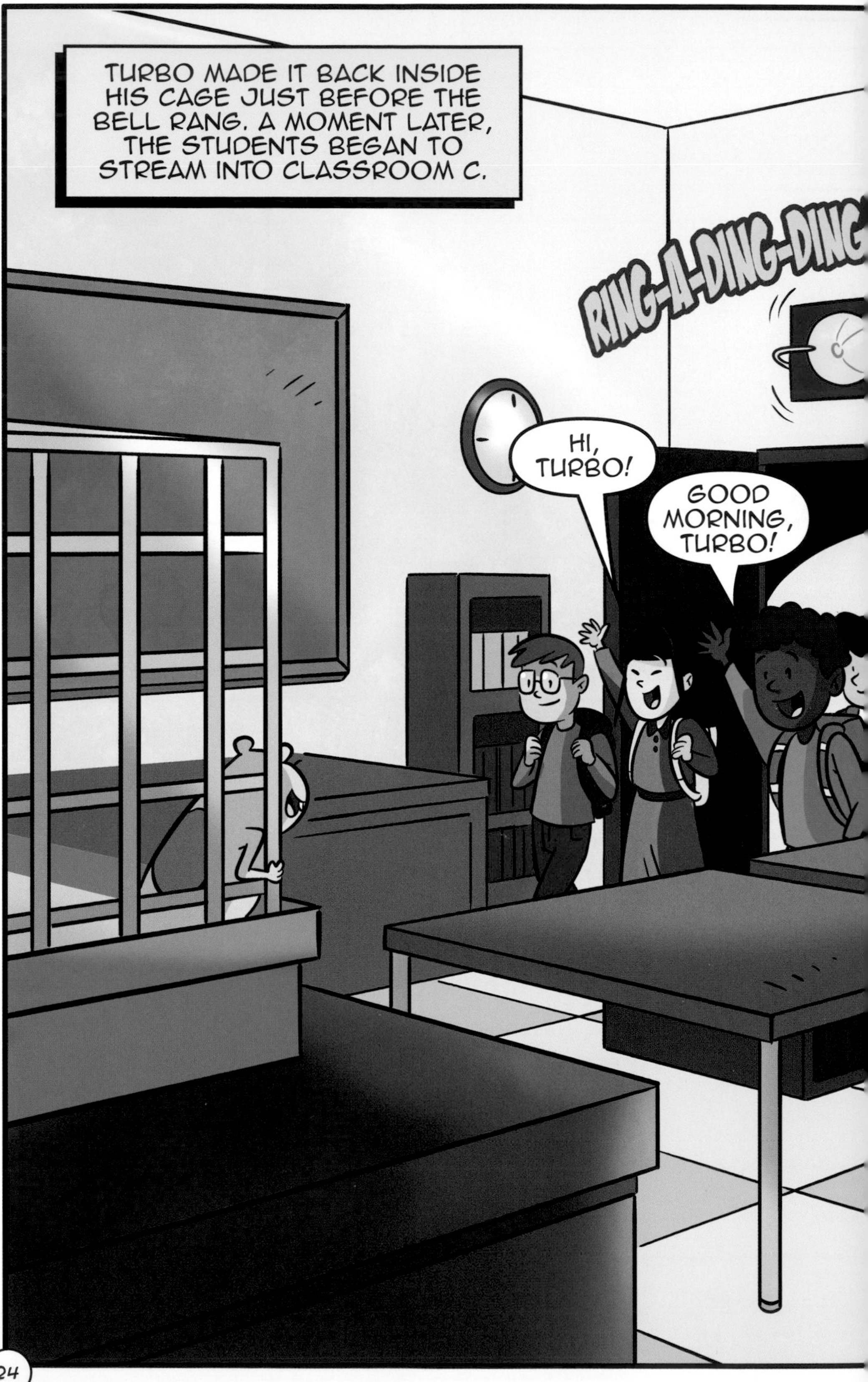
TURBO MADE IT BACK INSIDE HIS CAGE JUST BEFORE THE BELL RANG. A MOMENT LATER, THE STUDENTS BEGAN TO STREAM INTO CLASSROOM C.
RING-A-DING-DING
HI, TURBO!
GOOD MORNING, TURBO!

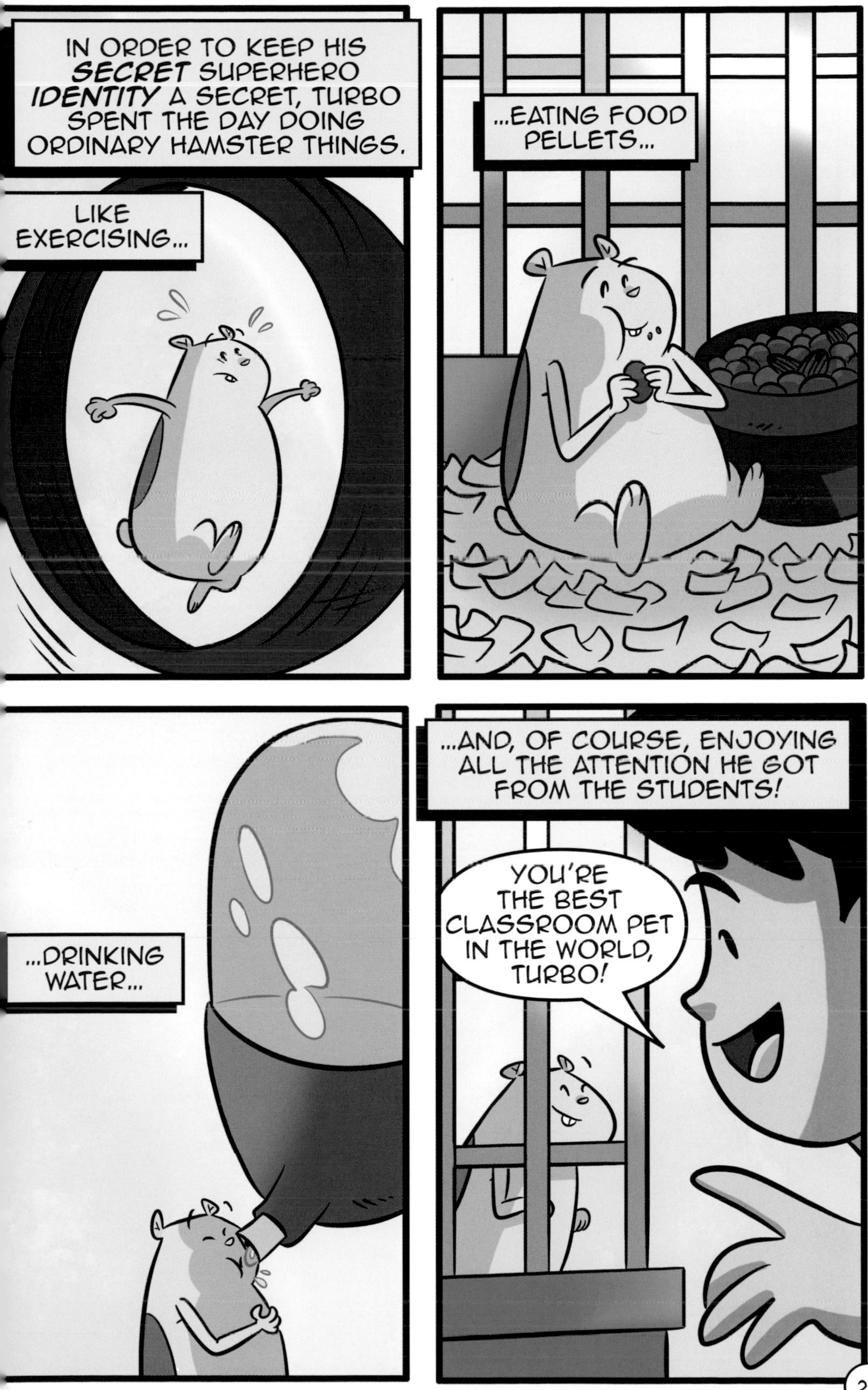
IN ORDER TO KEEP HIS SECRET SUPERHERO IDENTITY A SECRET, TURBO SPENT THE DAY DOING ORDINARY HAMSTER THINGS.
LIKE EXERCISING...
...EATING FOOD PELLETS...
...DRINKING WATER...
...AND, OF COURSE, ENJOYING ALL THE ATTENTION HE GOT FROM THE STUDENTS!
YOU'RE THE BEST CLASSROOM PET IN THE WORLD, TURBO!

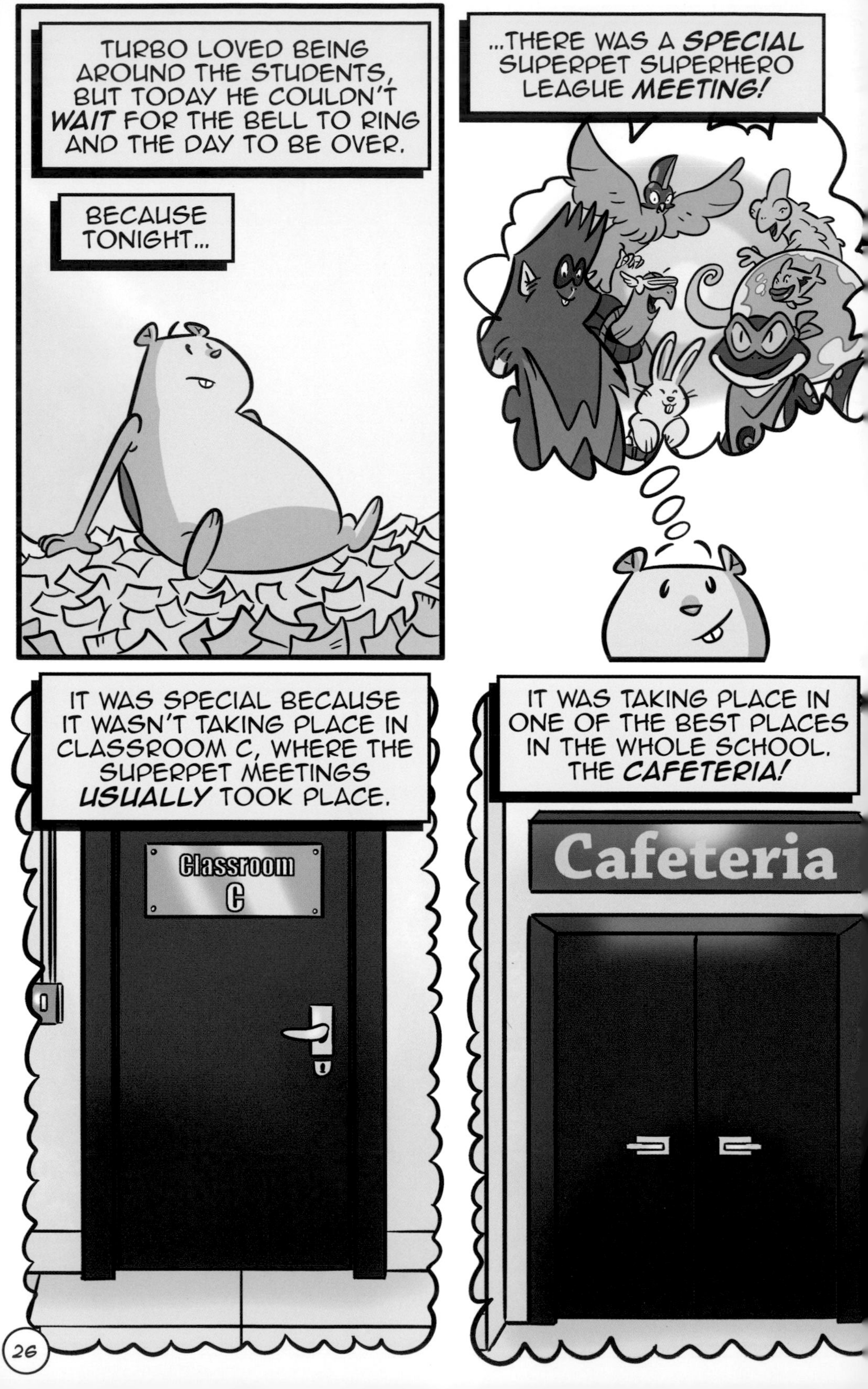
TURBO LOVED BEING AROUND THE STUDENTS, BUT TODAY HE COULDN'T WAIT FOR THE BELL TO RING AND THE DAY TO BE OVER.
BECAUSE TONIGHT...
...THERE WAS A SPECIAL SUPERPET SUPERHERO LEAGUE MEETING!
IT WAS SPECIAL BECAUSE IT WASN'T TAKING PLACE IN CLASSROOM C, WHERE THE SUPERPET MEETINGS USUALLY TOOK PLACE.
Classroom C
IT WAS TAKING PLACE IN ONE OF THE BEST PLACES IN THE WHOLE SCHOOL. THE CAFETERIA!
Cafeteria

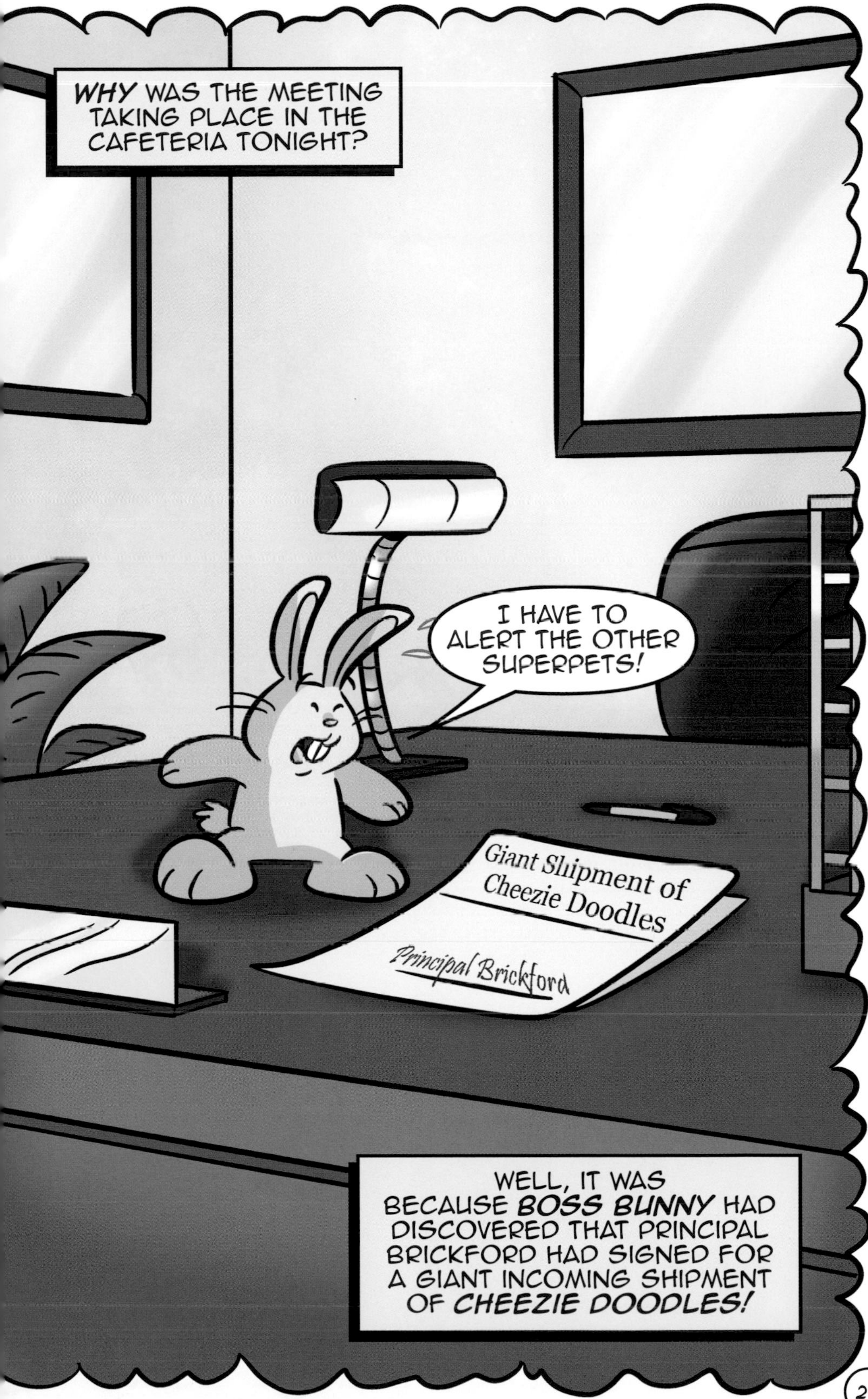
WHY WAS THE MEETING TAKING PLACE IN THE CAFETERIA TONIGHT?
I HAVE TO ALERT THE OTHER SUPERPETS!
Giant Shipment of Cheezie Doodles
Principal Brickford
WELL, IT WAS BECAUSE BOSS BUNNY HAD DISCOVERED THAT PRINCIPAL BRICKFORD HAD SIGNED FOR A GIANT INCOMING SHIPMENT OF CHEEZIE DOODLES!

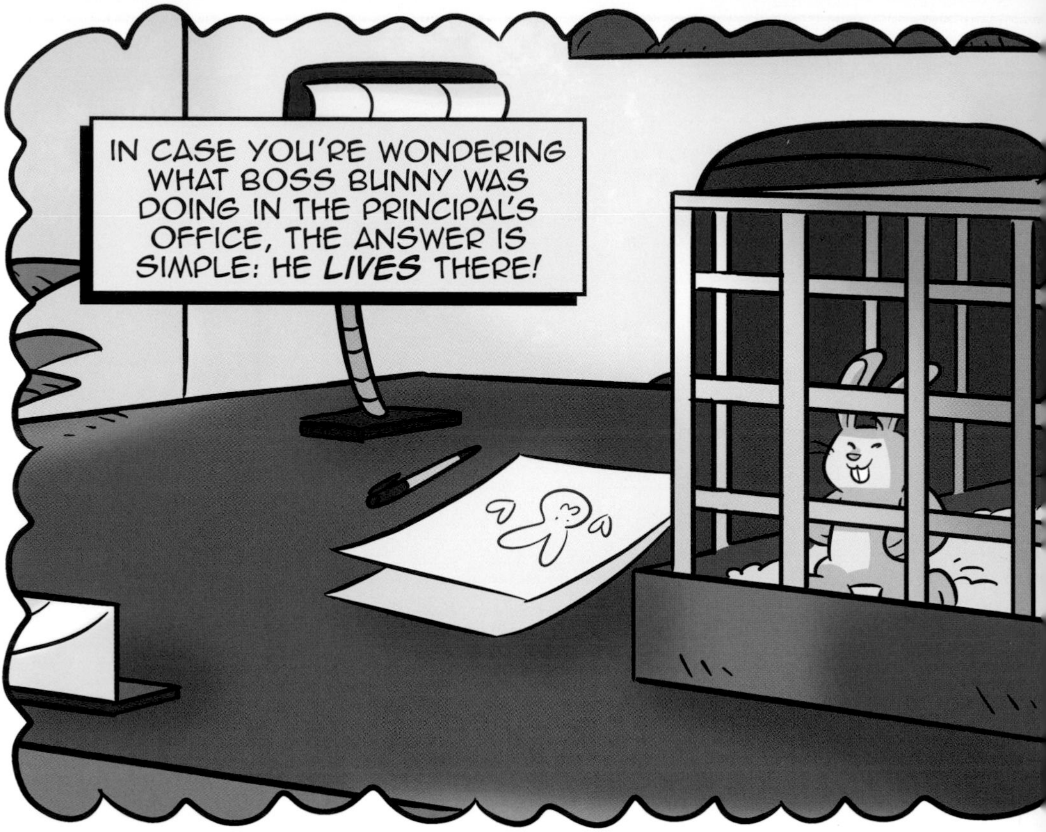
IN CASE YOU'RE WONDERING WHAT BOSS BUNNY WAS DOING IN THE PRINCIPAL'S OFFICE, THE ANSWER IS SIMPLE: HE *LIVES* THERE!

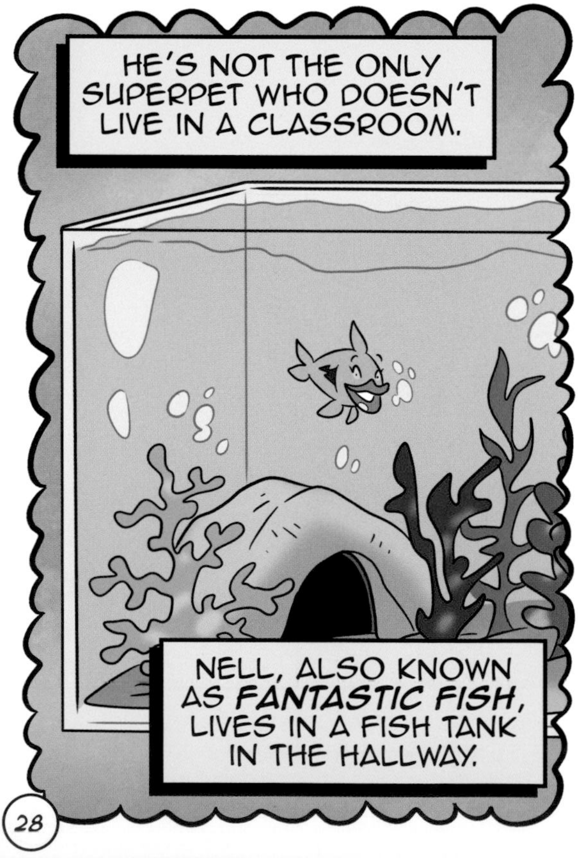
HE'S NOT THE ONLY SUPERPET WHO DOESN'T LIVE IN A CLASSROOM.
NELL, ALSO KNOWN AS *FANTASTIC FISH*, LIVES IN A FISH TANK IN THE HALLWAY.

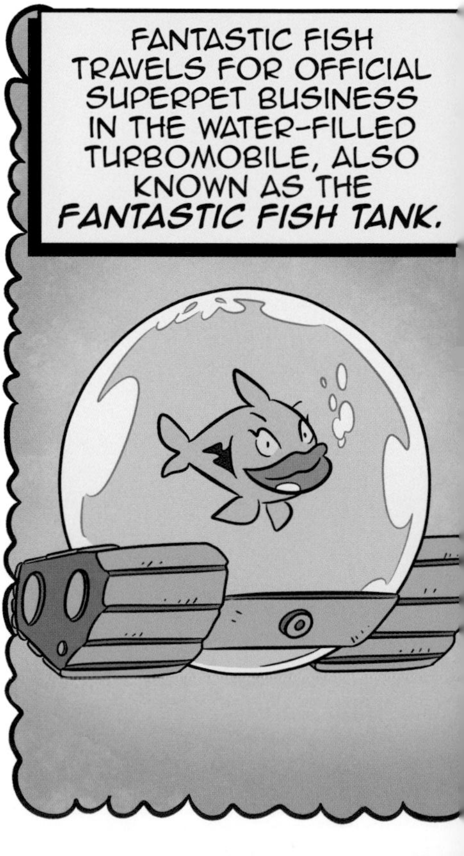
FANTASTIC FISH TRAVELS FOR OFFICIAL SUPERPET BUSINESS IN THE WATER-FILLED TURBOMOBILE, ALSO KNOWN AS THE *FANTASTIC FISH TANK.*

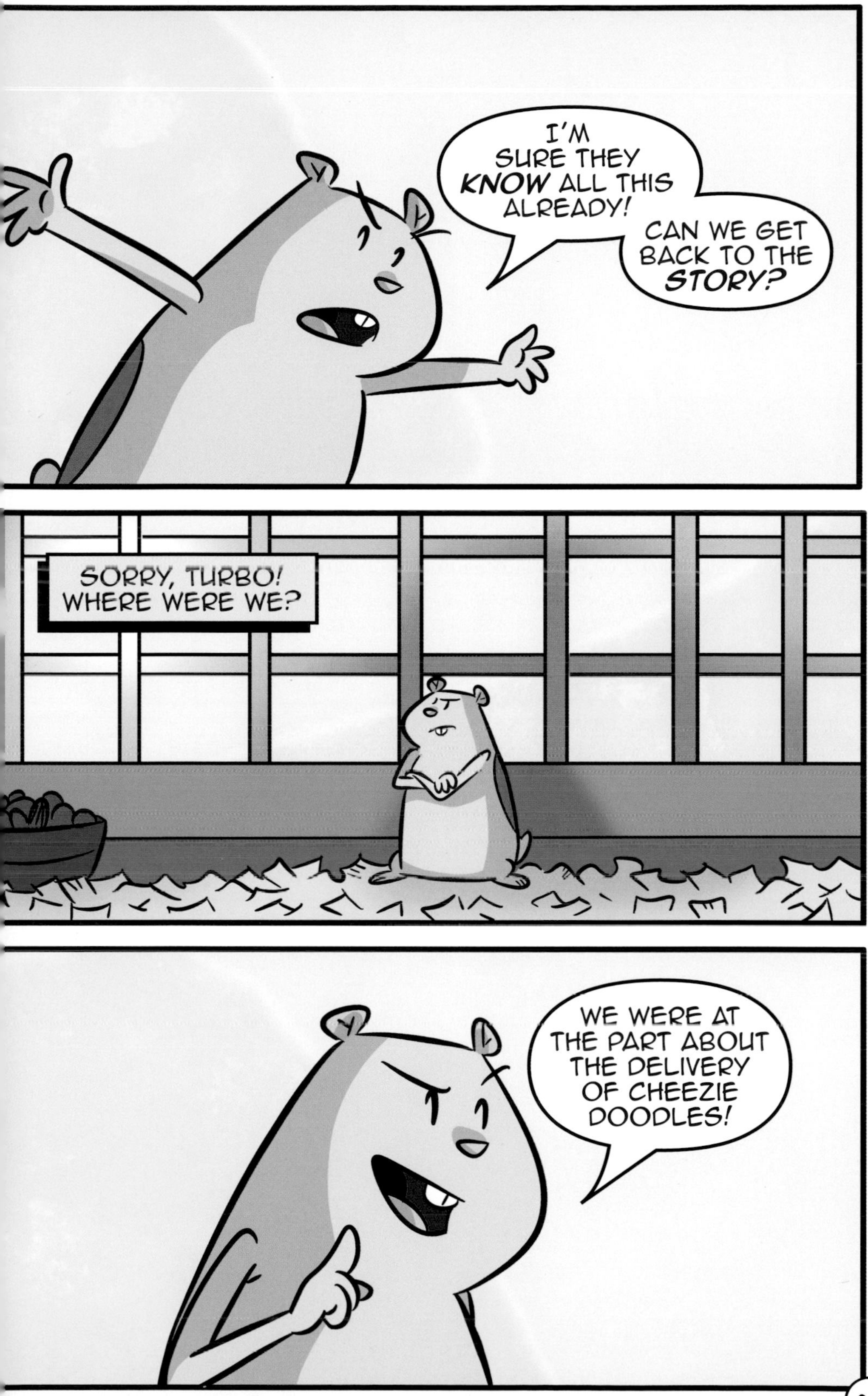
I'M SURE THEY *KNOW* ALL THIS ALREADY!
CAN WE GET BACK TO THE *STORY?*
SORRY, TURBO! WHERE WERE WE?
WE WERE AT THE PART ABOUT THE DELIVERY OF CHEEZIE DOODLES!

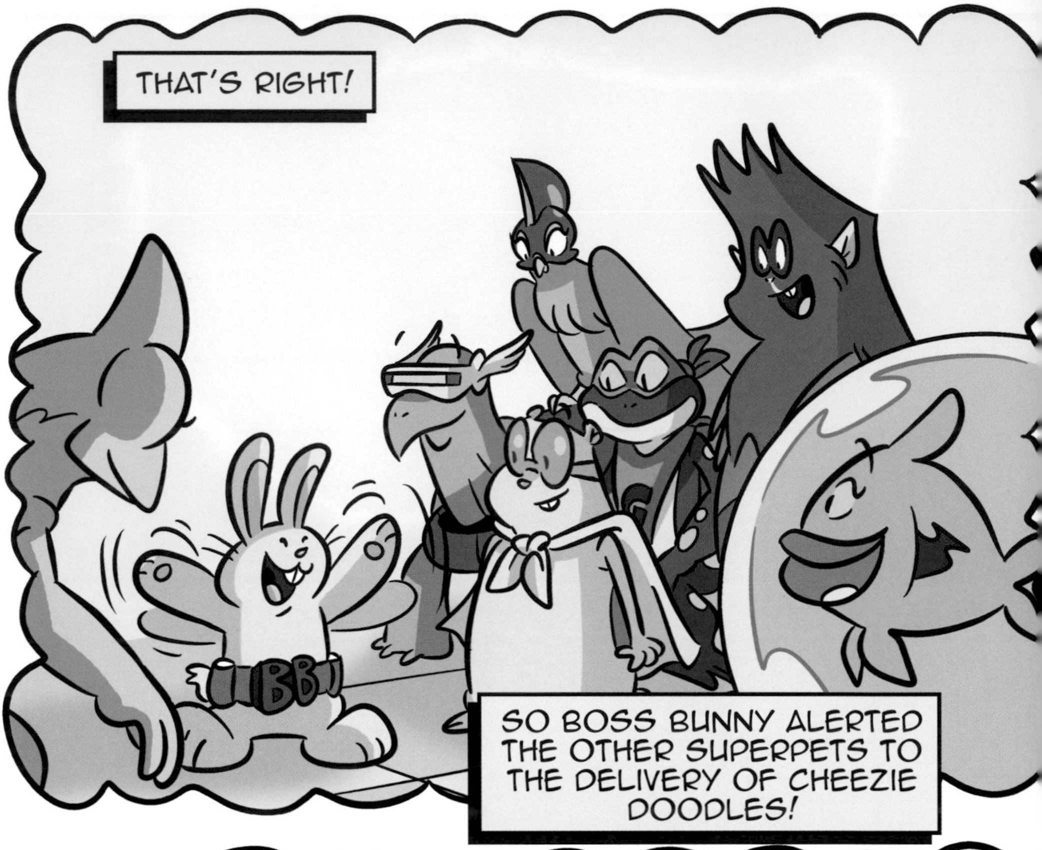
THAT'S RIGHT!
SO BOSS BUNNY ALERTED THE OTHER SUPERPETS TO THE DELIVERY OF CHEEZIE DOODLES!

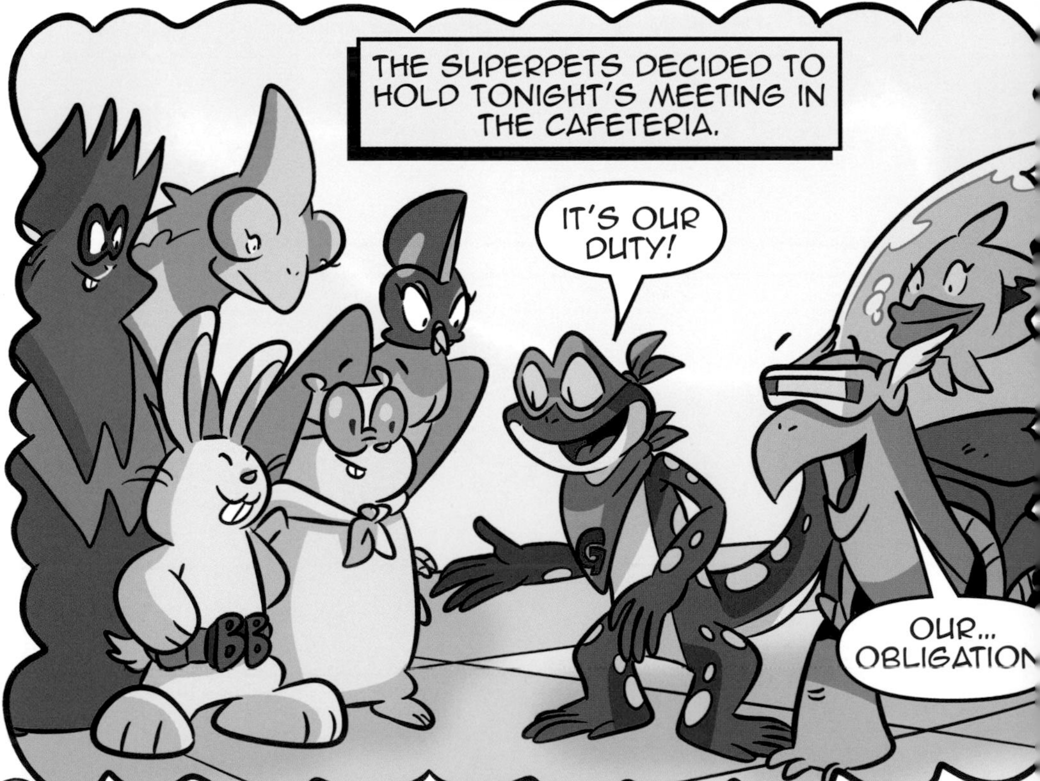
THE SUPERPETS DECIDED TO HOLD TONIGHT'S MEETING IN THE CAFETERIA.
IT'S OUR DUTY!
OUR... OBLIGATION

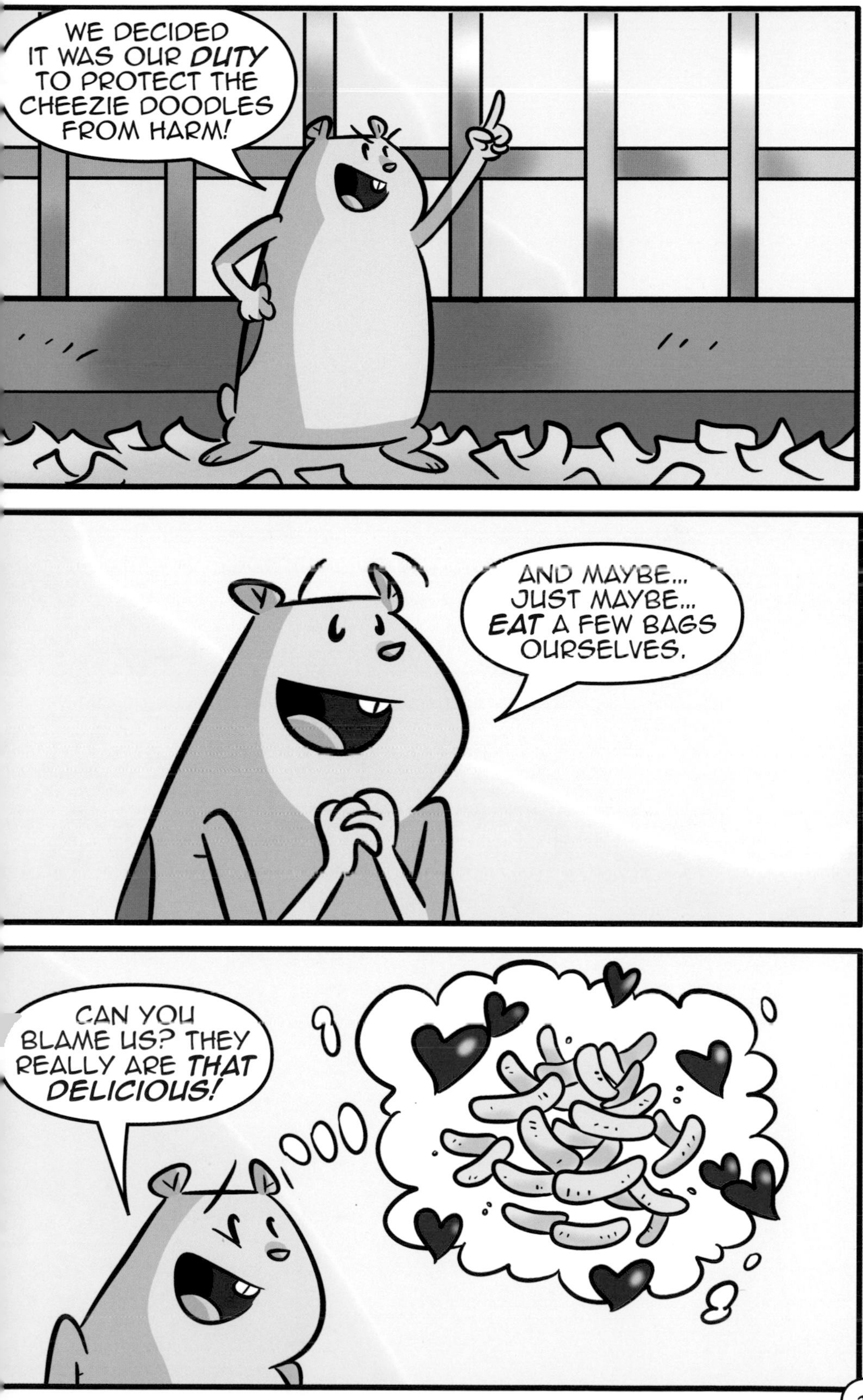
WE DECIDED IT WAS OUR DUTY TO PROTECT THE CHEEZIE DOODLES FROM HARM!
AND MAYBE... JUST MAYBE... EAT A FEW BAGS OURSELVES.
CAN YOU BLAME US? THEY REALLY ARE THAT DELICIOUS!

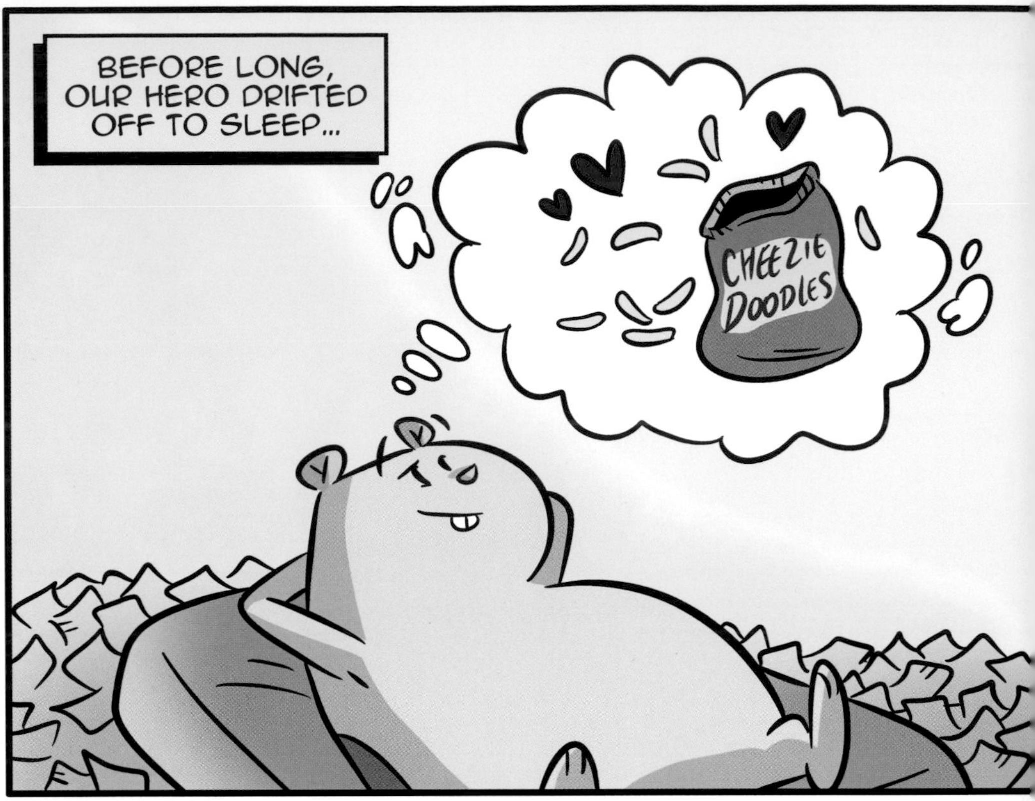
BEFORE LONG, OUR HERO DRIFTED OFF TO SLEEP...
CHEEZIE DOODLES

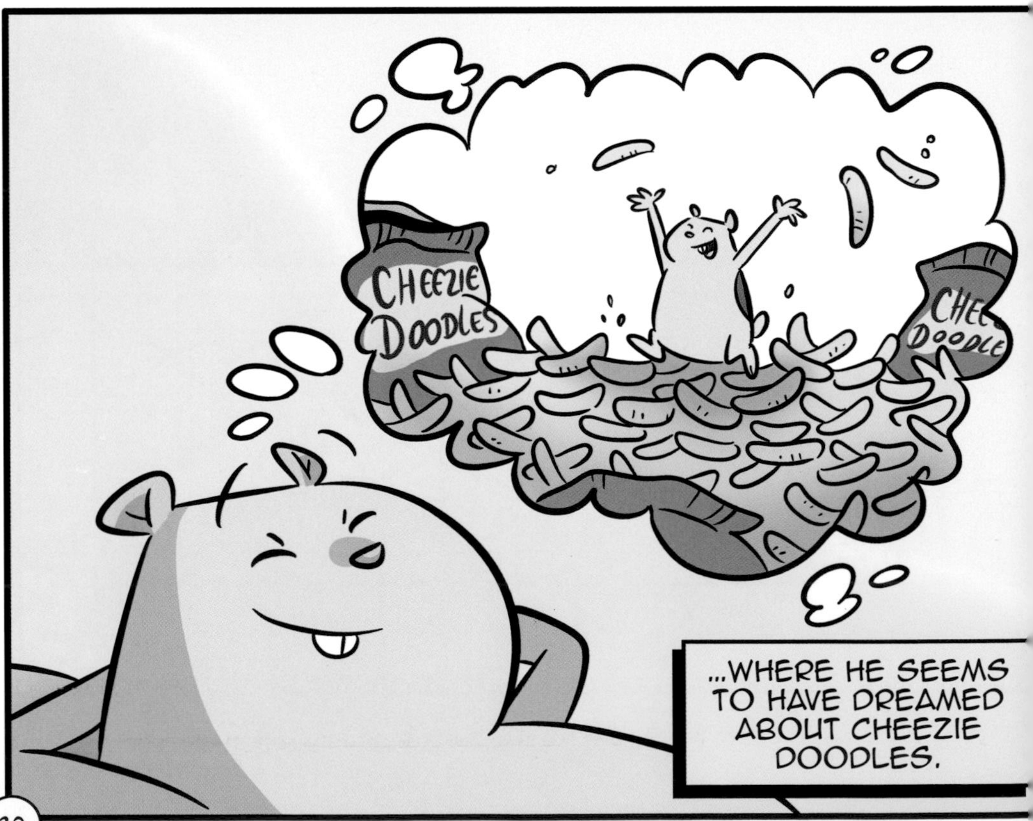
CHEEZIE DOODLES
...WHERE HE SEEMS TO HAVE DREAMED ABOUT CHEEZIE DOODLES.

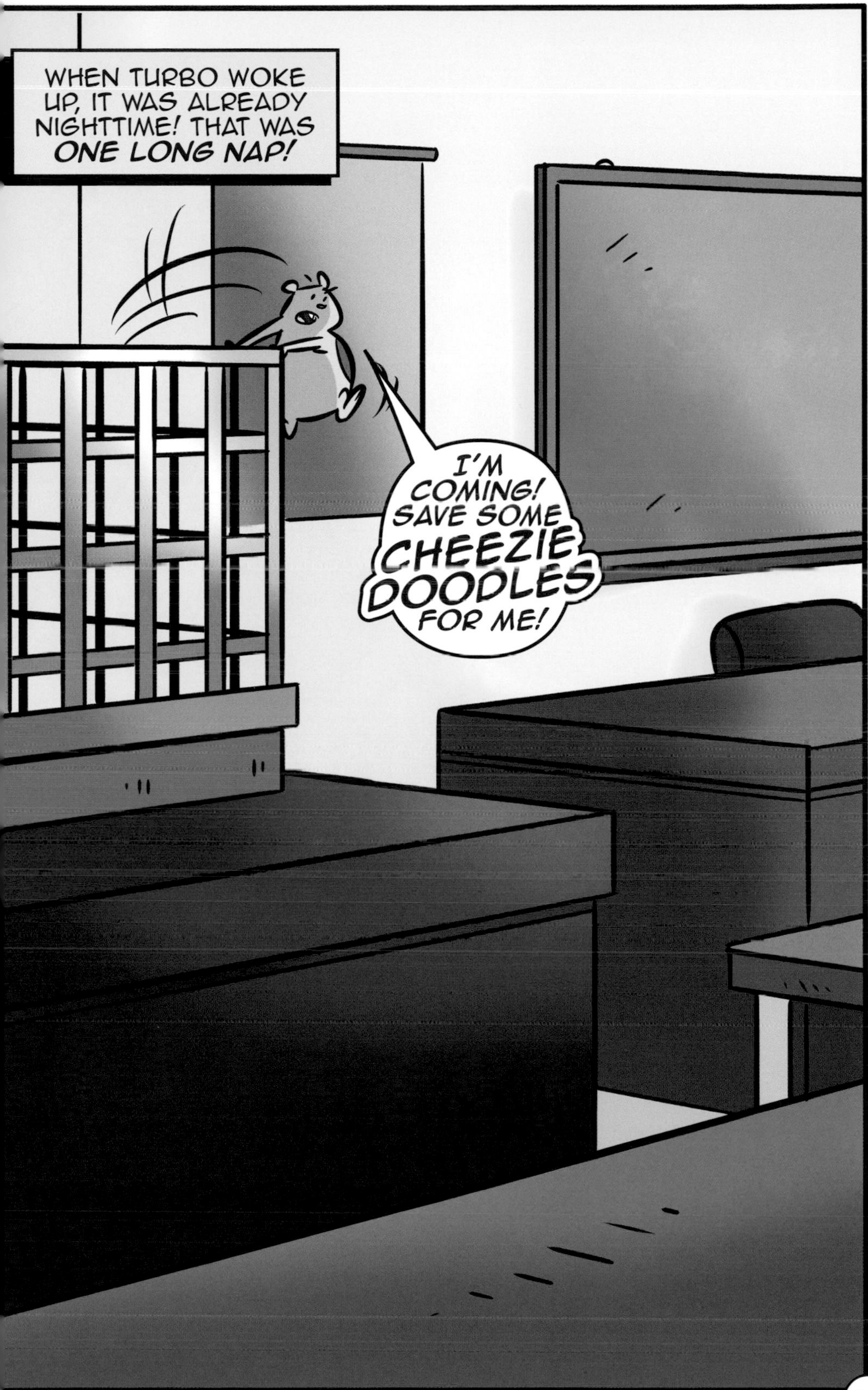
WHEN TURBO WOKE UP, IT WAS ALREADY NIGHTTIME! THAT WAS *ONE LONG NAP!*
I'M COMING! SAVE SOME CHEEZIE DOODLES FOR ME!

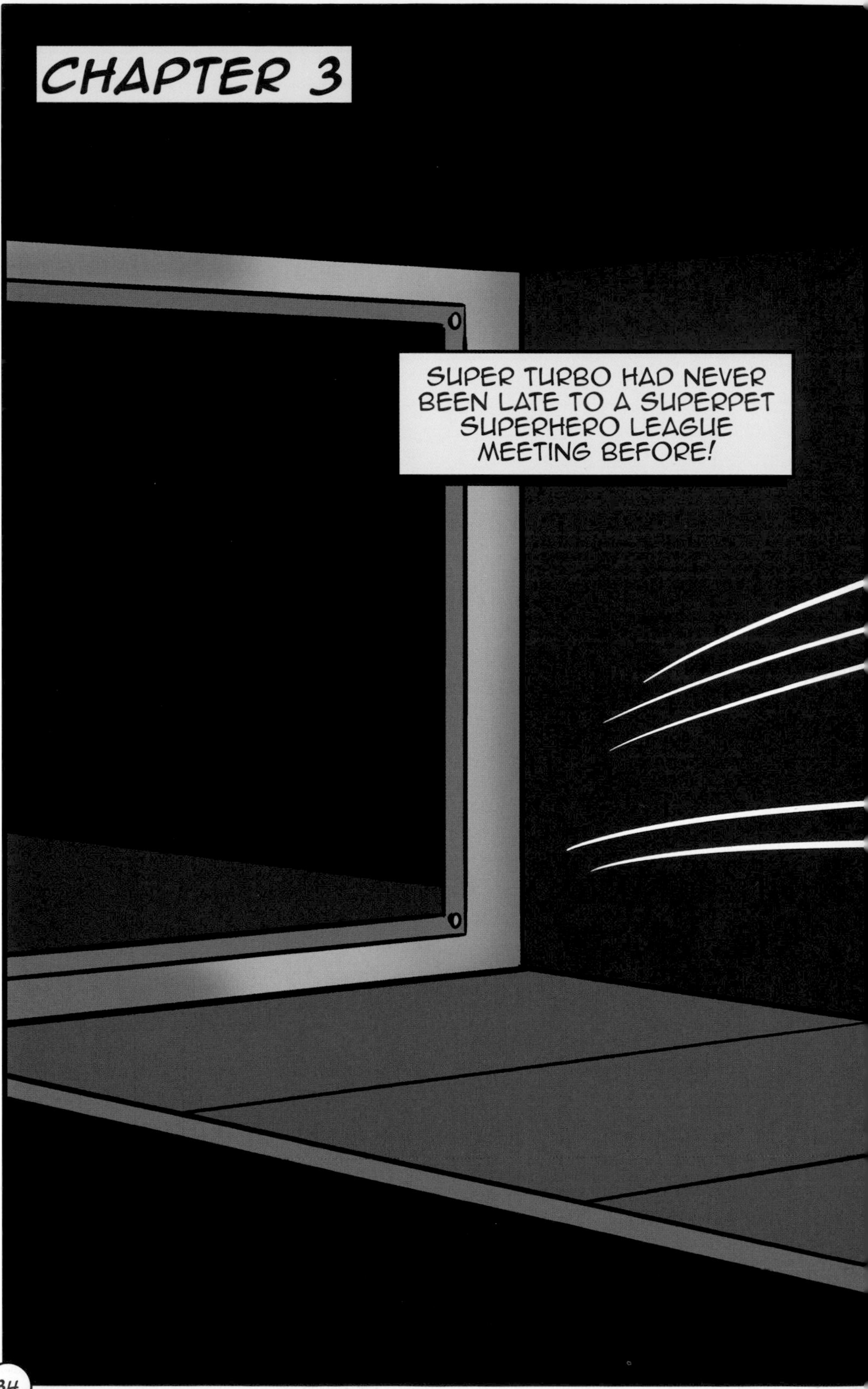
CHAPTER 3
SUPER TURBO HAD NEVER BEEN LATE TO A SUPERPET SUPERHERO LEAGUE MEETING BEFORE!

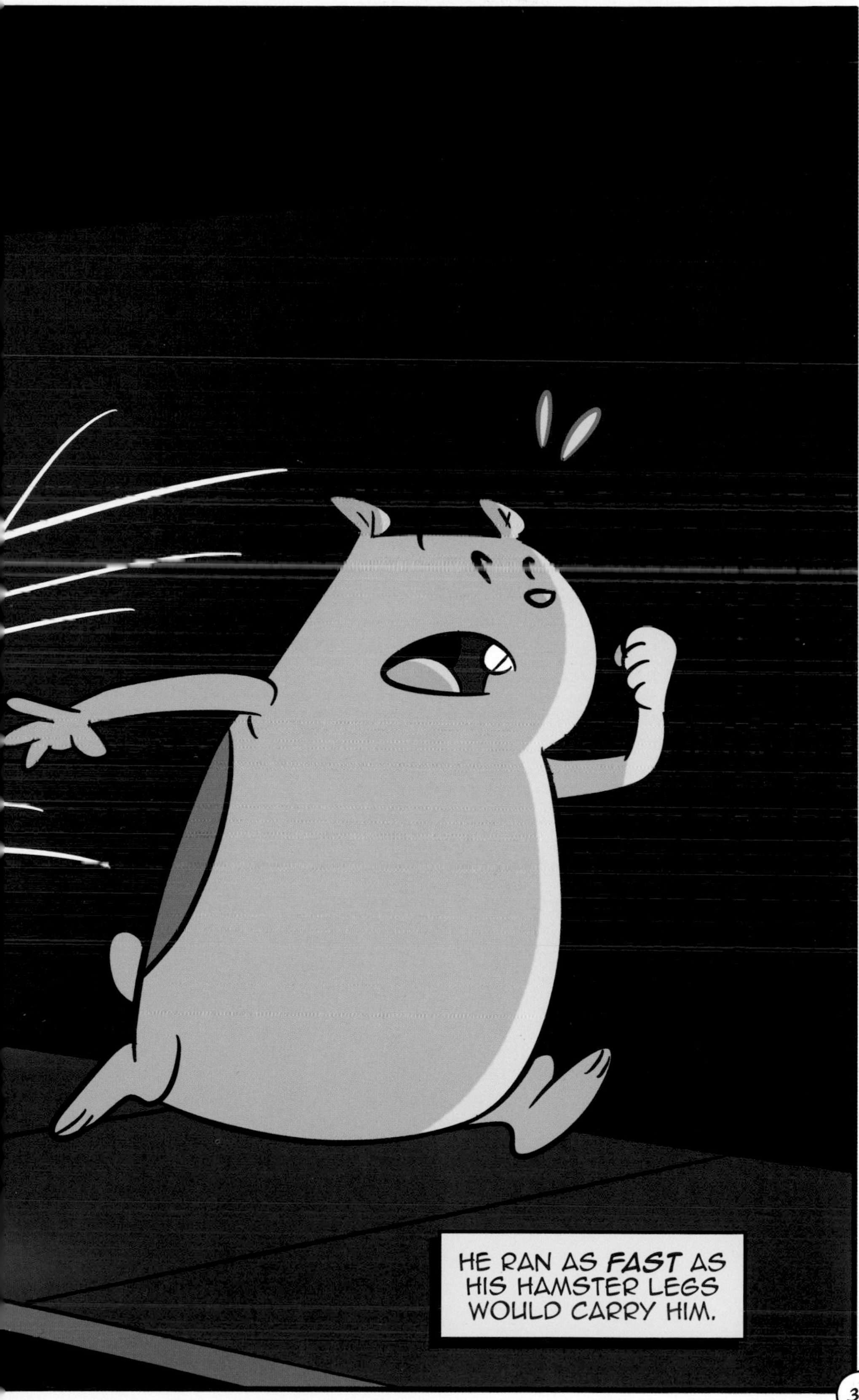
HE RAN AS ***FAST*** AS HIS HAMSTER LEGS WOULD CARRY HIM.

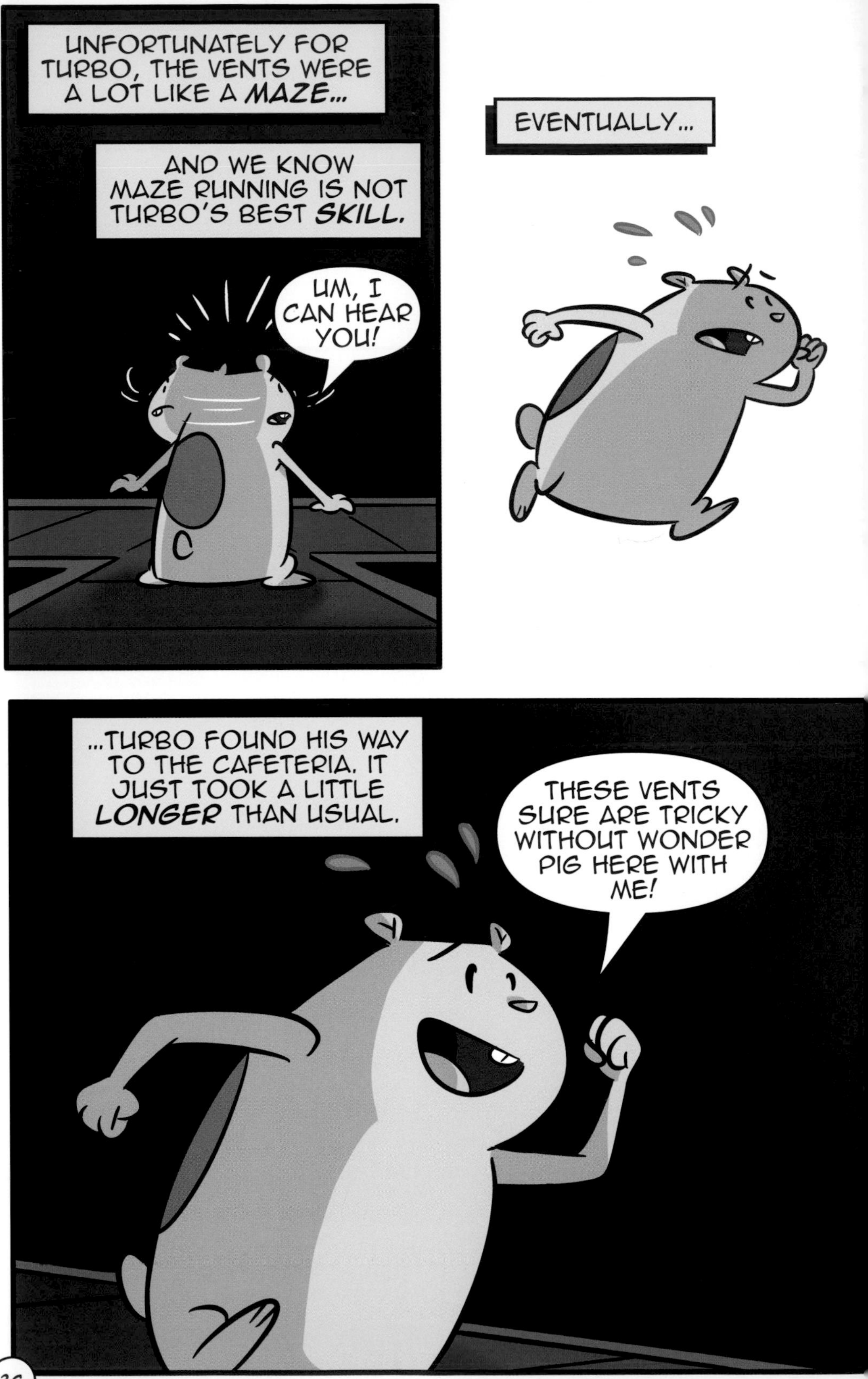
UNFORTUNATELY FOR TURBO, THE VENTS WERE A LOT LIKE A MAZE...
AND WE KNOW MAZE RUNNING IS NOT TURBO'S BEST SKILL.
UM, I CAN HEAR YOU!
EVENTUALLY...
...TURBO FOUND HIS WAY TO THE CAFETERIA. IT JUST TOOK A LITTLE LONGER THAN USUAL.
THESE VENTS SURE ARE TRICKY WITHOUT WONDER PIG HERE WITH ME!

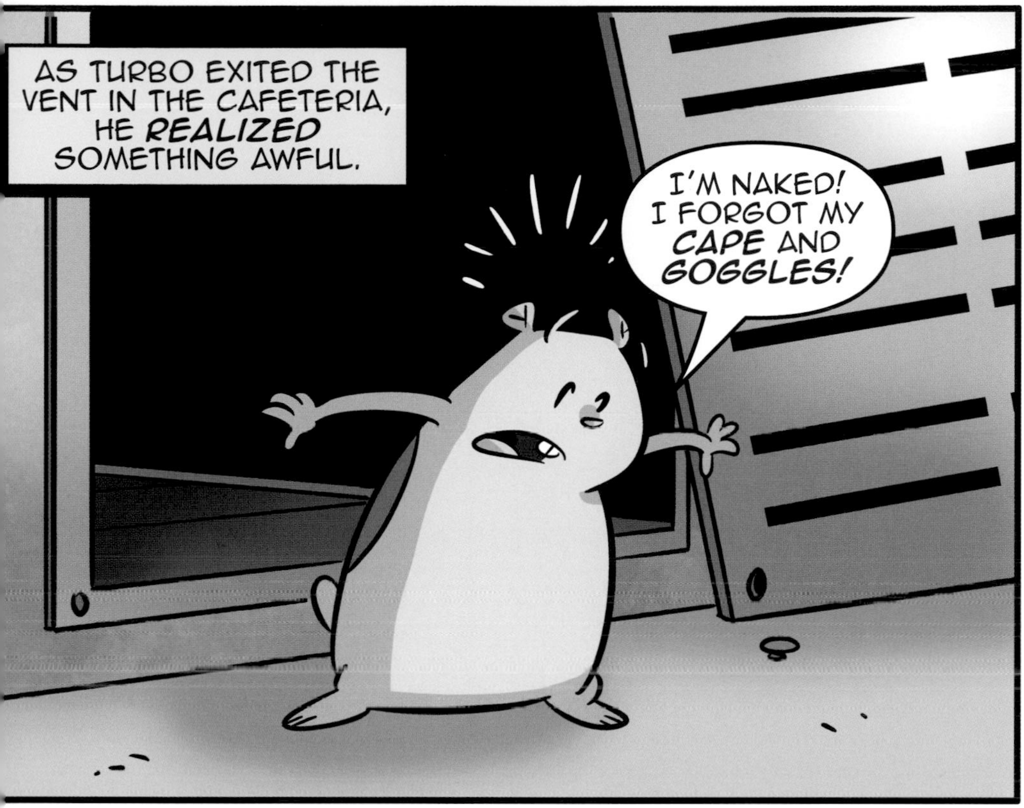
AS TURBO EXITED THE VENT IN THE CAFETERIA, HE *REALIZED* SOMETHING AWFUL.
I'M NAKED! I FORGOT MY *CAPE* AND *GOGGLES!*

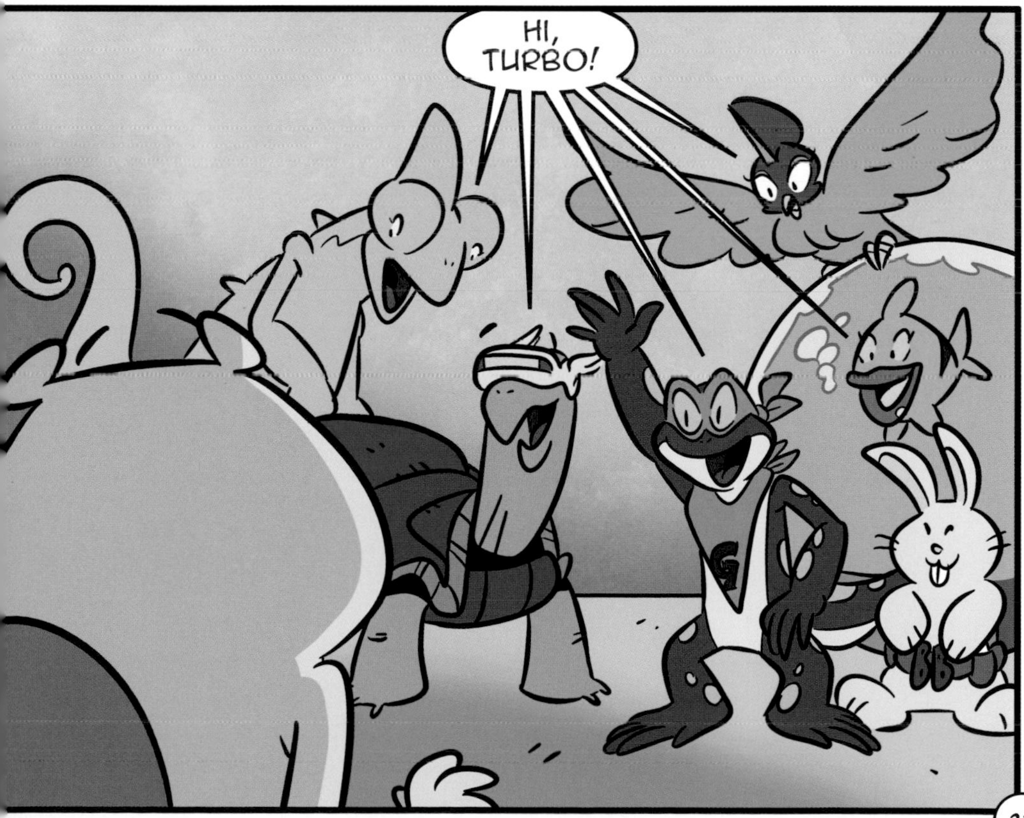
HI, TURBO!

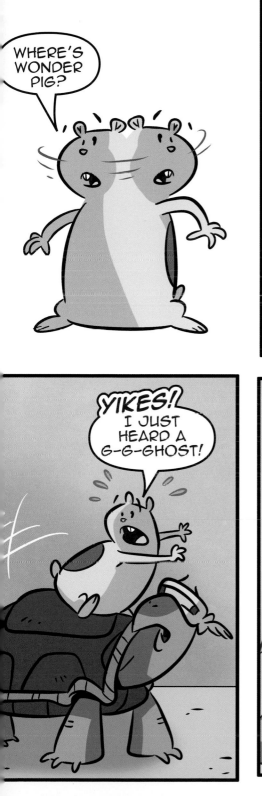

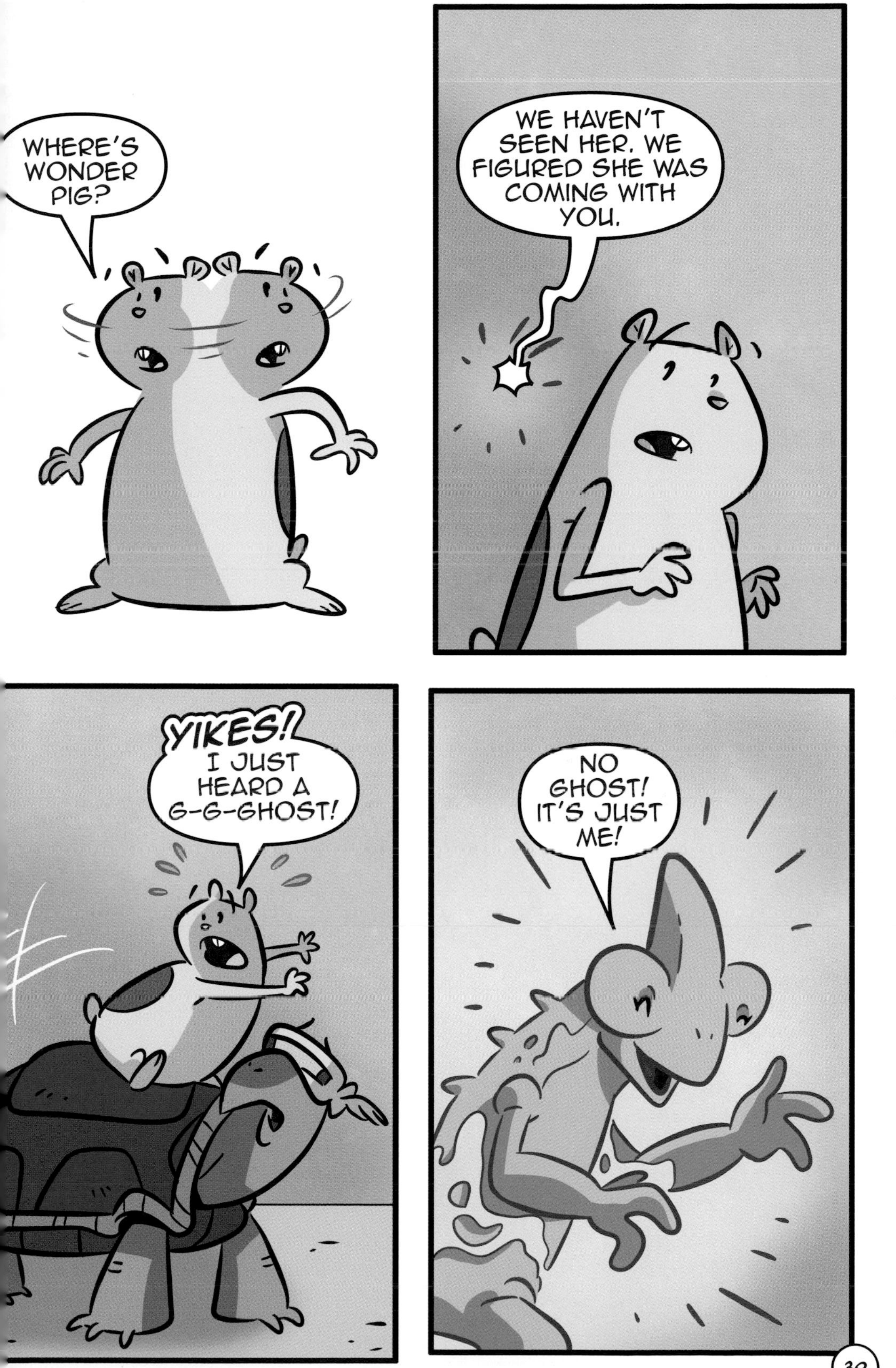
WHERE'S WONDER PIG?
WE HAVEN'T SEEN HER. WE FIGURED SHE WAS COMING WITH YOU.
YIKES! I JUST HEARD A G-G-GHOST!
NO GHOST! IT'S JUST ME!

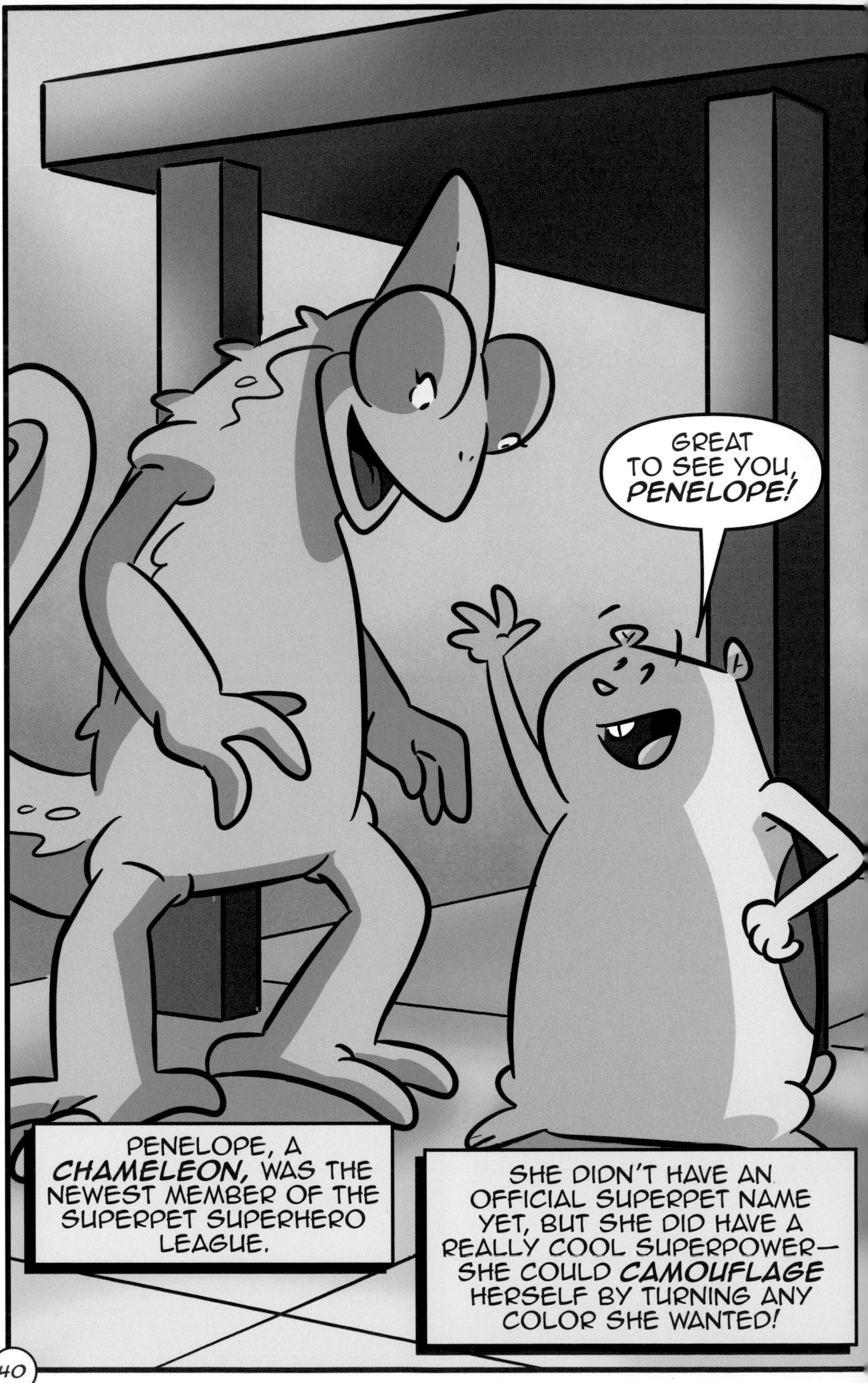
GREAT TO SEE YOU, PENELOPE!
PENELOPE, A CHAMELEON, WAS THE NEWEST MEMBER OF THE SUPERPET SUPERHERO LEAGUE.
SHE DIDN'T HAVE AN OFFICIAL SUPERPET NAME YET, BUT SHE DID HAVE A REALLY COOL SUPERPOWER—SHE COULD CAMOUFLAGE HERSELF BY TURNING ANY COLOR SHE WANTED!

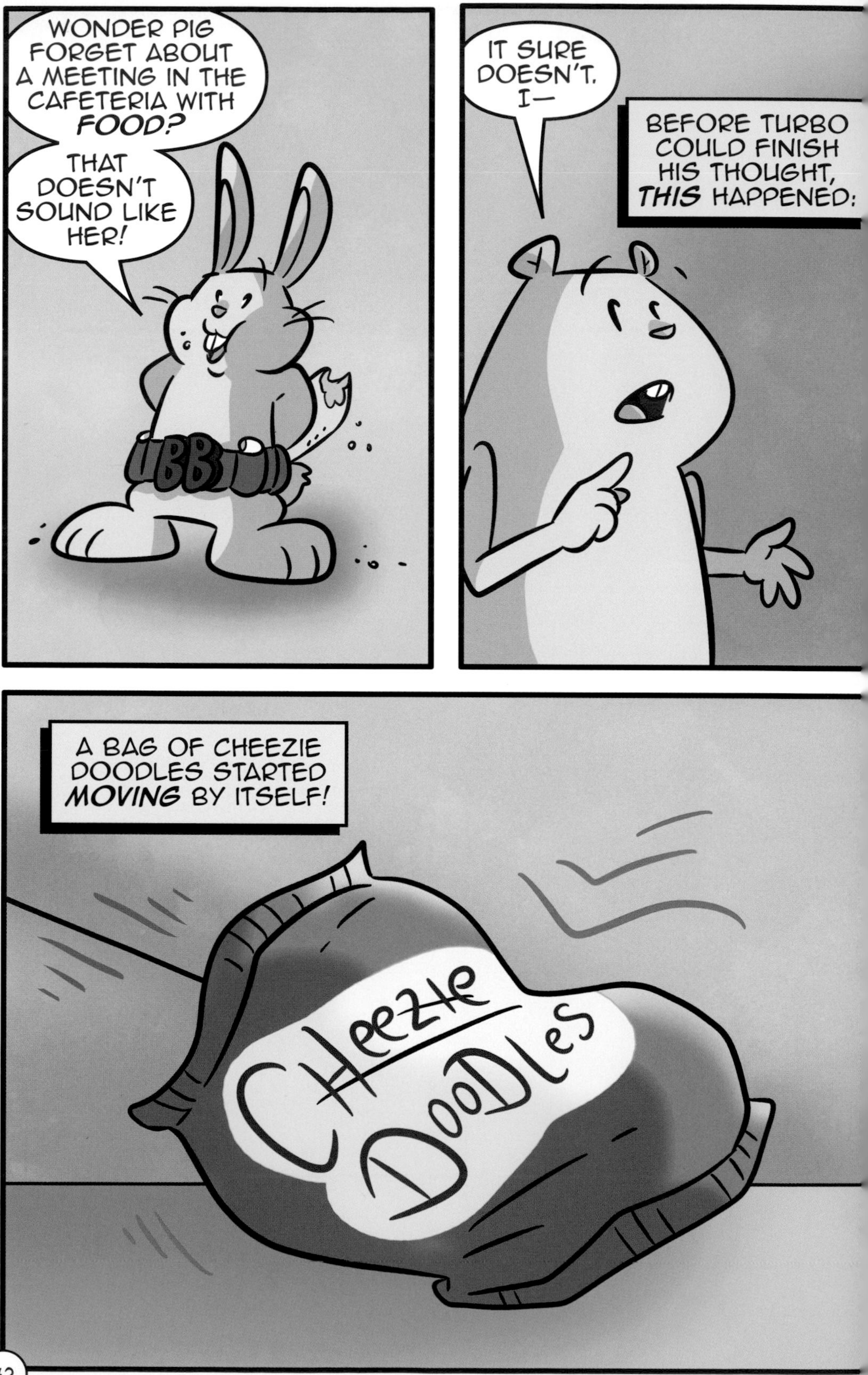
WONDER PIG FORGET ABOUT A MEETING IN THE CAFETERIA WITH *FOOD?*
THAT DOESN'T SOUND LIKE HER!
BB
IT SURE DOESN'T. I—
BEFORE TURBO COULD FINISH HIS THOUGHT, *THIS* HAPPENED:
A BAG OF CHEEZIE DOODLES STARTED *MOVING* BY ITSELF!
Cheezie Doodles

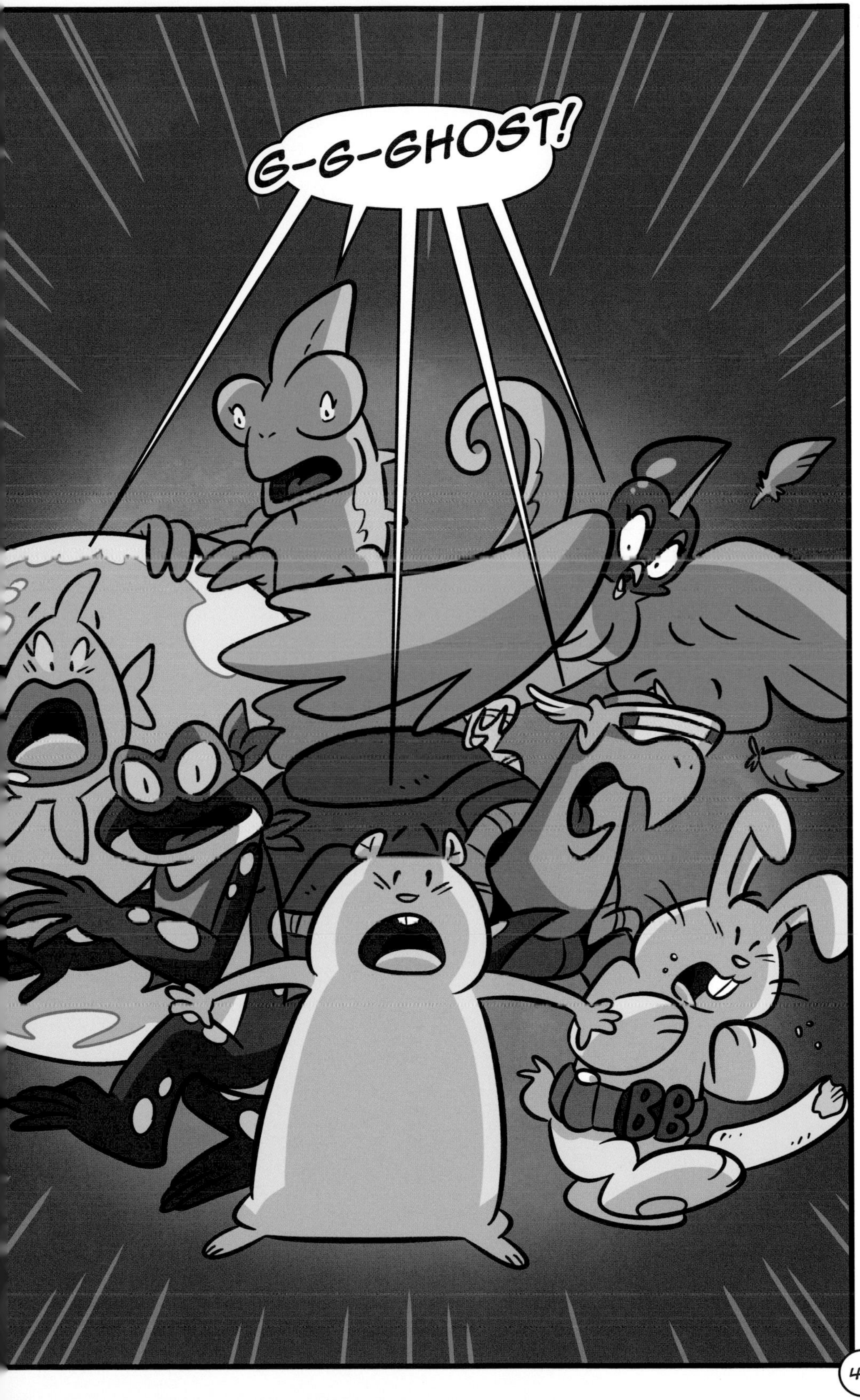
G-G-GHOST!

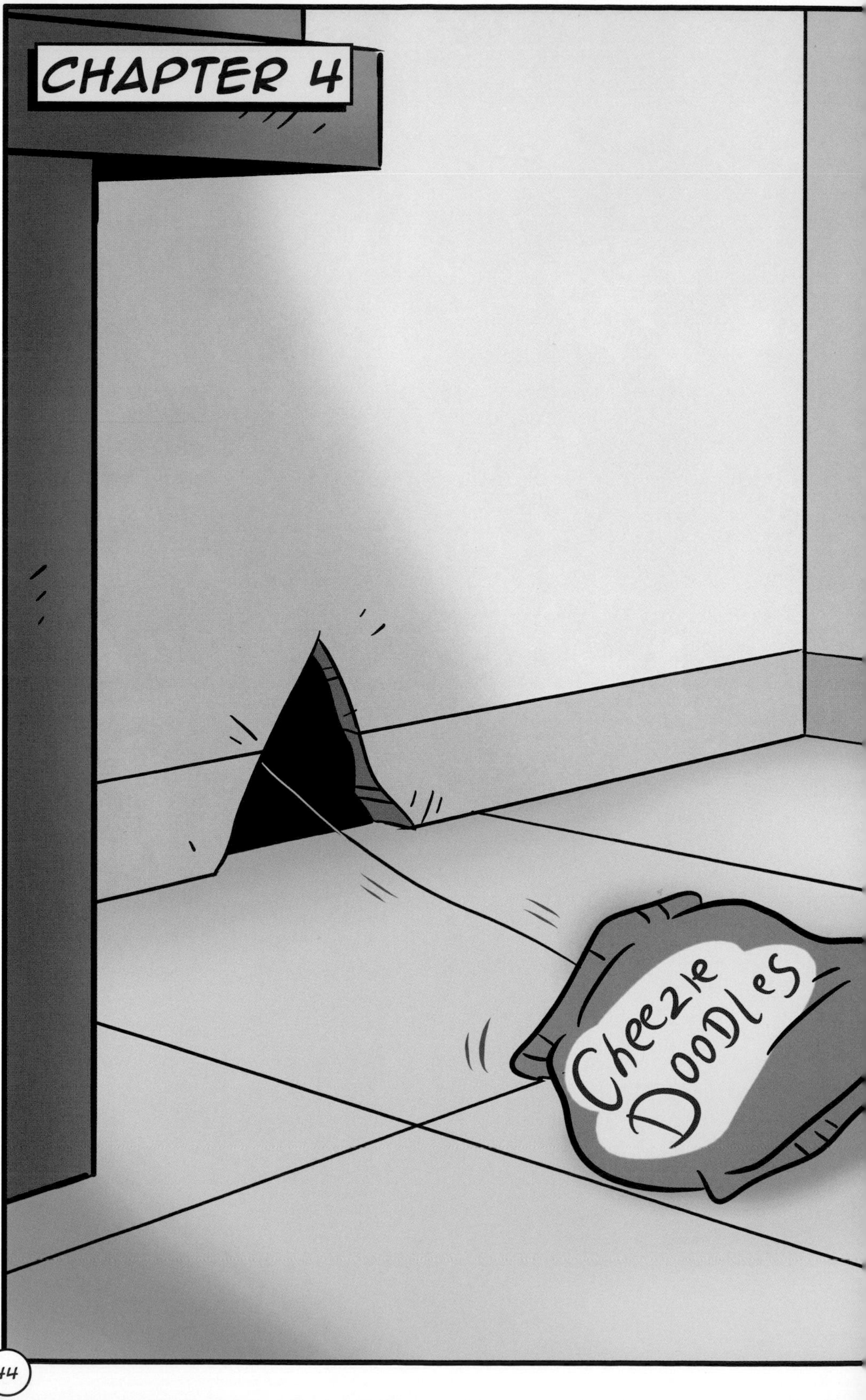
CHAPTER 4
Cheezie Doodles

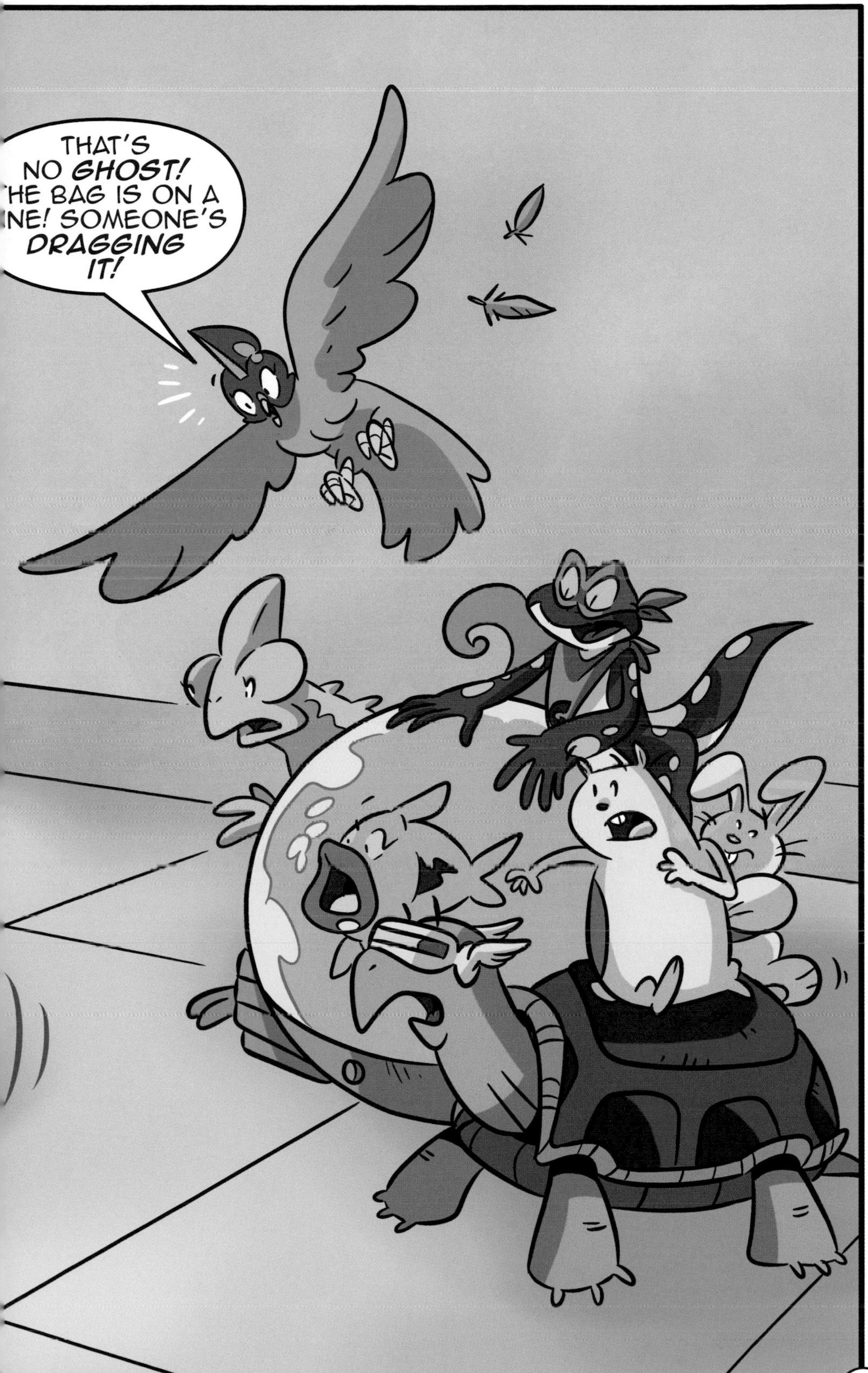
THAT'S NO *GHOST!* 'HE BAG IS ON A NE! SOMEONE'S *DRAGGING* *IT!*

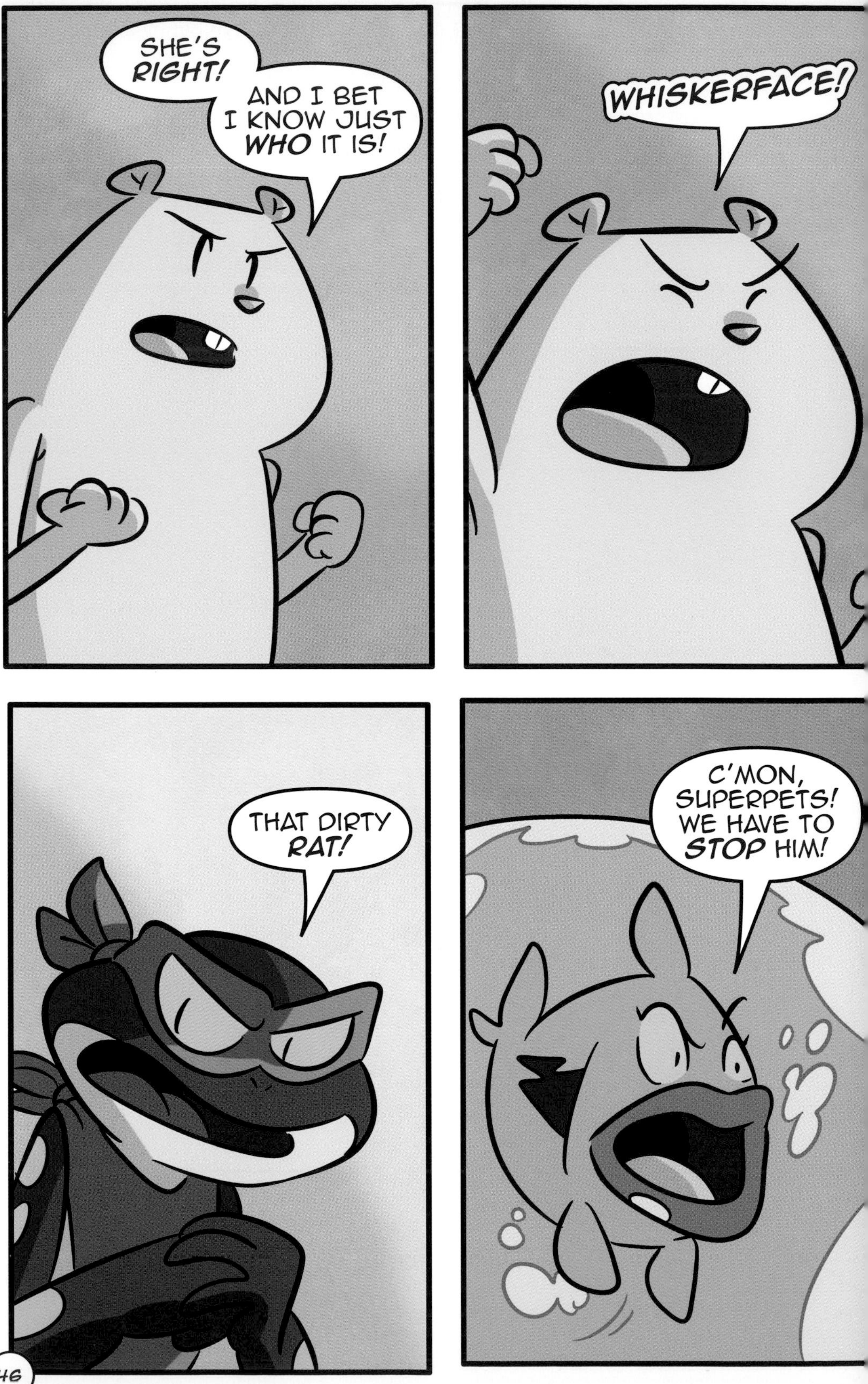

SHE'S RIGHT!
AND I BET I KNOW JUST WHO IT IS!
WHISKERFACE!
THAT DIRTY RAT!
C'MON, SUPERPETS! WE HAVE TO STOP HIM!

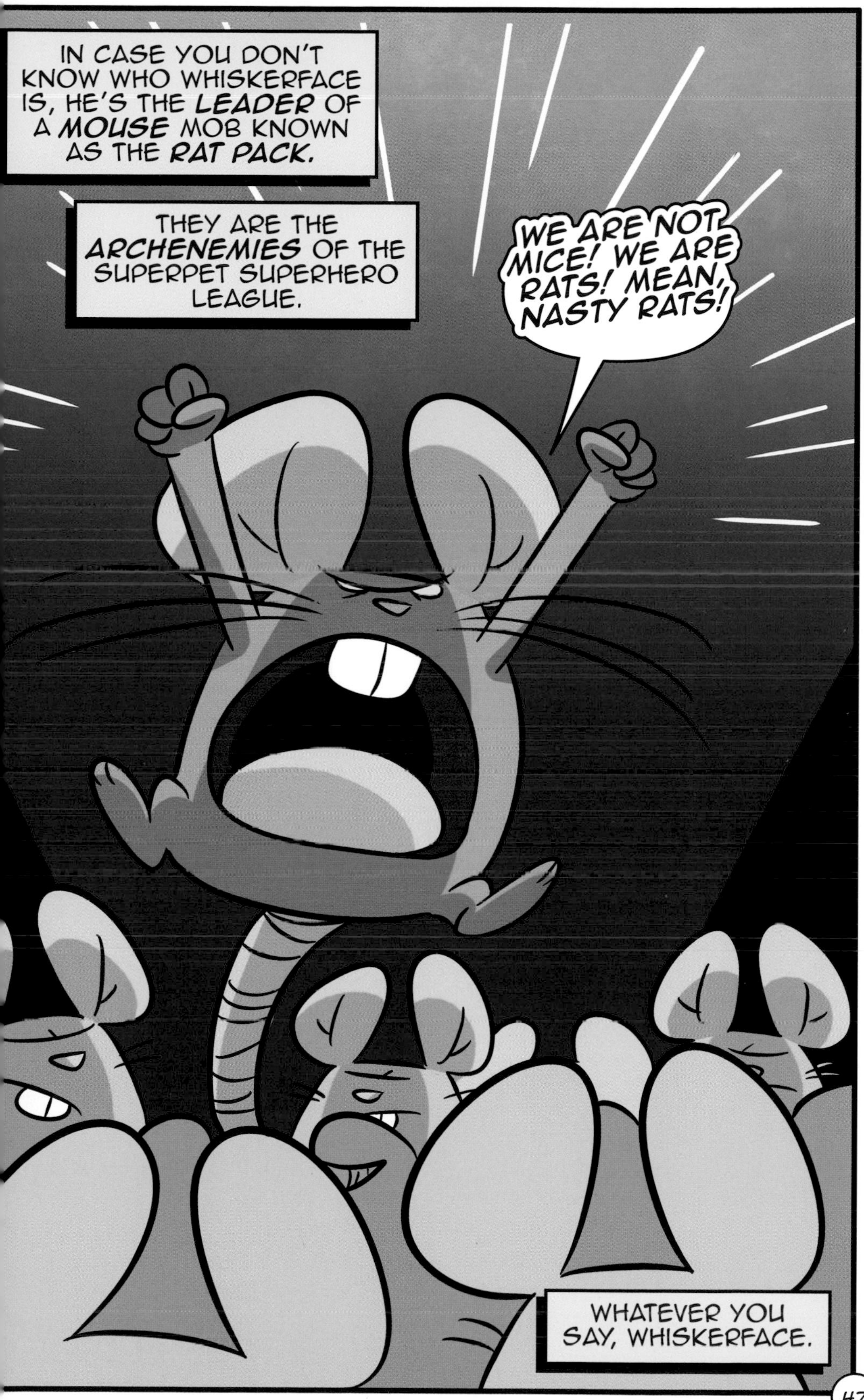
IN CASE YOU DON'T KNOW WHO WHISKERFACE IS, HE'S THE LEADER OF A MOUSE MOB KNOWN AS THE RAT PACK.
THEY ARE THE ARCHENEMIES OF THE SUPERPET SUPERHERO LEAGUE.
WE ARE NOT MICE! WE ARE RATS! MEAN, NASTY RATS!
WHATEVER YOU SAY, WHISKERFACE.

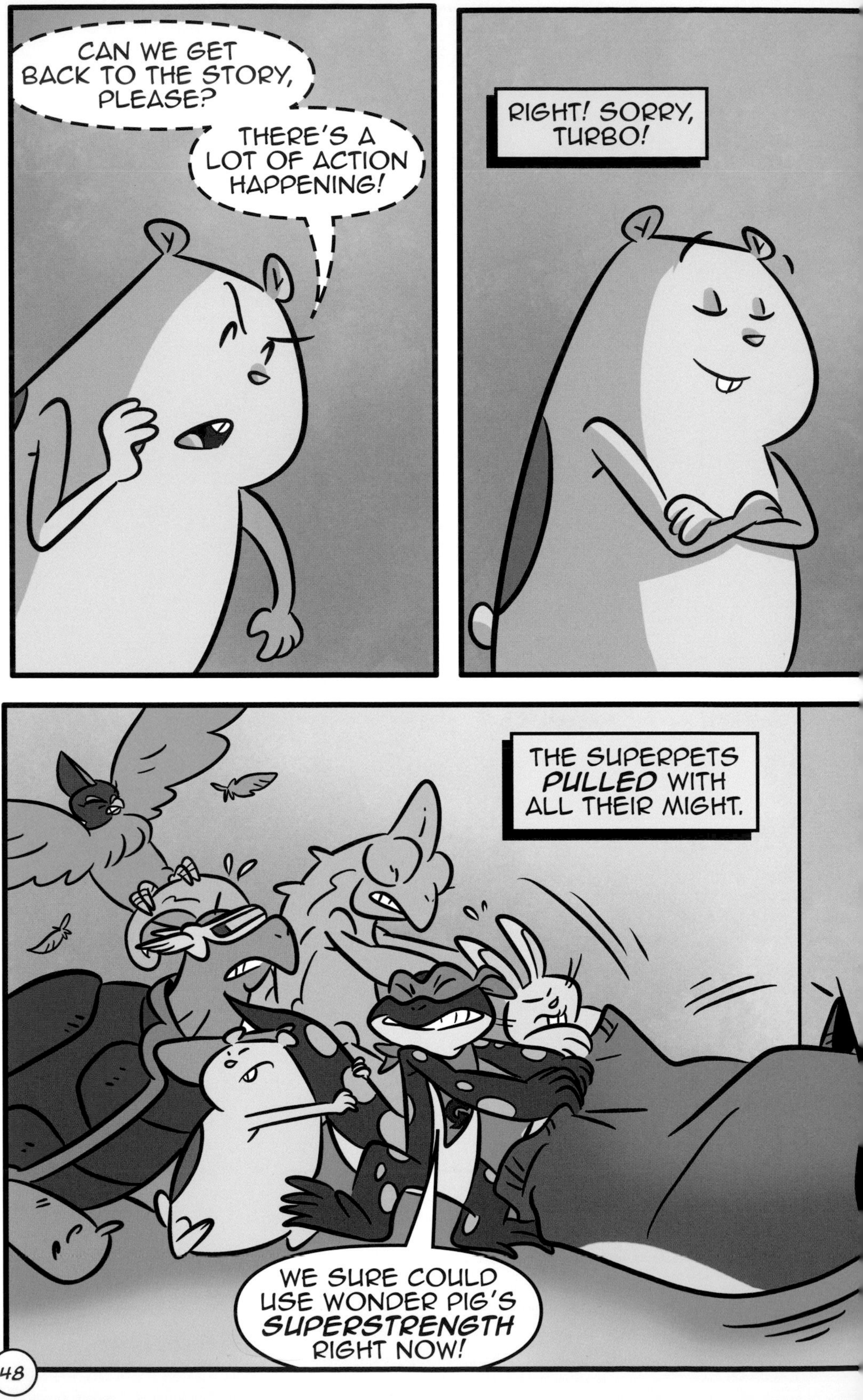
CAN WE GET BACK TO THE STORY, PLEASE?
THERE'S A LOT OF ACTION HAPPENING!
RIGHT! SORRY, TURBO!
THE SUPERPETS PULLED WITH ALL THEIR MIGHT.
WE SURE COULD USE WONDER PIG'S SUPERSTRENGTH RIGHT NOW!

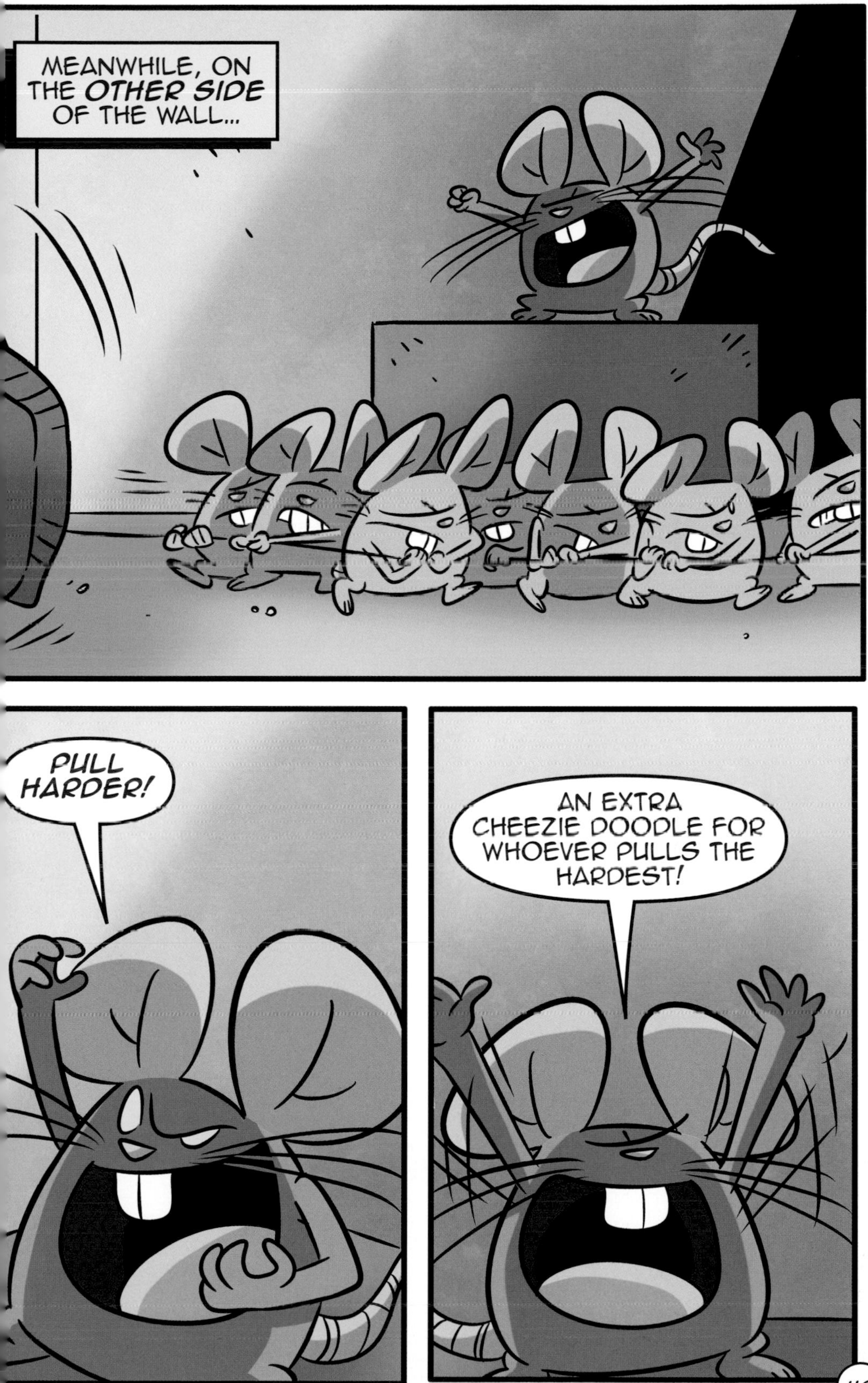
MEANWHILE, ON THE *OTHER SIDE* OF THE WALL...
PULL HARDER!
AN EXTRA CHEEZIE DOODLE FOR WHOEVER PULLS THE HARDEST!

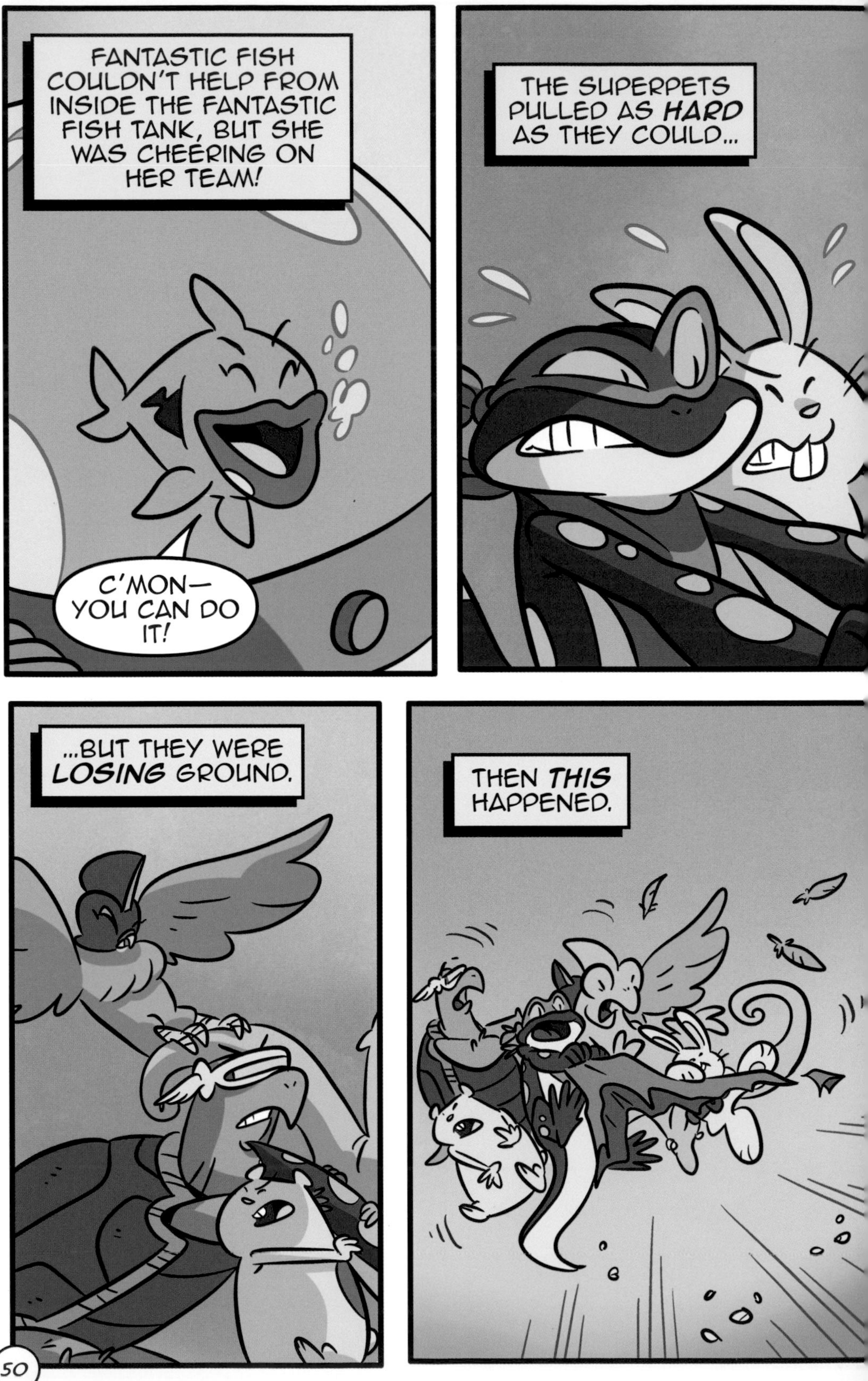
FANTASTIC FISH COULDN'T HELP FROM INSIDE THE FANTASTIC FISH TANK, BUT SHE WAS CHEERING ON HER TEAM!
C'MON— YOU CAN DO IT!
THE SUPERPETS PULLED AS HARD AS THEY COULD...
...BUT THEY WERE LOSING GROUND.
THEN THIS HAPPENED.

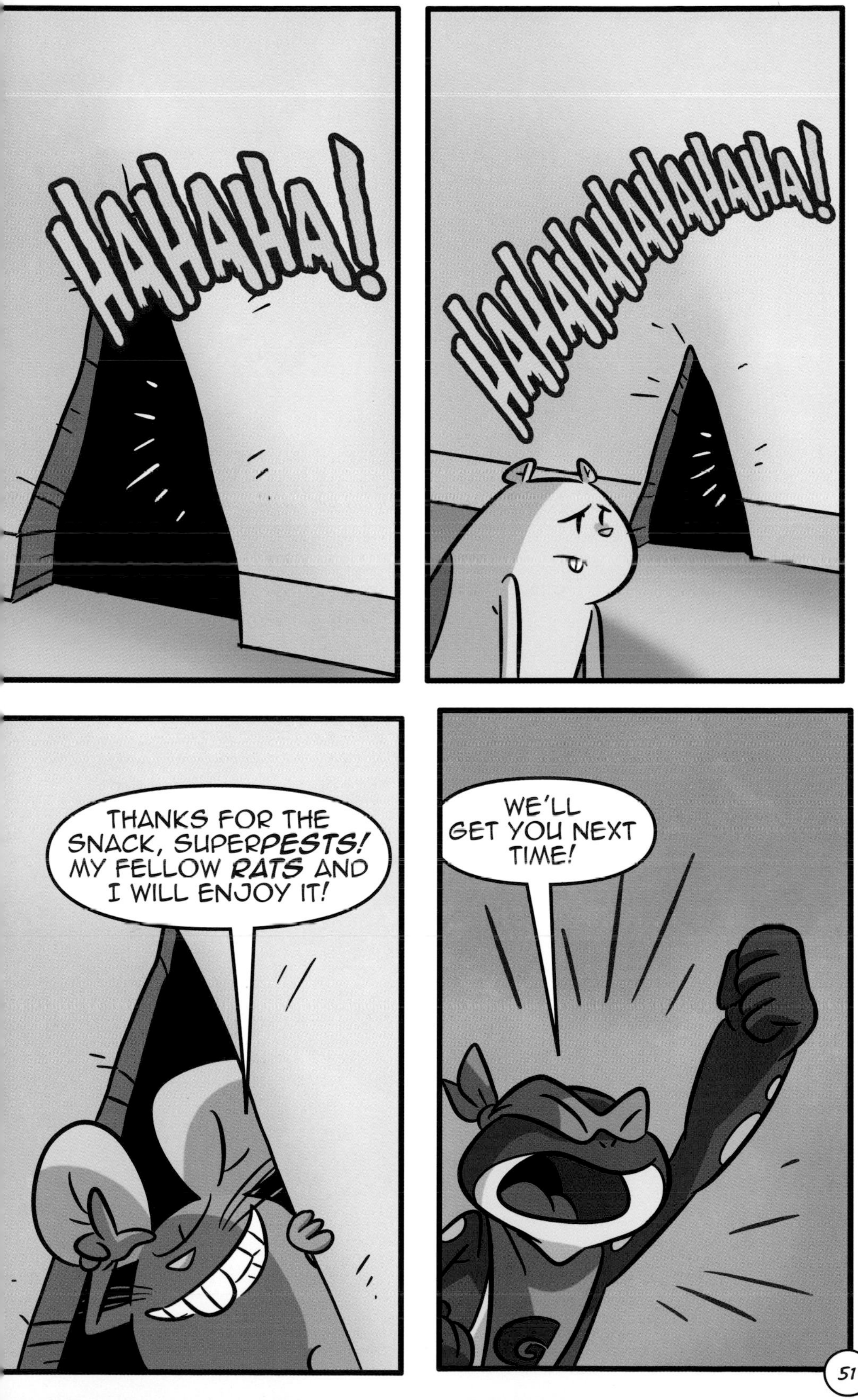
HAHAHA!
HAHAHAHAHAHAHA!
THANKS FOR THE SNACK, SUPERPESTS! MY FELLOW RATS AND I WILL ENJOY IT!
WE'LL GET YOU NEXT TIME!

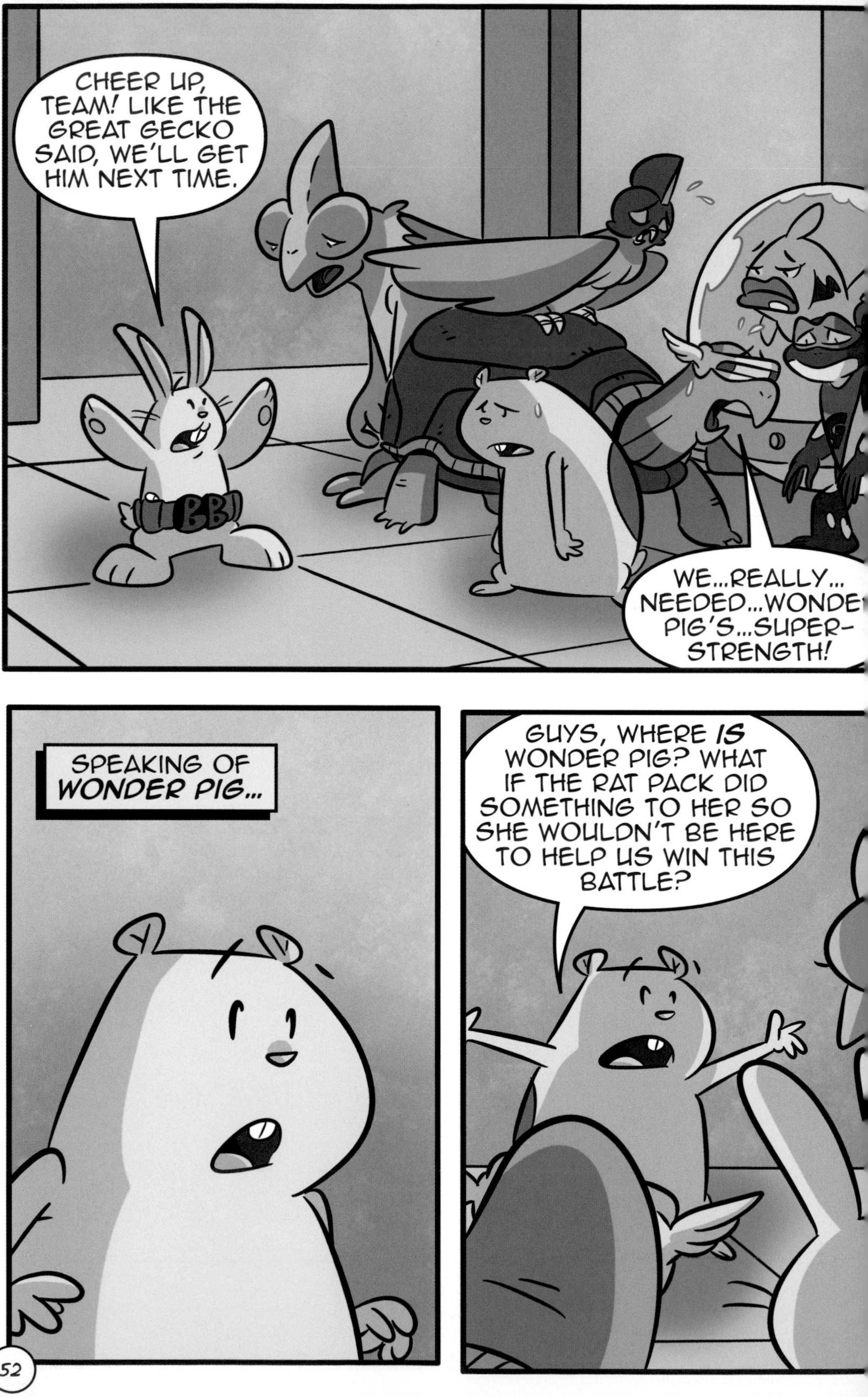
CHEER UP, TEAM! LIKE THE GREAT GECKO SAID, WE'LL GET HIM NEXT TIME.
WE...REALLY... NEEDED...WONDE PIG'S...SUPER-STRENGTH!
SPEAKING OF *WONDER PIG*...
GUYS, WHERE *IS* WONDER PIG? WHAT IF THE RAT PACK DID SOMETHING TO HER SO SHE WOULDN'T BE HERE TO HELP US WIN THIS BATTLE?

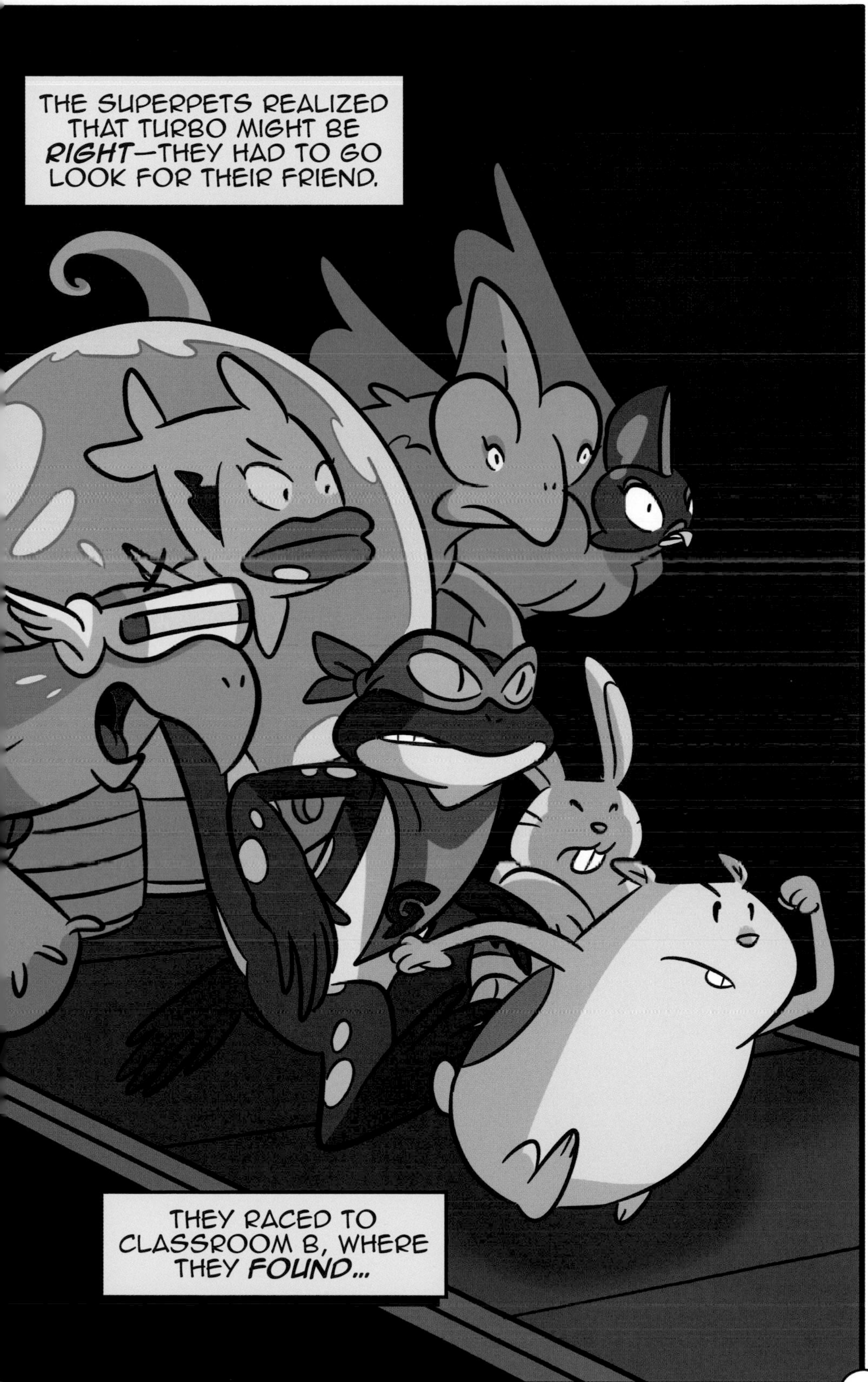
THE SUPERPETS REALIZED THAT TURBO MIGHT BE *RIGHT*—THEY HAD TO GO LOOK FOR THEIR FRIEND.
THEY RACED TO CLASSROOM B, WHERE THEY ***FOUND...***

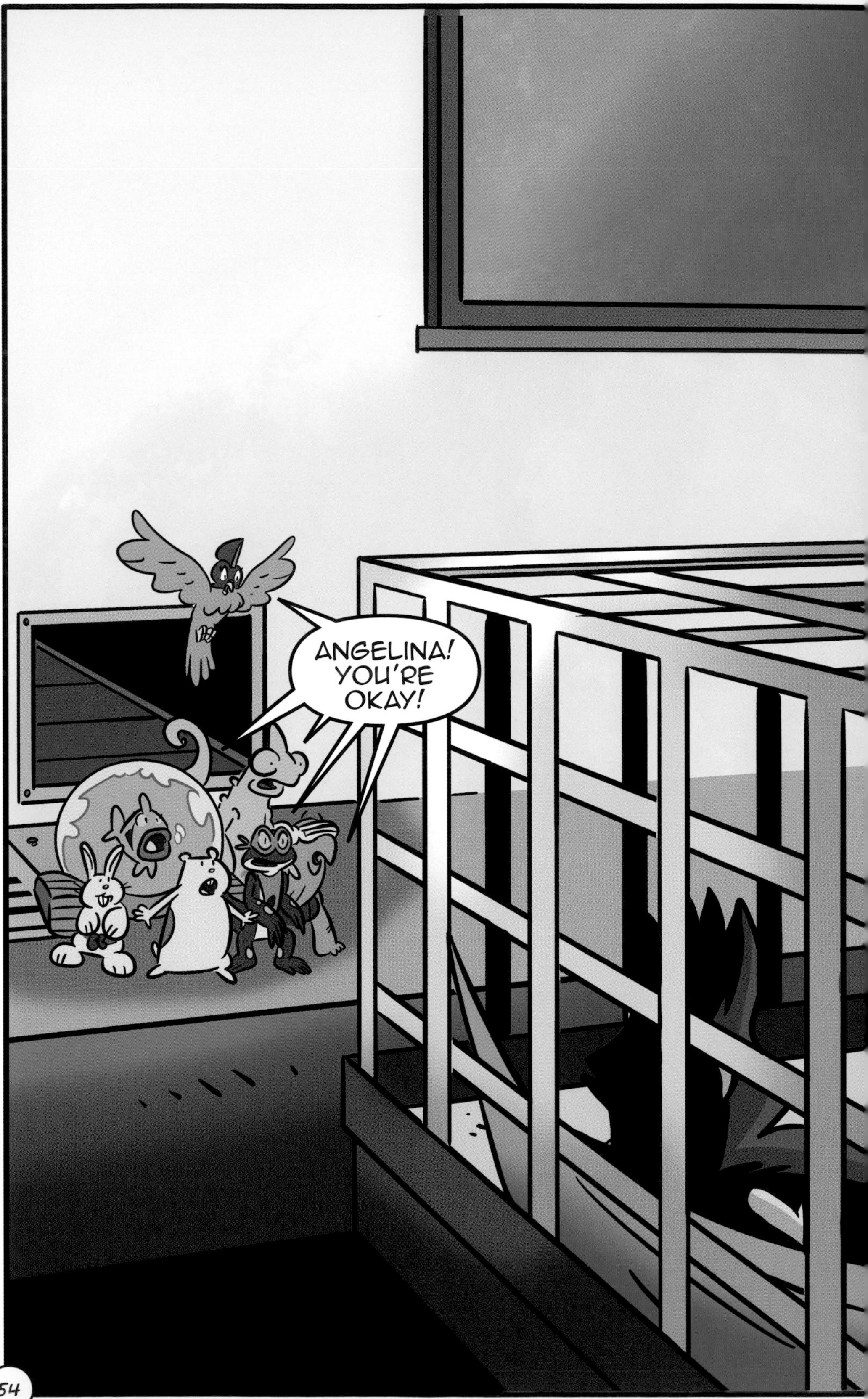
ANGELINA! YOU'RE OKAY!

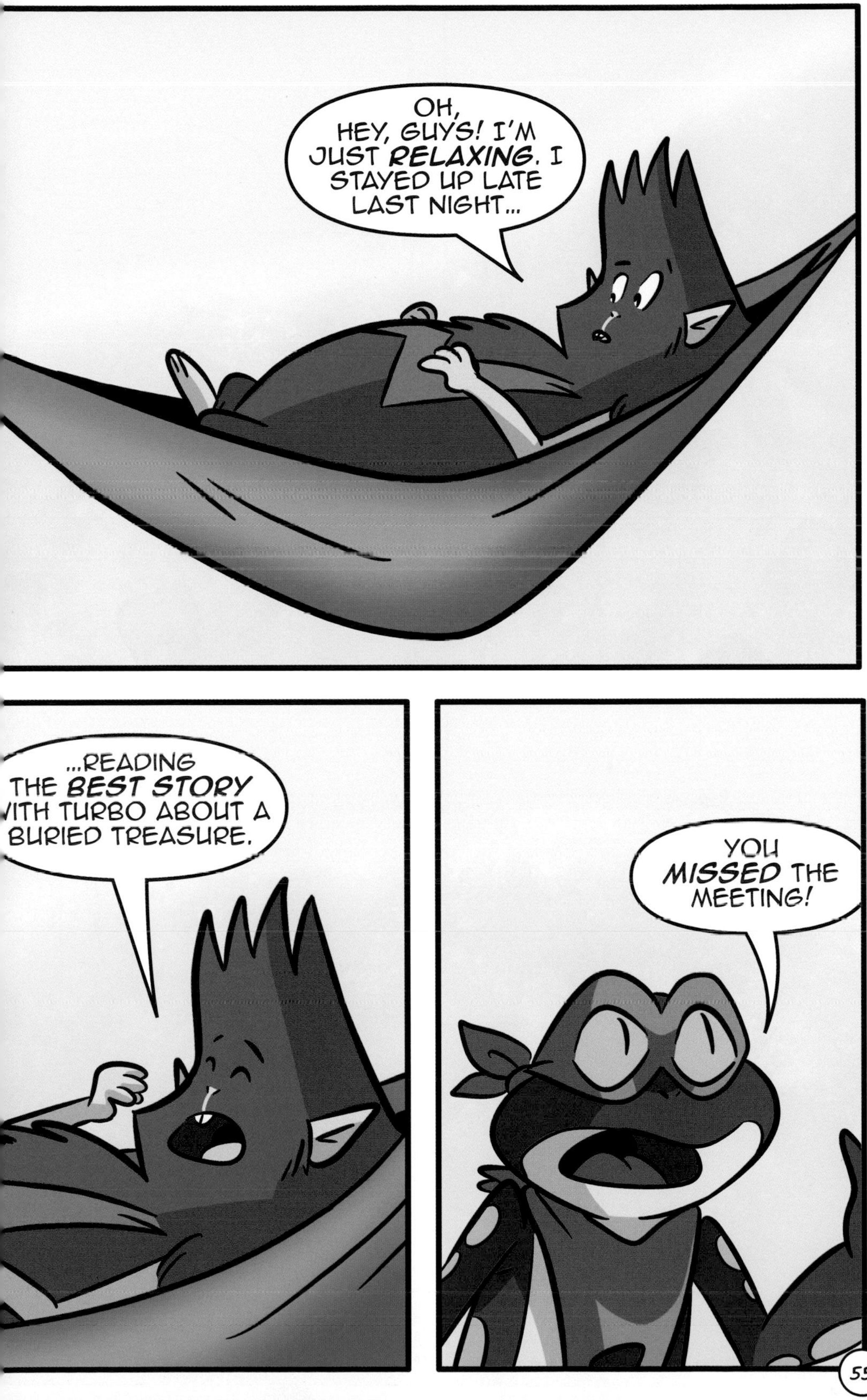
OH, HEY, GUYS! I'M JUST *RELAXING*. I STAYED UP LATE LAST NIGHT...
...READING THE *BEST STORY* WITH TURBO ABOUT A BURIED TREASURE.
YOU *MISSED* THE MEETING!

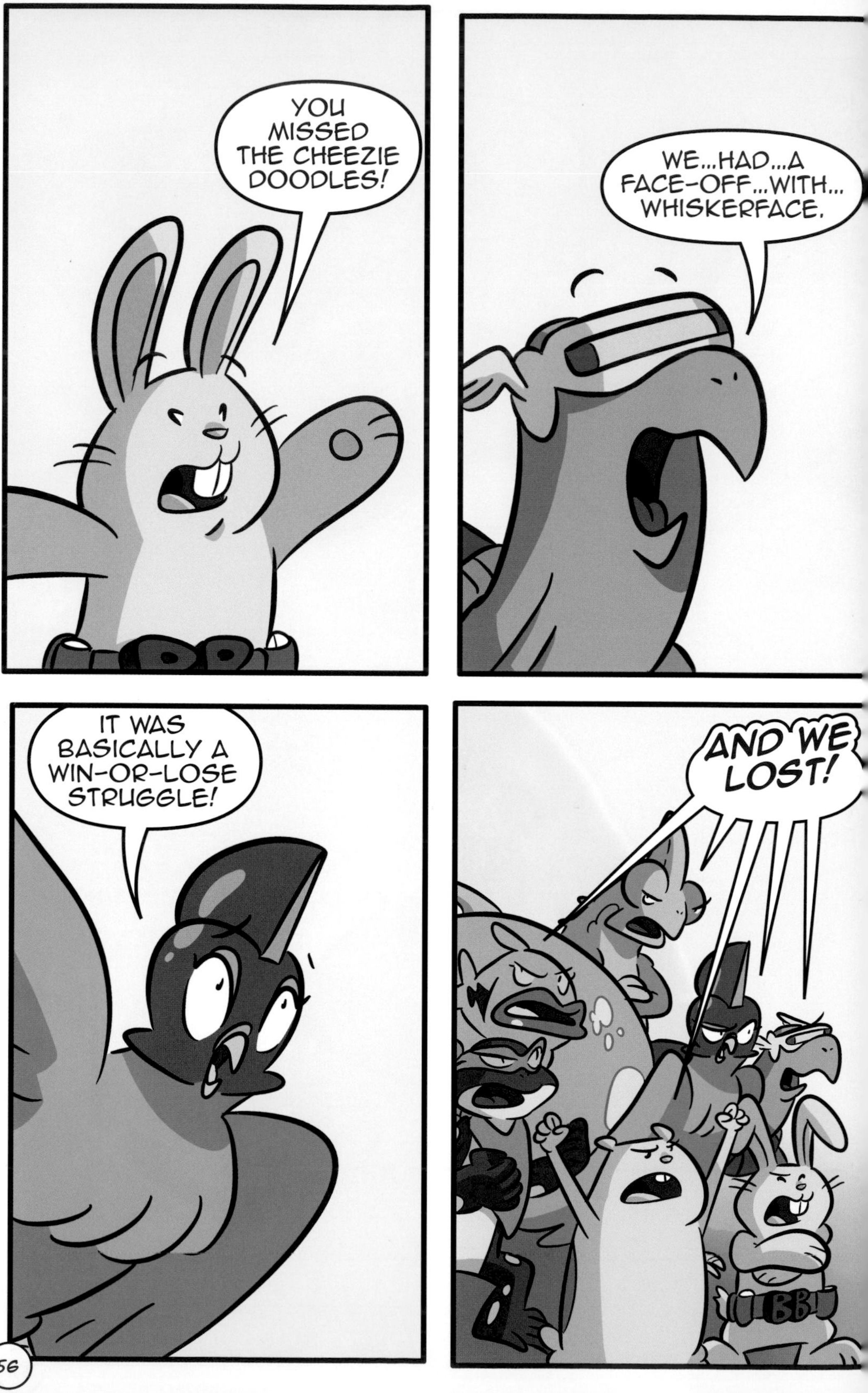
YOU MISSED THE CHEEZIE DOODLES!
WE...HAD...A FACE-OFF...WITH... WHISKERFACE.
IT WAS BASICALLY A WIN-OR-LOSE STRUGGLE!
AND WE LOST!
BB

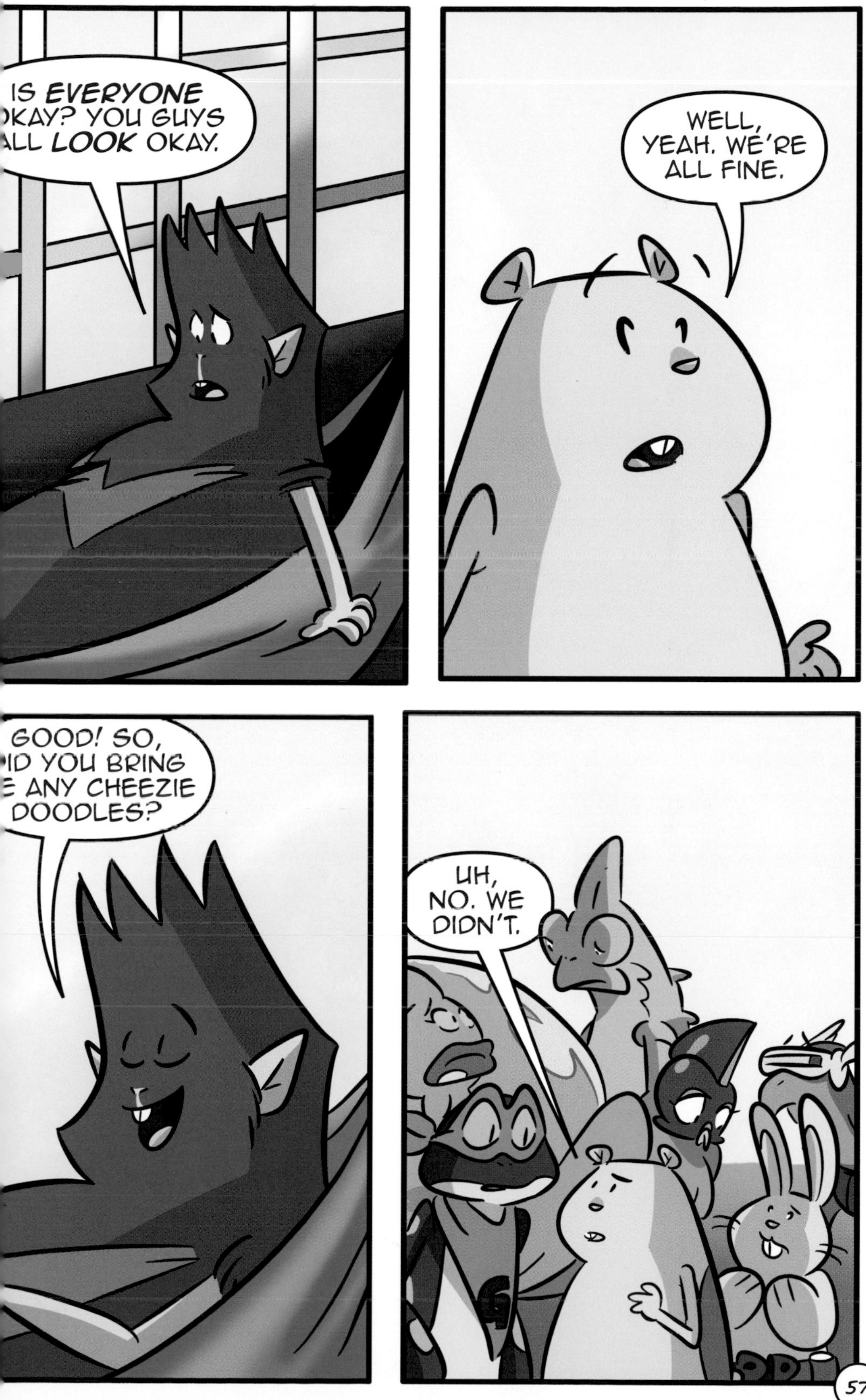
IS EVERYONE
KAY? YOU GUYS
LL LOOK OKAY.
WELL, YEAH. WE'RE ALL FINE.
GOOD! SO,
ID YOU BRING
E ANY CHEEZIE
DOODLES?
UH, NO. WE DIDN'T.

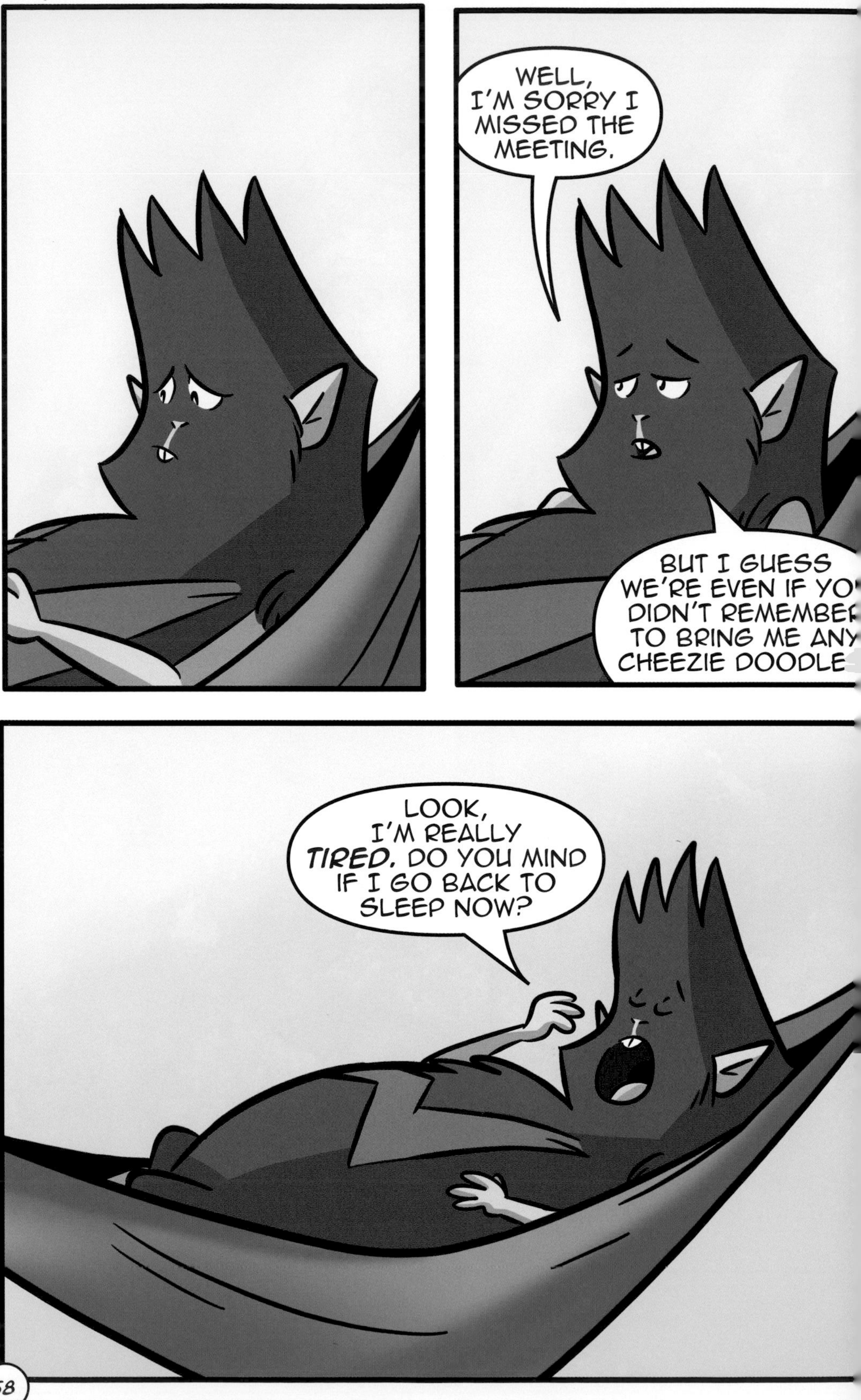
WELL, I'M SORRY I MISSED THE MEETING.
BUT I GUESS WE'RE EVEN IF YO DIDN'T REMEMBER TO BRING ME ANY CHEEZIE DOODLE
LOOK, I'M REALLY *TIRED.* DO YOU MIND IF I GO BACK TO SLEEP NOW?

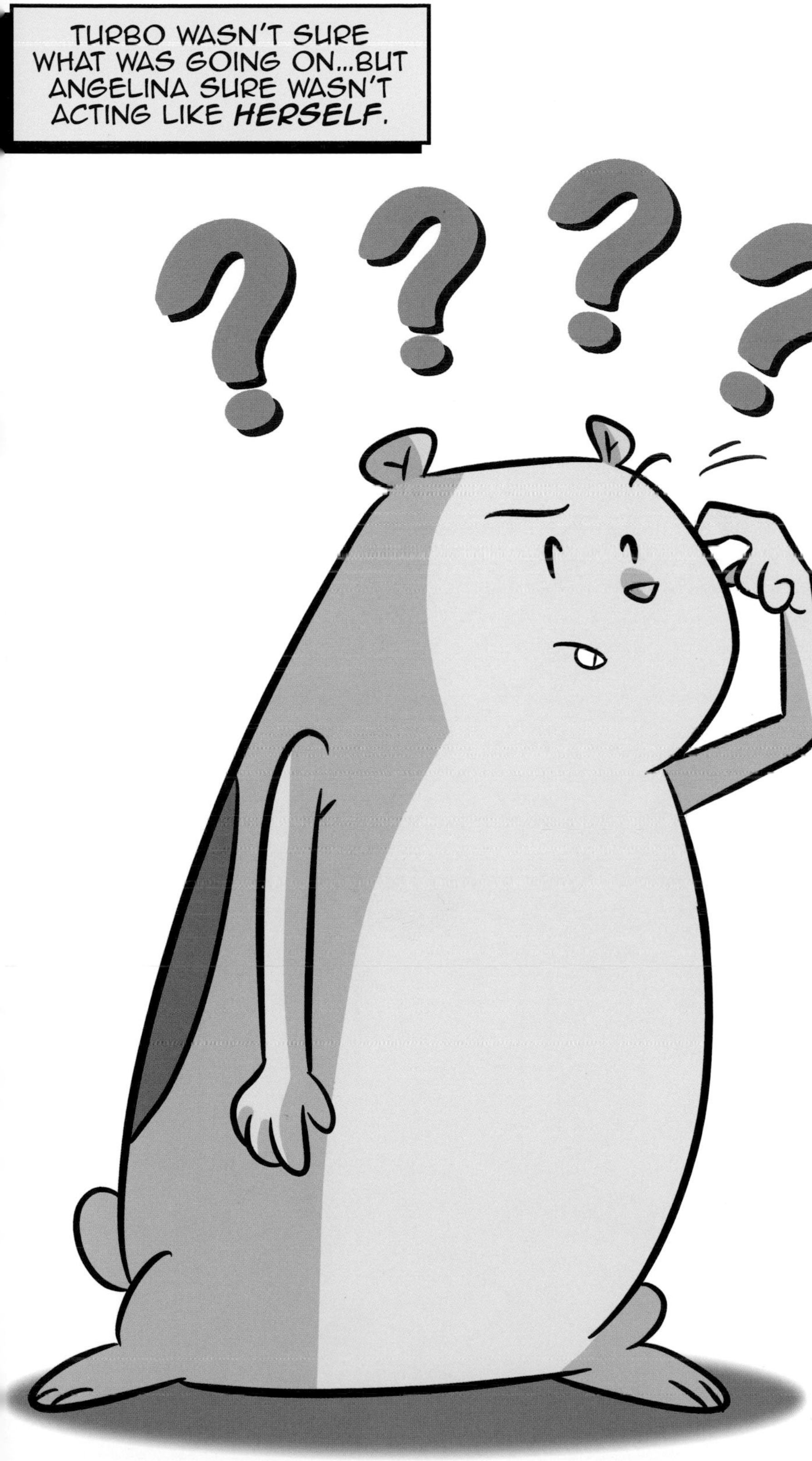
TURBO WASN'T SURE WHAT WAS GOING ON...BUT ANGELINA SURE WASN'T ACTING LIKE *HERSELF*.

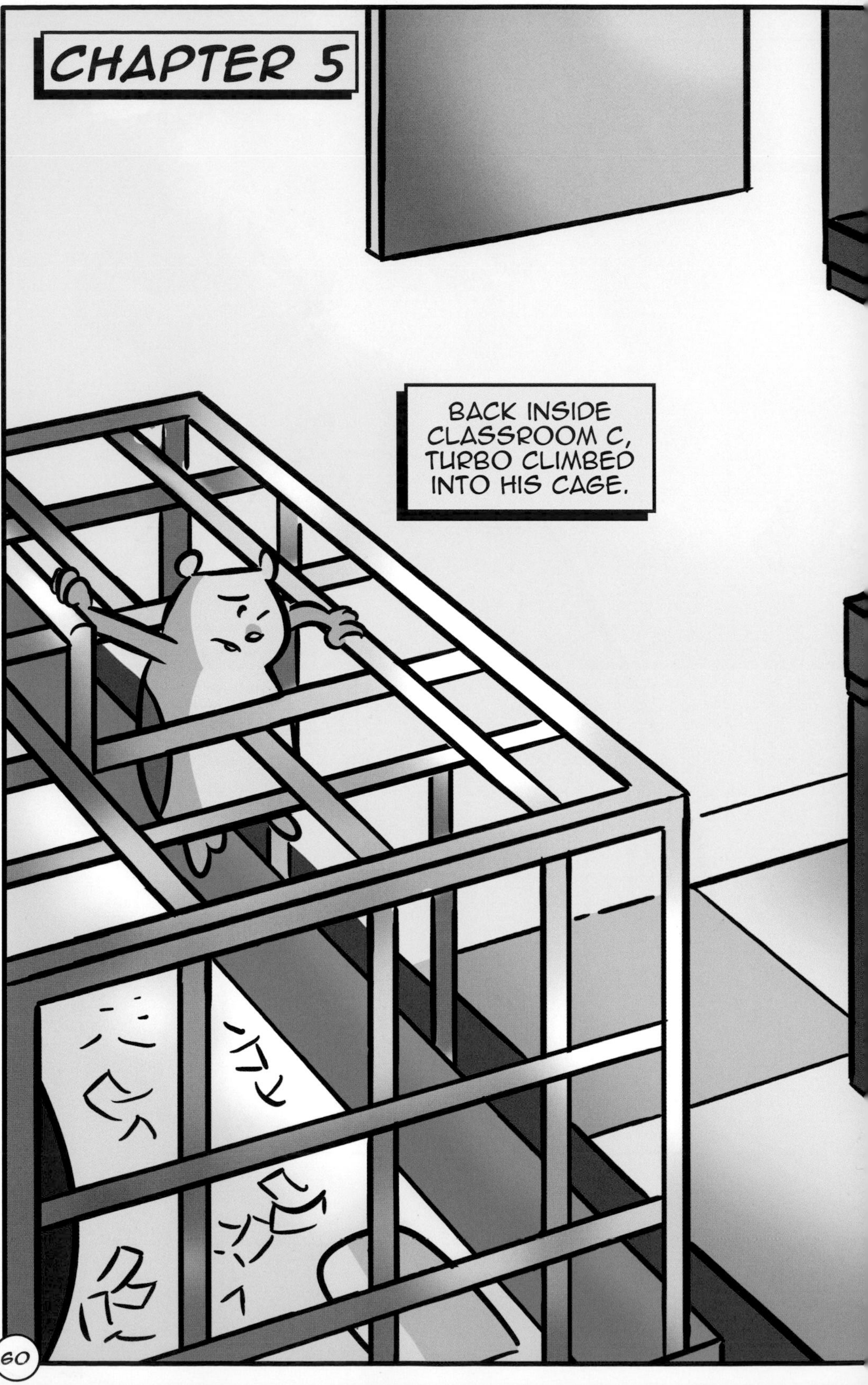
CHAPTER 5
BACK INSIDE CLASSROOM C, TURBO CLIMBED INTO HIS CAGE.

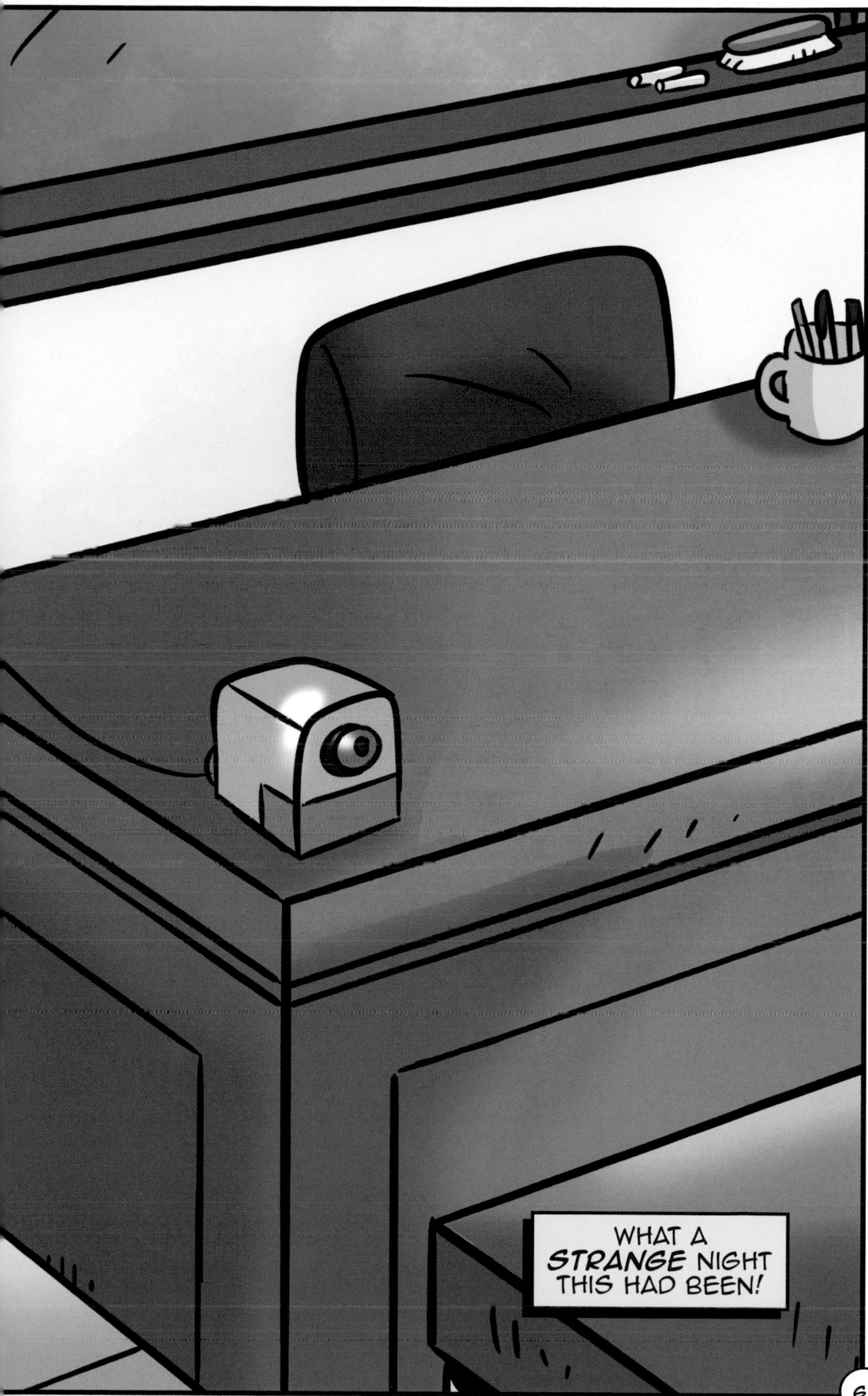
WHAT A STRANGE NIGHT THIS HAD BEEN!

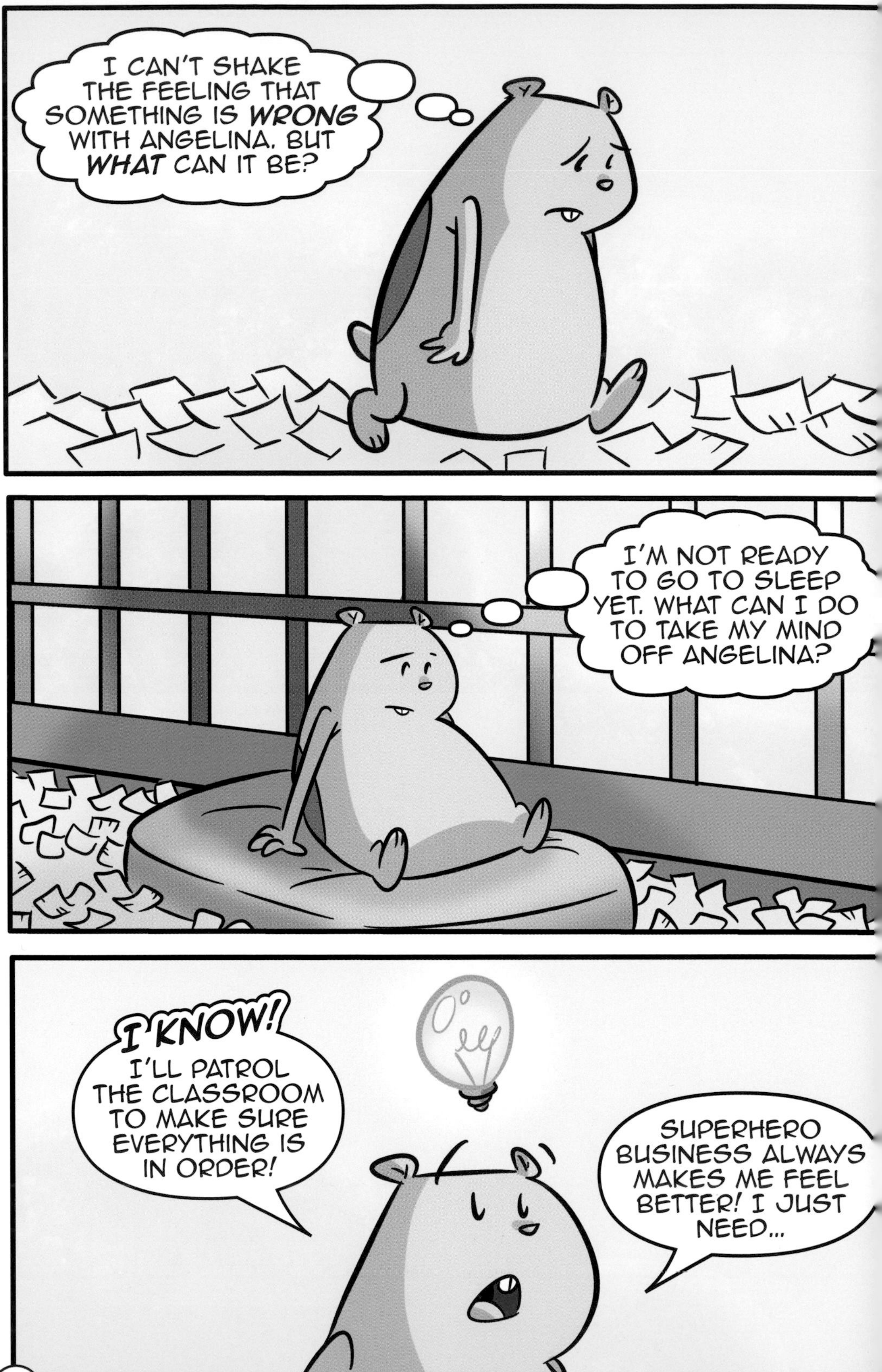
I CAN'T SHAKE THE FEELING THAT SOMETHING IS WRONG WITH ANGELINA. BUT WHAT CAN IT BE?
I'M NOT READY TO GO TO SLEEP YET. WHAT CAN I DO TO TAKE MY MIND OFF ANGELINA?
I KNOW! I'LL PATROL THE CLASSROOM TO MAKE SURE EVERYTHING IS IN ORDER!
SUPERHERO BUSINESS ALWAYS MAKES ME FEEL BETTER! I JUST NEED...

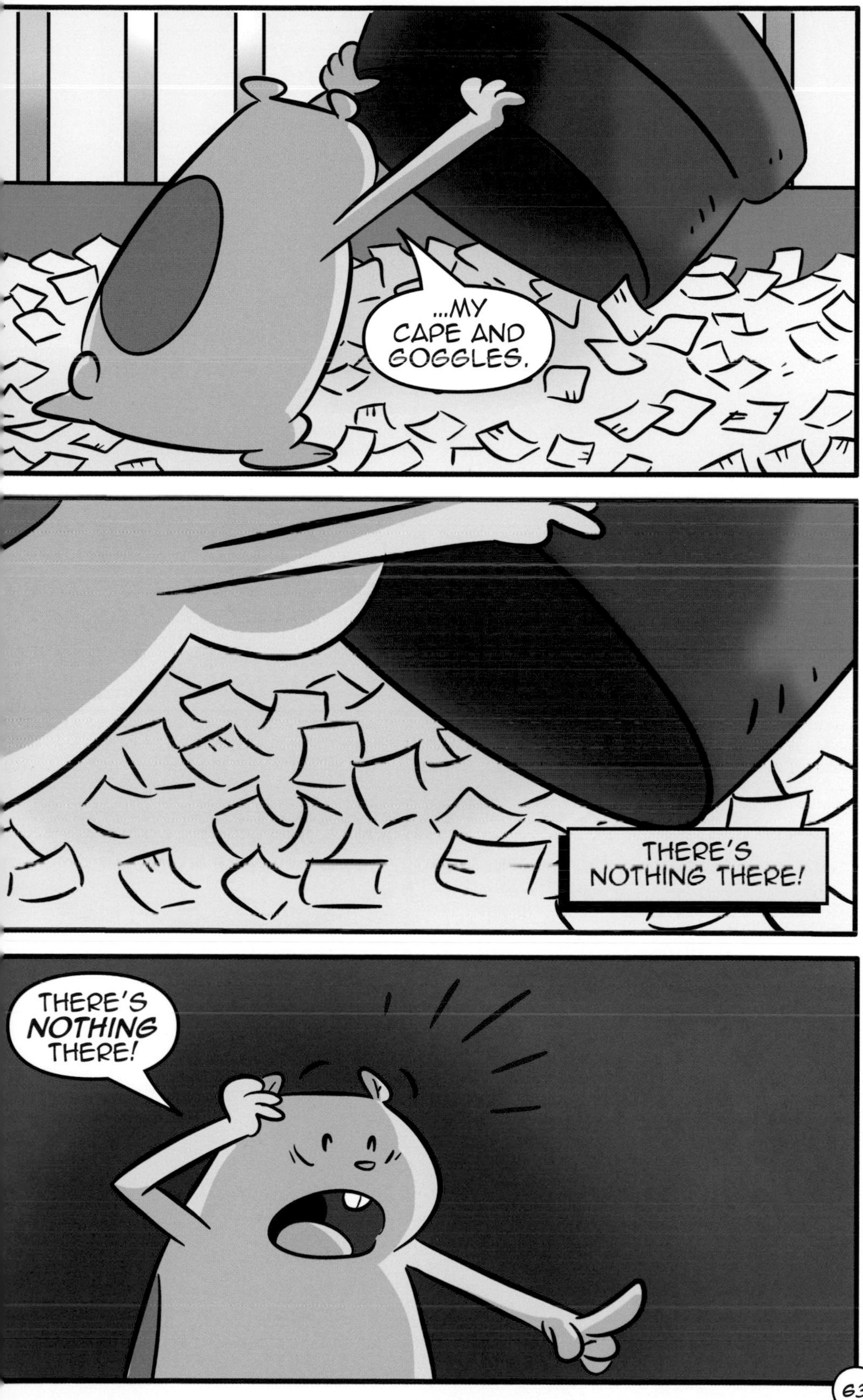

...MY CAPE AND GOGGLES.
THERE'S NOTHING THERE!
THERE'S NOTHING THERE!

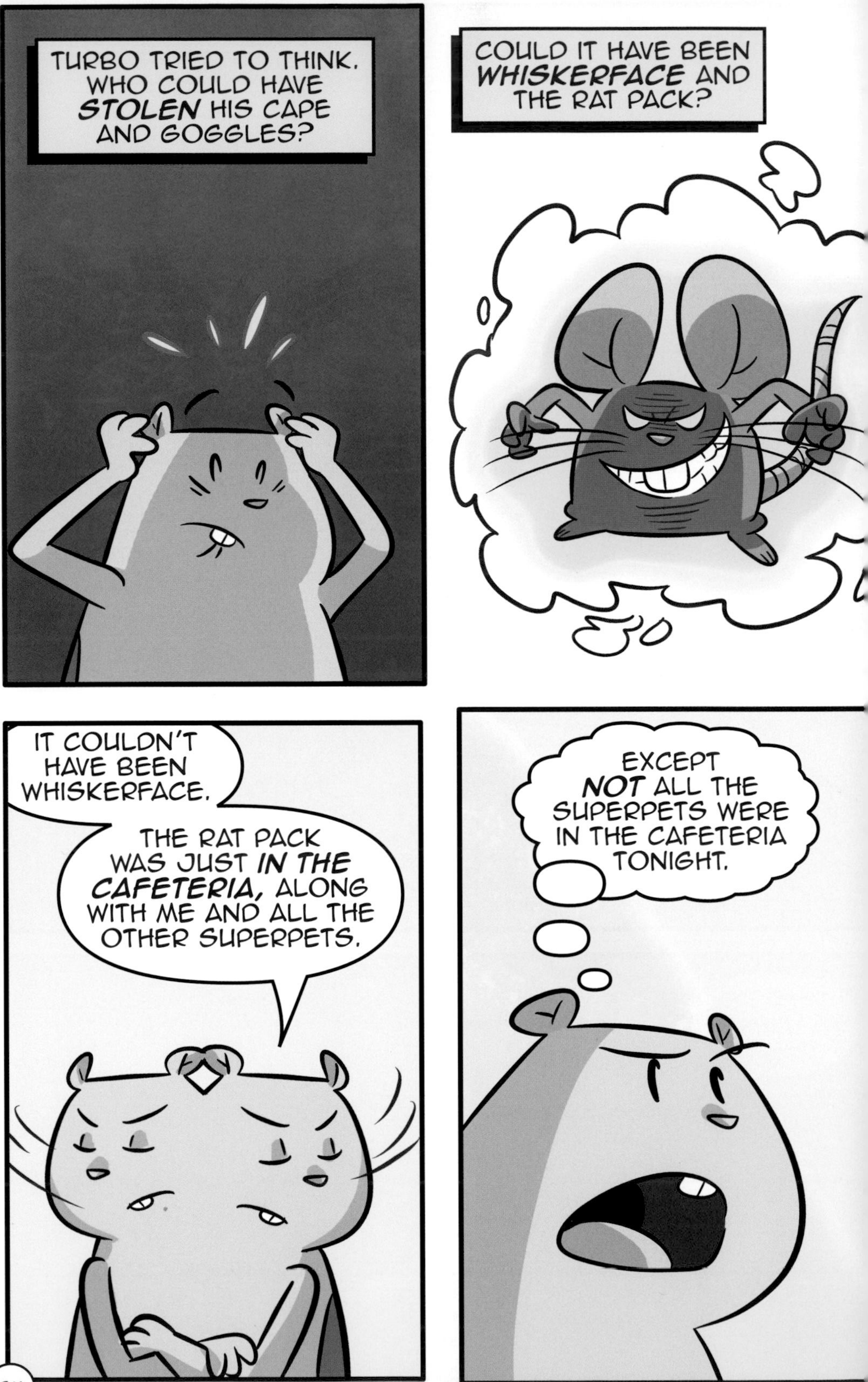
TURBO TRIED TO THINK. WHO COULD HAVE *STOLEN* HIS CAPE AND GOGGLES?
COULD IT HAVE BEEN *WHISKERFACE* AND THE RAT PACK?
IT COULDN'T HAVE BEEN WHISKERFACE.
THE RAT PACK WAS JUST *IN THE CAFETERIA,* ALONG WITH ME AND ALL THE OTHER SUPERPETS.
EXCEPT *NOT* ALL THE SUPERPETS WERE IN THE CAFETERIA TONIGHT.

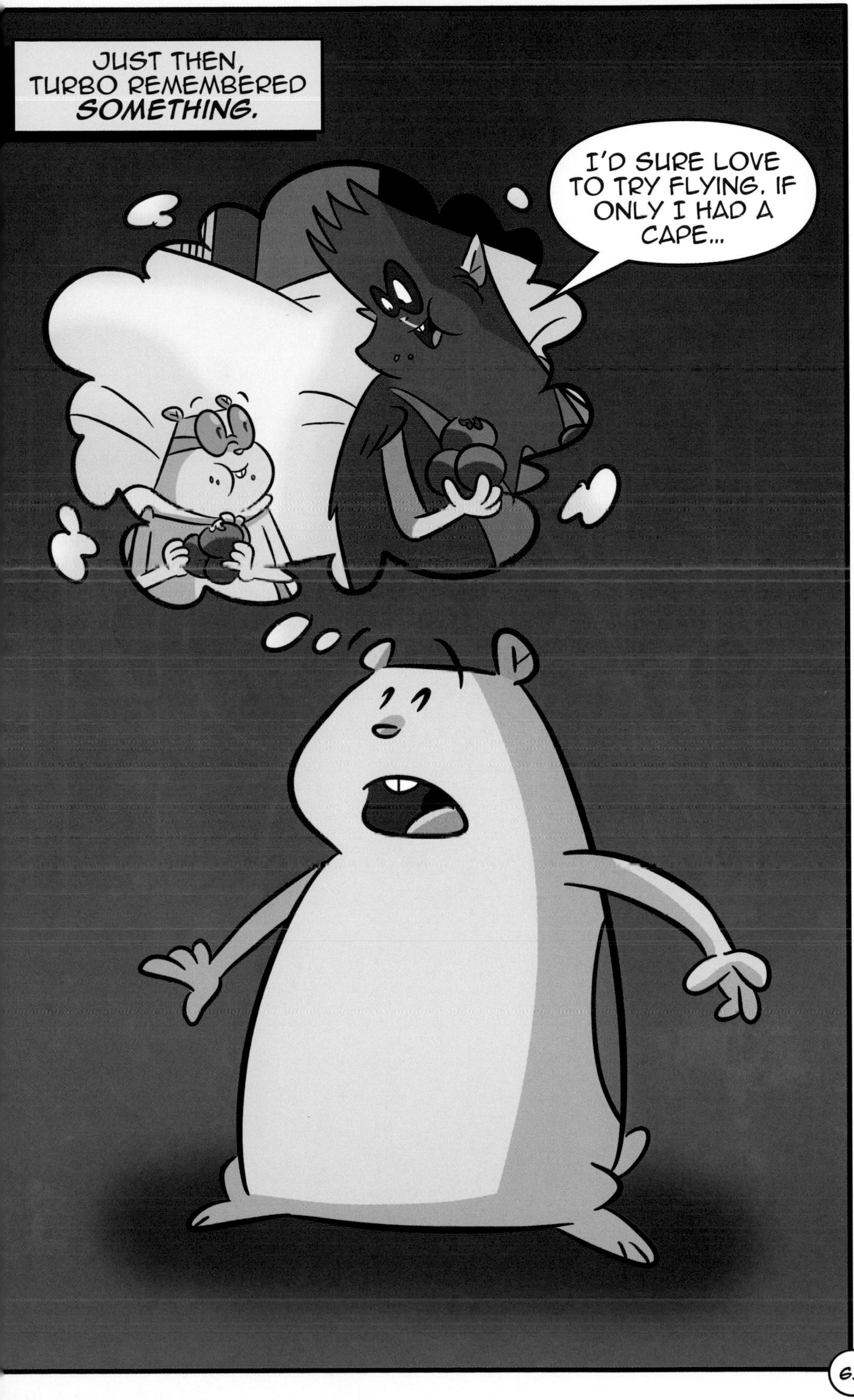
JUST THEN, TURBO REMEMBERED *SOMETHING.*
I'D SURE LOVE TO TRY FLYING. IF ONLY I HAD A CAPE...

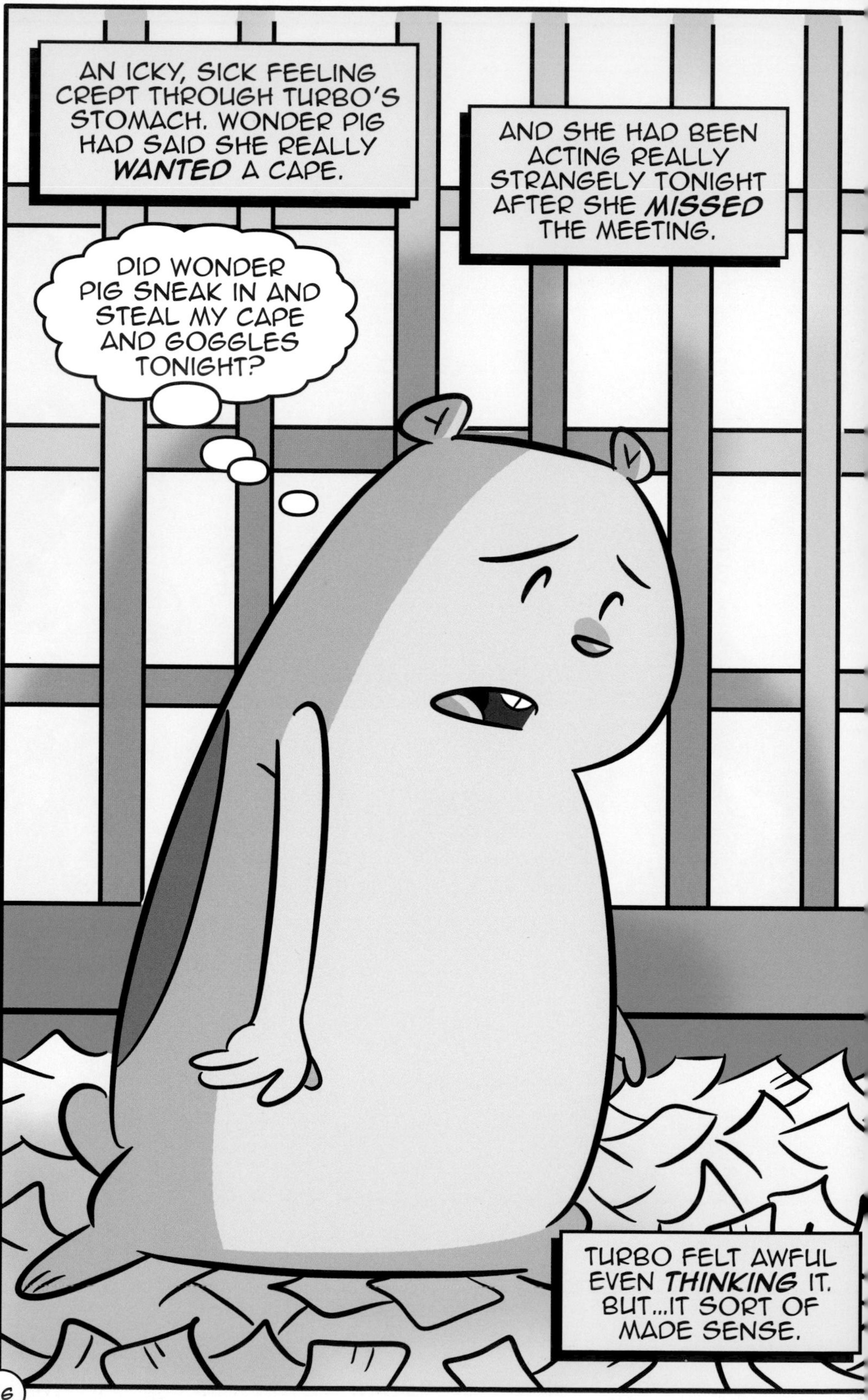

AN ICKY, SICK FEELING CREPT THROUGH TURBO'S STOMACH. WONDER PIG HAD SAID SHE REALLY *WANTED* A CAPE.
AND SHE HAD BEEN ACTING REALLY STRANGELY TONIGHT AFTER SHE *MISSED* THE MEETING.
DID WONDER PIG SNEAK IN AND STEAL MY CAPE AND GOGGLES TONIGHT?
TURBO FELT AWFUL EVEN *THINKING* IT. BUT...IT SORT OF MADE SENSE.

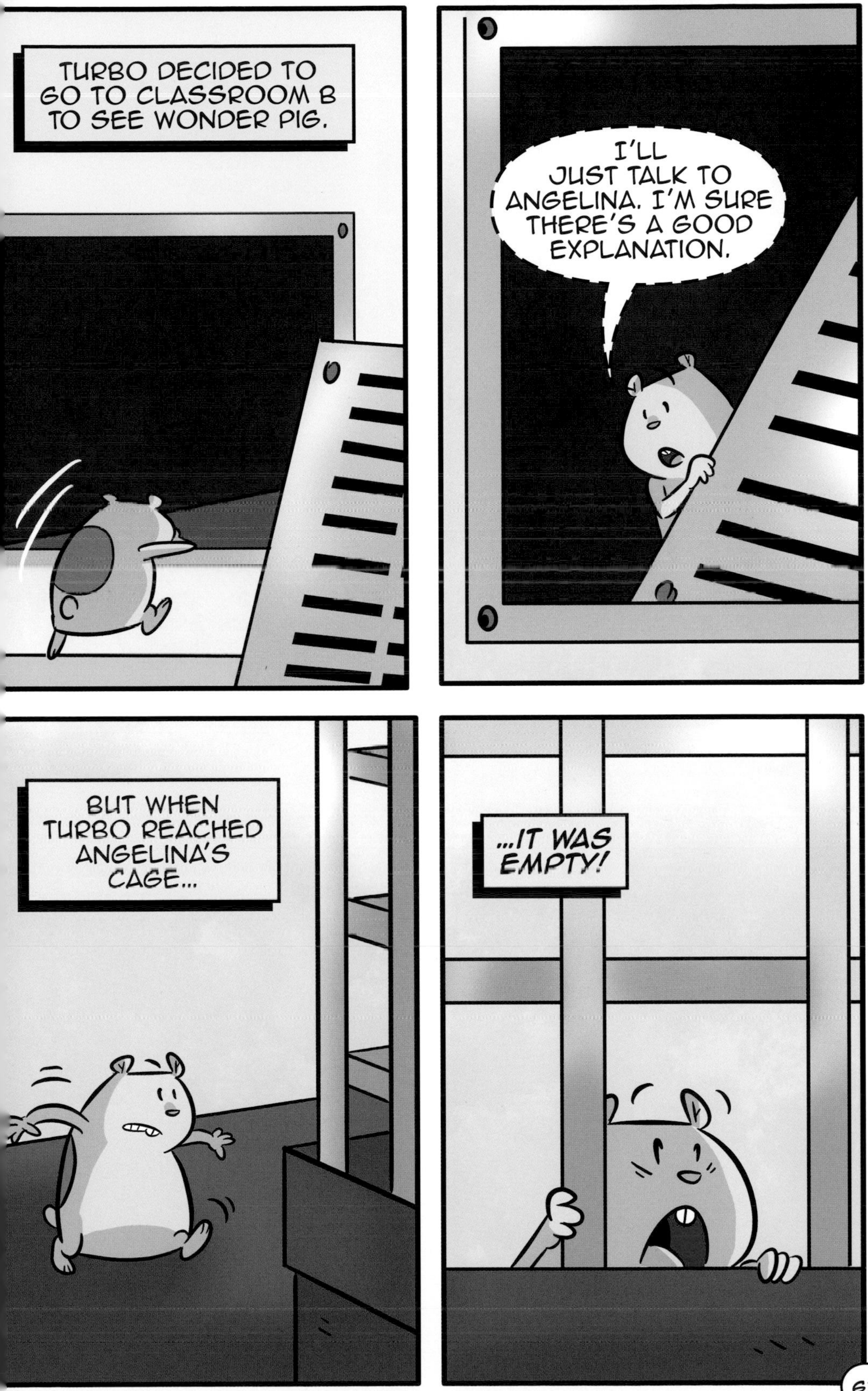

TURBO DECIDED TO GO TO CLASSROOM B TO SEE WONDER PIG.
I'LL JUST TALK TO ANGELINA. I'M SURE THERE'S A GOOD EXPLANATION.
BUT WHEN TURBO REACHED ANGELINA'S CAGE...
...IT WAS EMPTY!

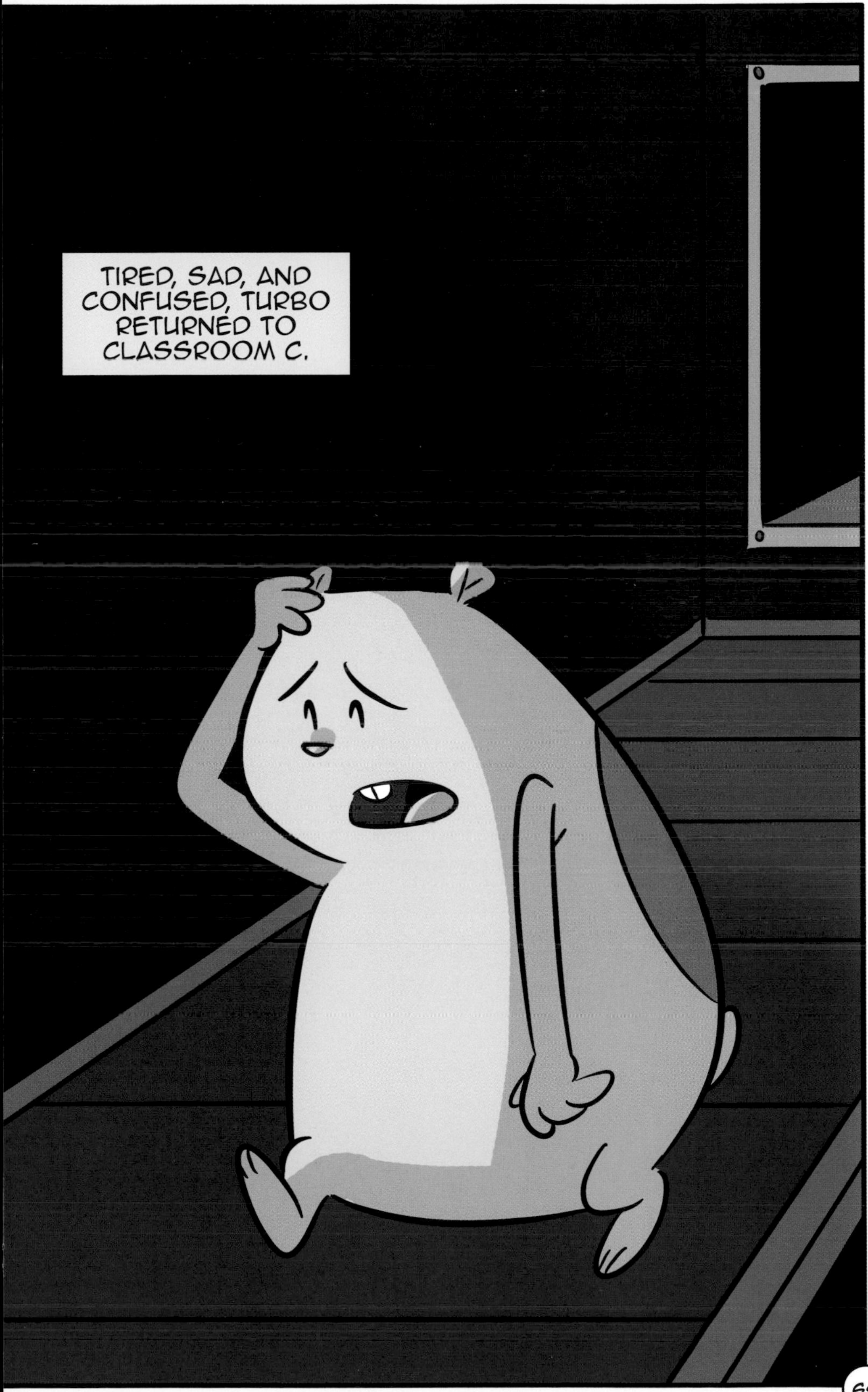
TIRED, SAD, AND CONFUSED, TURBO RETURNED TO CLASSROOM C.

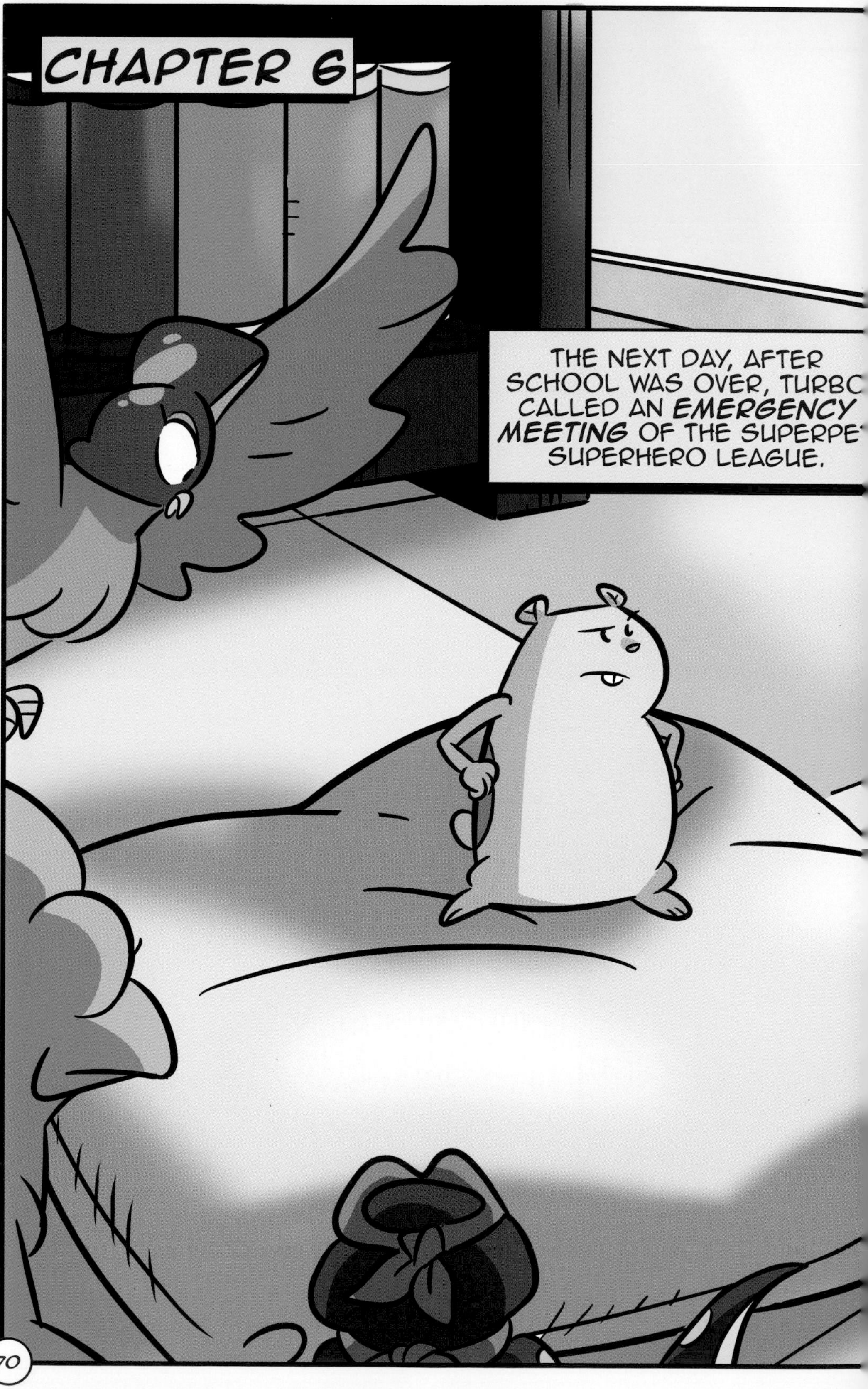
CHAPTER 6
THE NEXT DAY, AFTER SCHOOL WAS OVER, TURB CALLED AN *EMERGENCY MEETING* OF THE SUPERPE SUPERHERO LEAGUE.

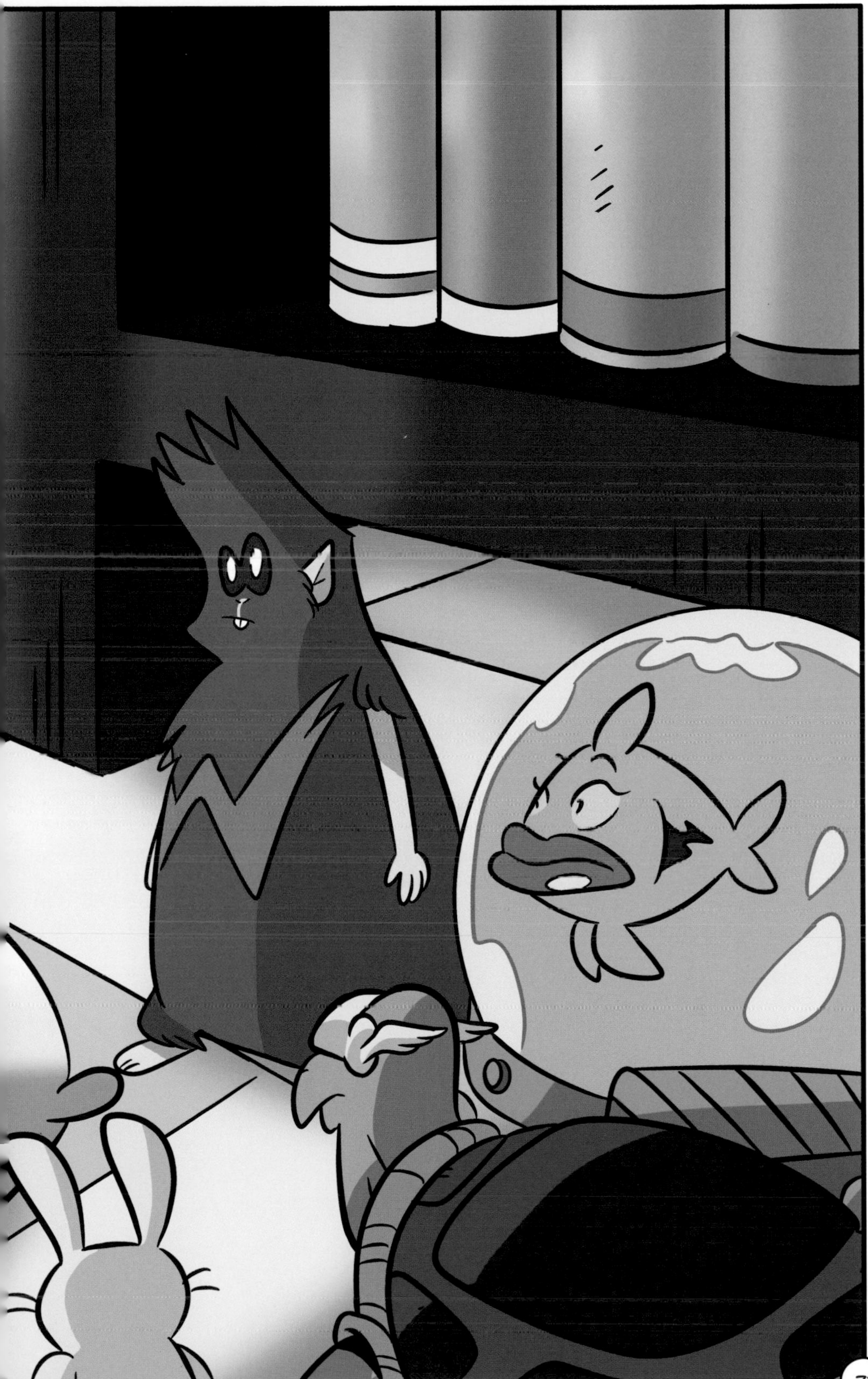

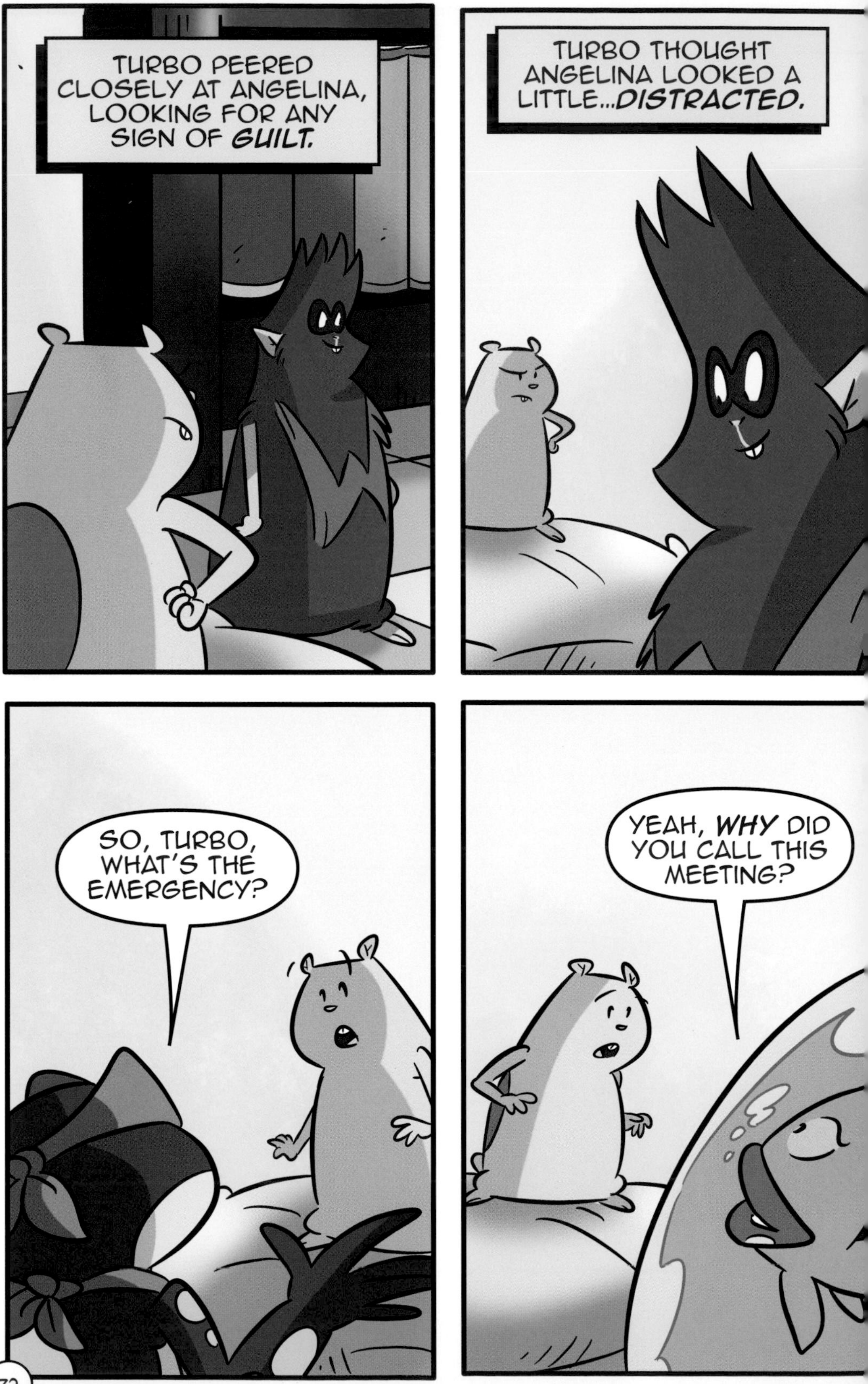
TURBO PEERED CLOSELY AT ANGELINA, LOOKING FOR ANY SIGN OF GUILT.
TURBO THOUGHT ANGELINA LOOKED A LITTLE...DISTRACTED.
SO, TURBO, WHAT'S THE EMERGENCY?
YEAH, WHY DID YOU CALL THIS MEETING?

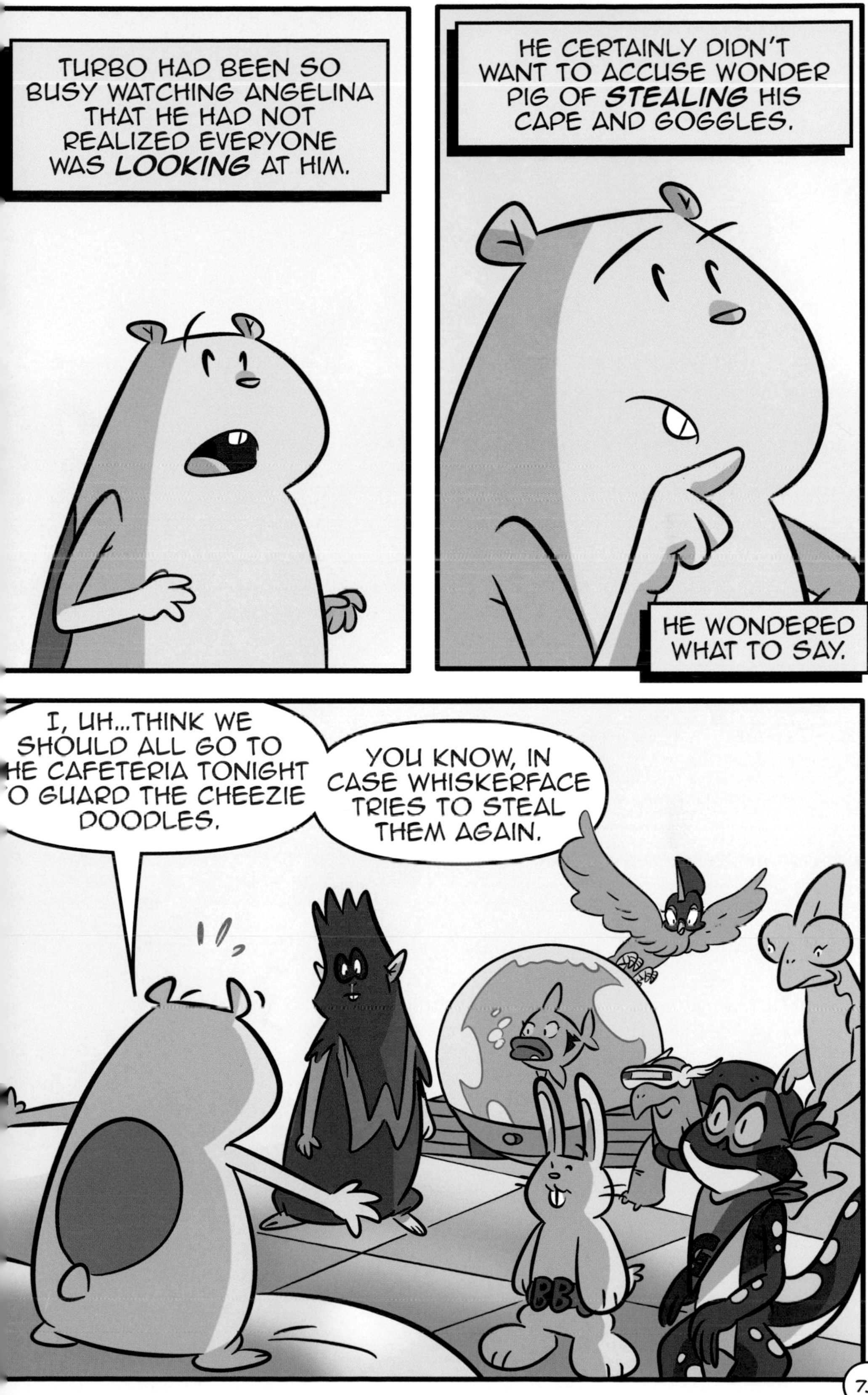
TURBO HAD BEEN SO BUSY WATCHING ANGELINA THAT HE HAD NOT REALIZED EVERYONE WAS ***LOOKING*** AT HIM.
HE CERTAINLY DIDN'T WANT TO ACCUSE WONDER PIG OF ***STEALING*** HIS CAPE AND GOGGLES.
HE WONDERED WHAT TO SAY.
I, UH...THINK WE SHOULD ALL GO TO HE CAFETERIA TONIGHT O GUARD THE CHEEZIE DOODLES.
YOU KNOW, IN CASE WHISKERFACE TRIES TO STEAL THEM AGAIN.
BB

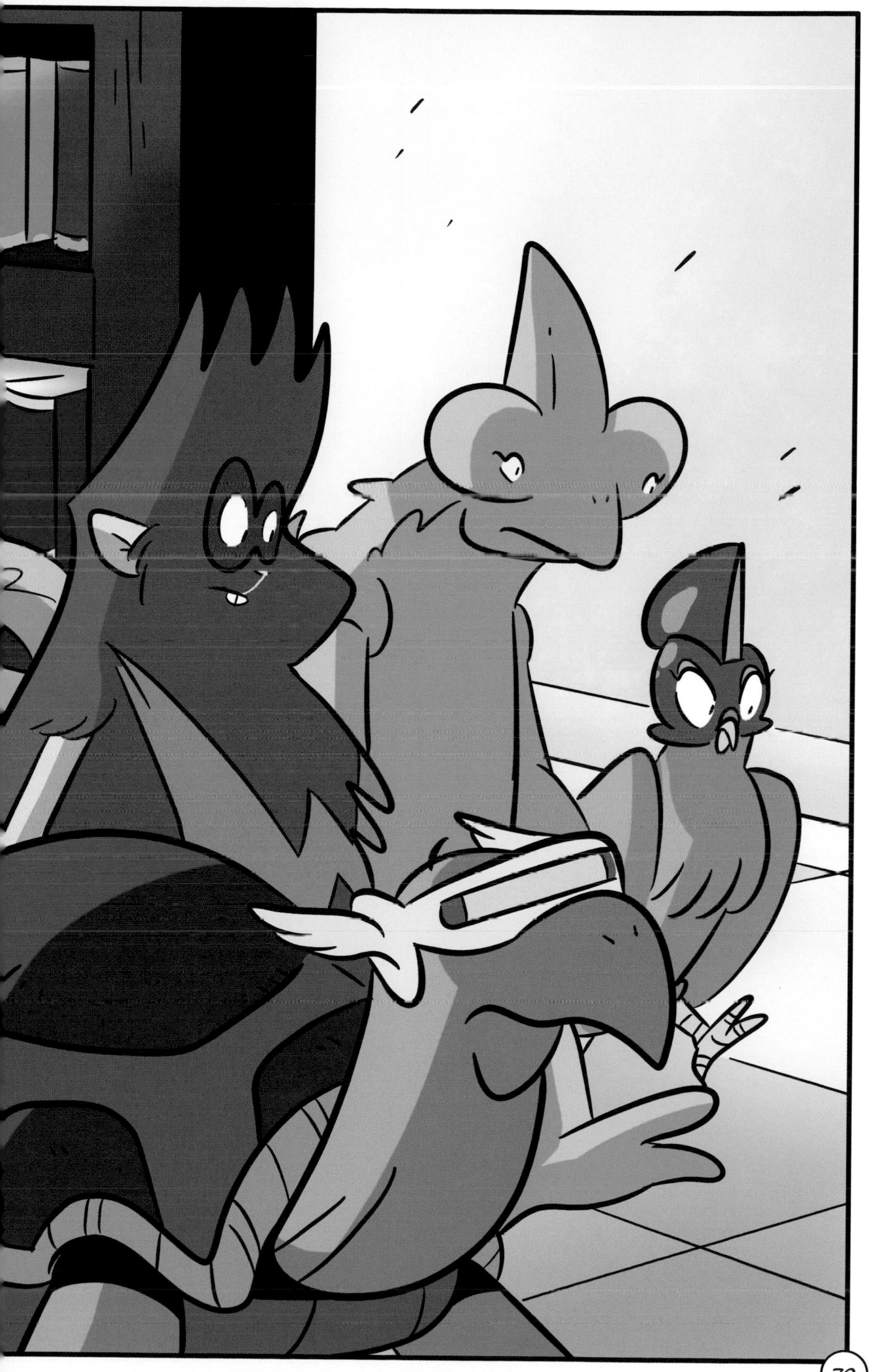

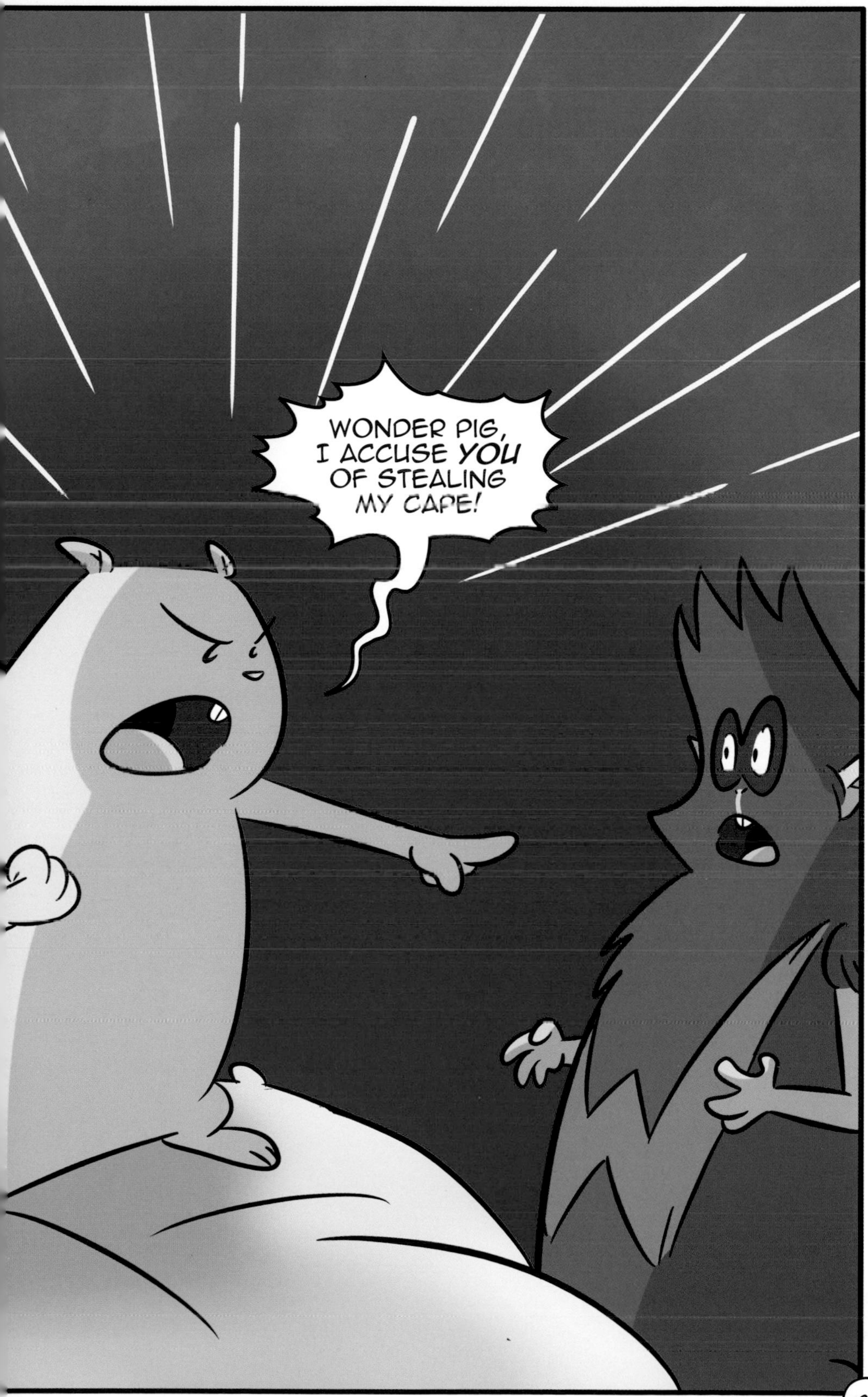
WONDER PIG, I ACCUSE YOU OF STEALING MY CAPE!

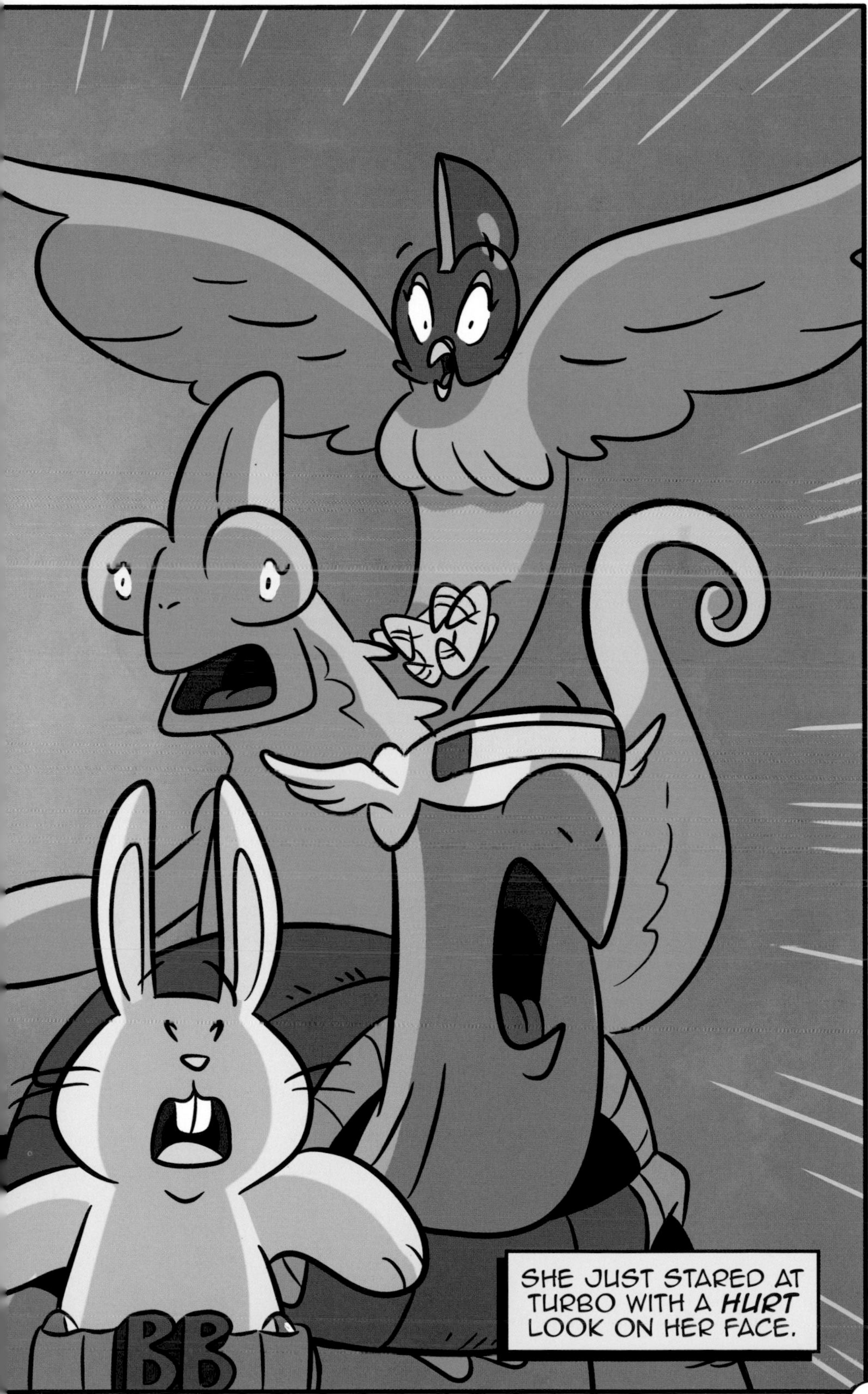
SHE JUST STARED AT TURBO WITH A *HURT* LOOK ON HER FACE.
BB

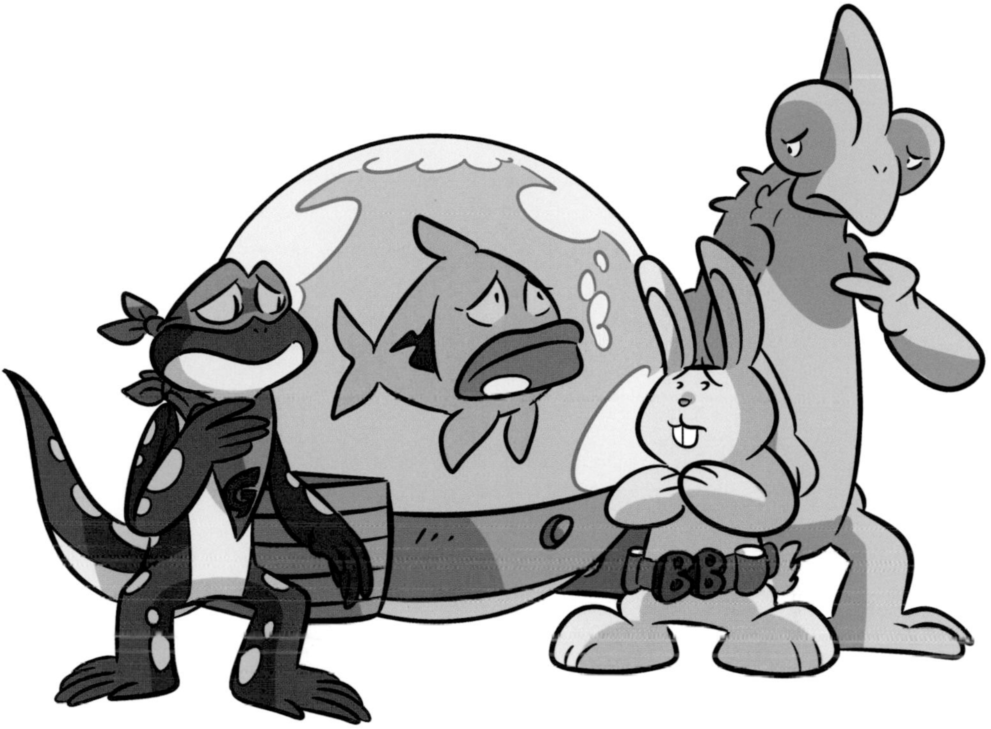

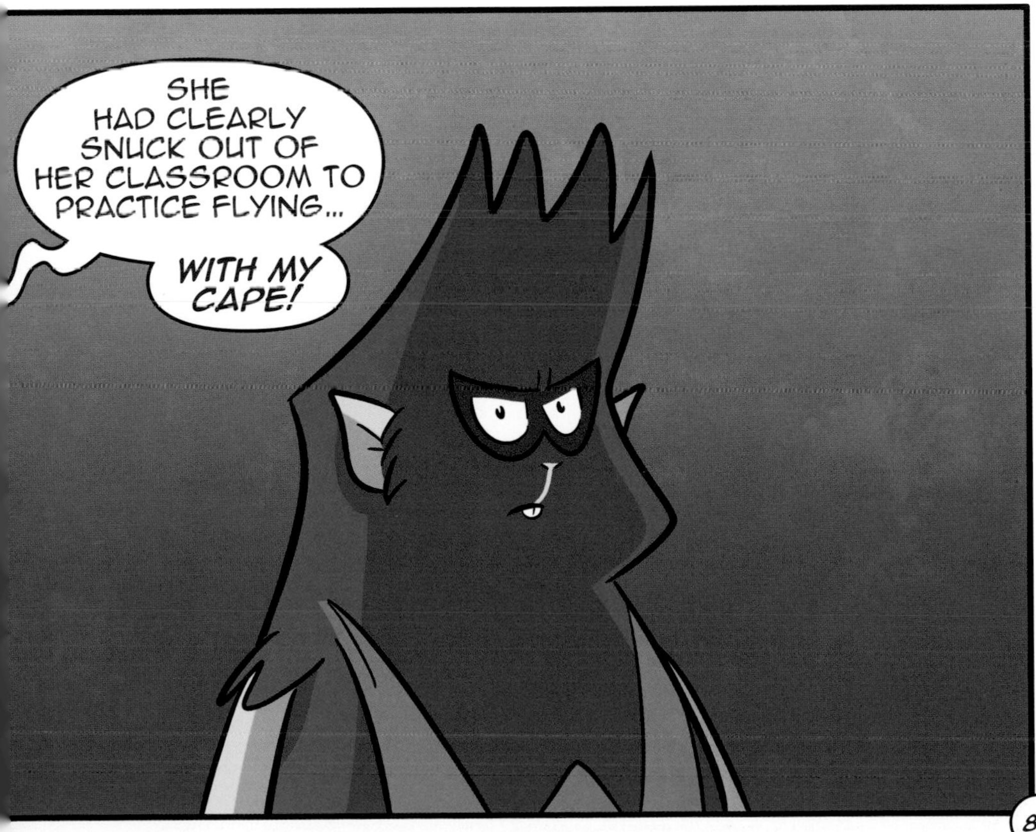
SHE HAD CLEARLY SNUCK OUT OF HER CLASSROOM TO PRACTICE FLYING...
WITH MY CAPE!

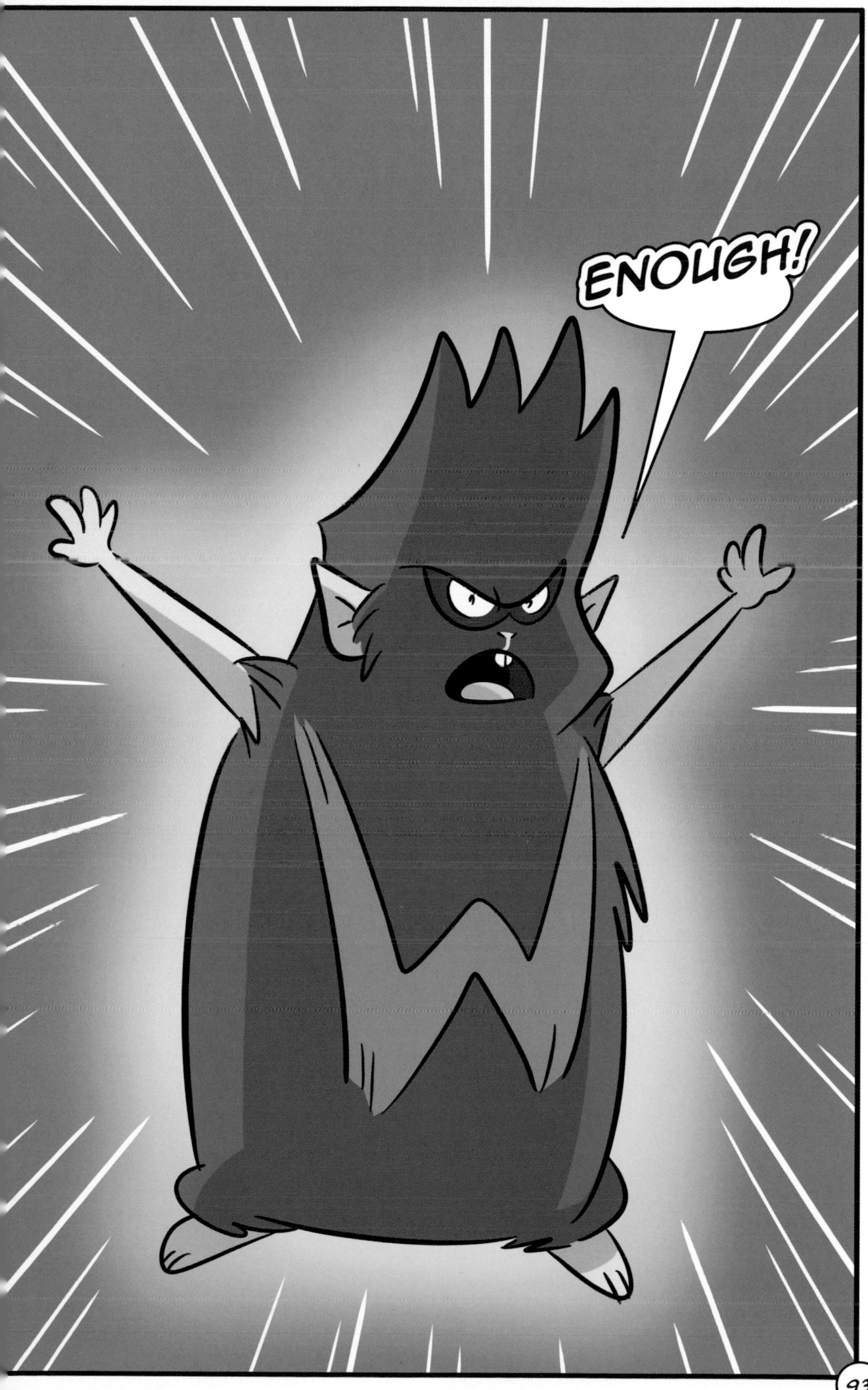
ENOUGH!

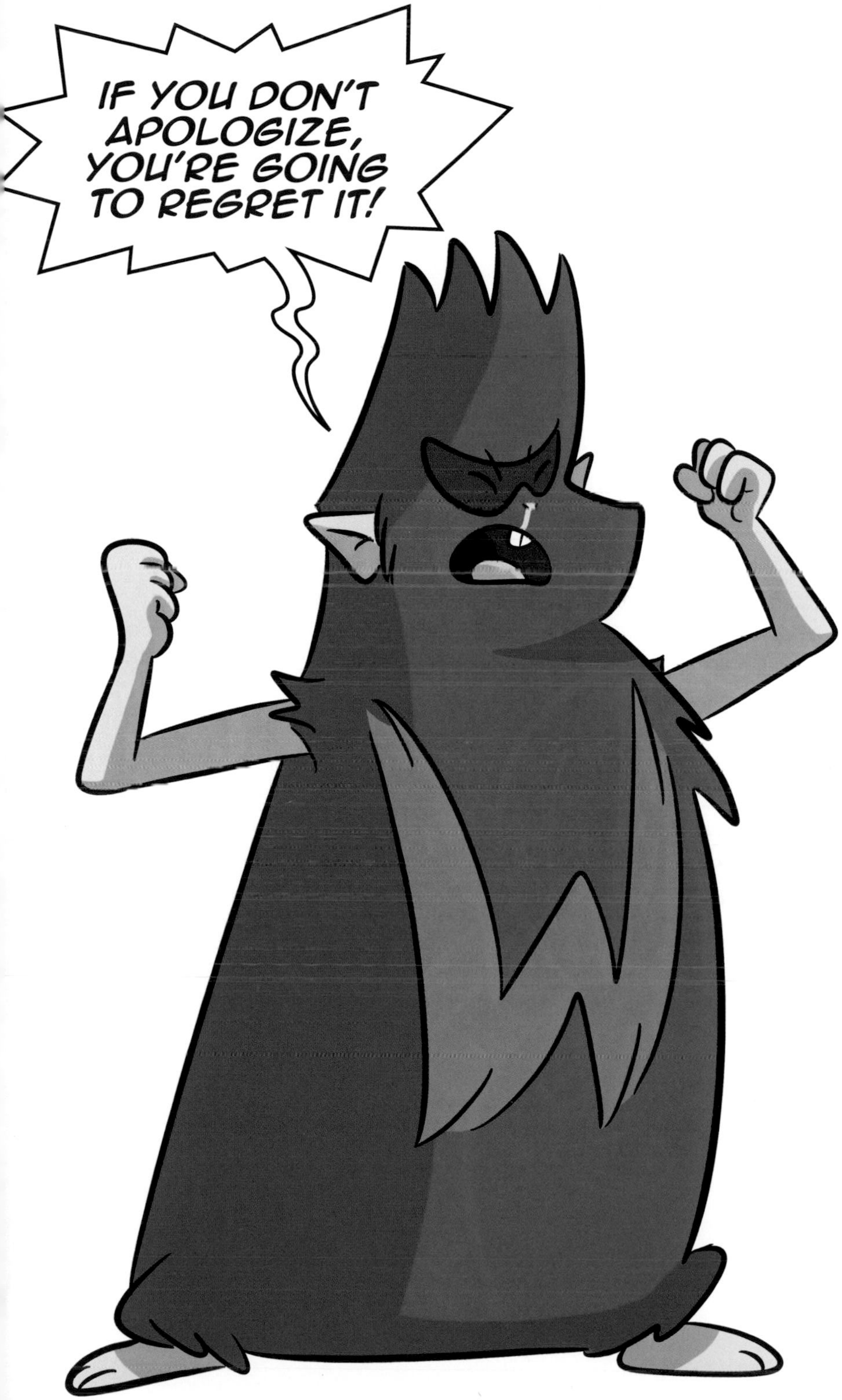
IF YOU DON'T APOLOGIZE, YOU'RE GOING TO REGRET IT!

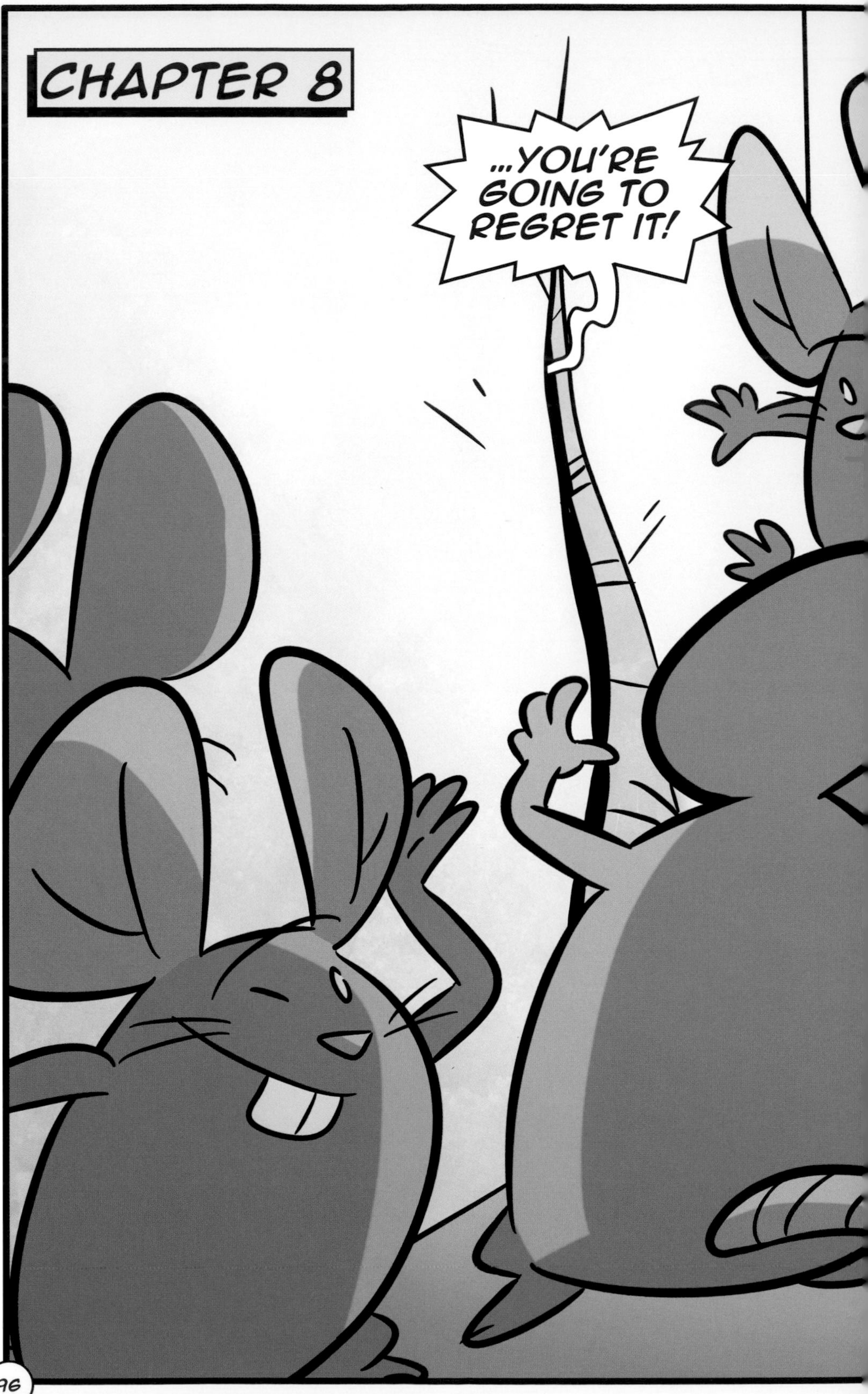
CHAPTER 8
...YOU'RE GOING TO REGRET IT!

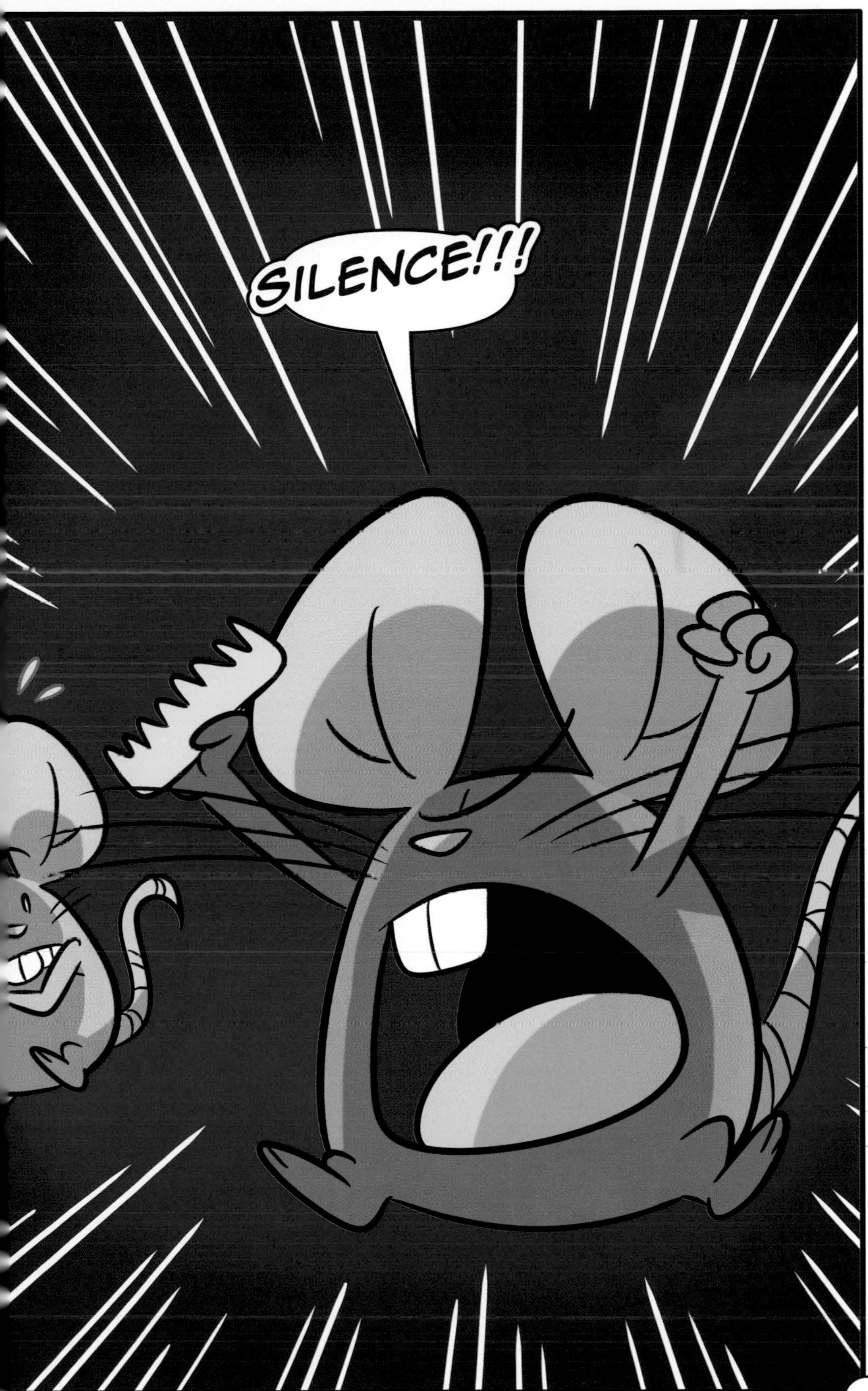
SILENCE!!!

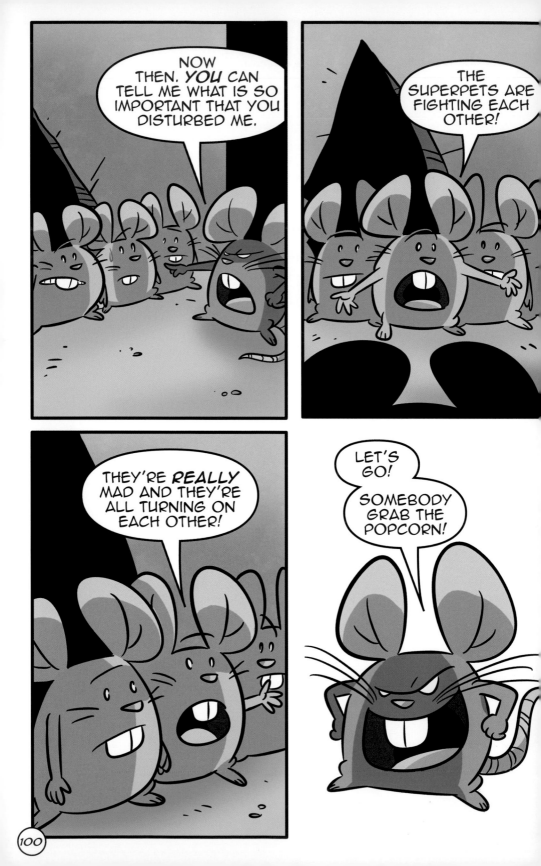

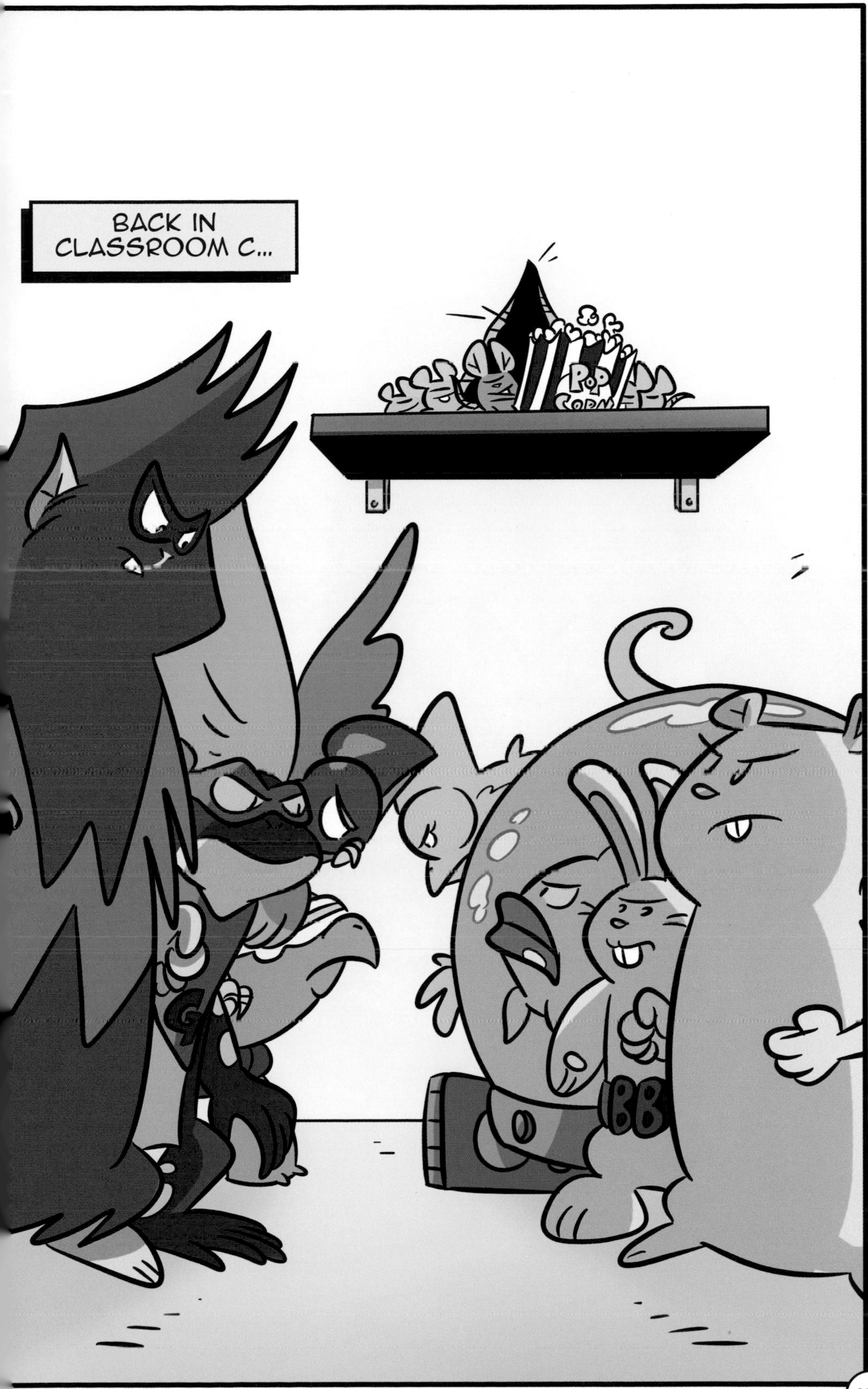
BACK IN
CLASSROOM C...
POP CORN
BB

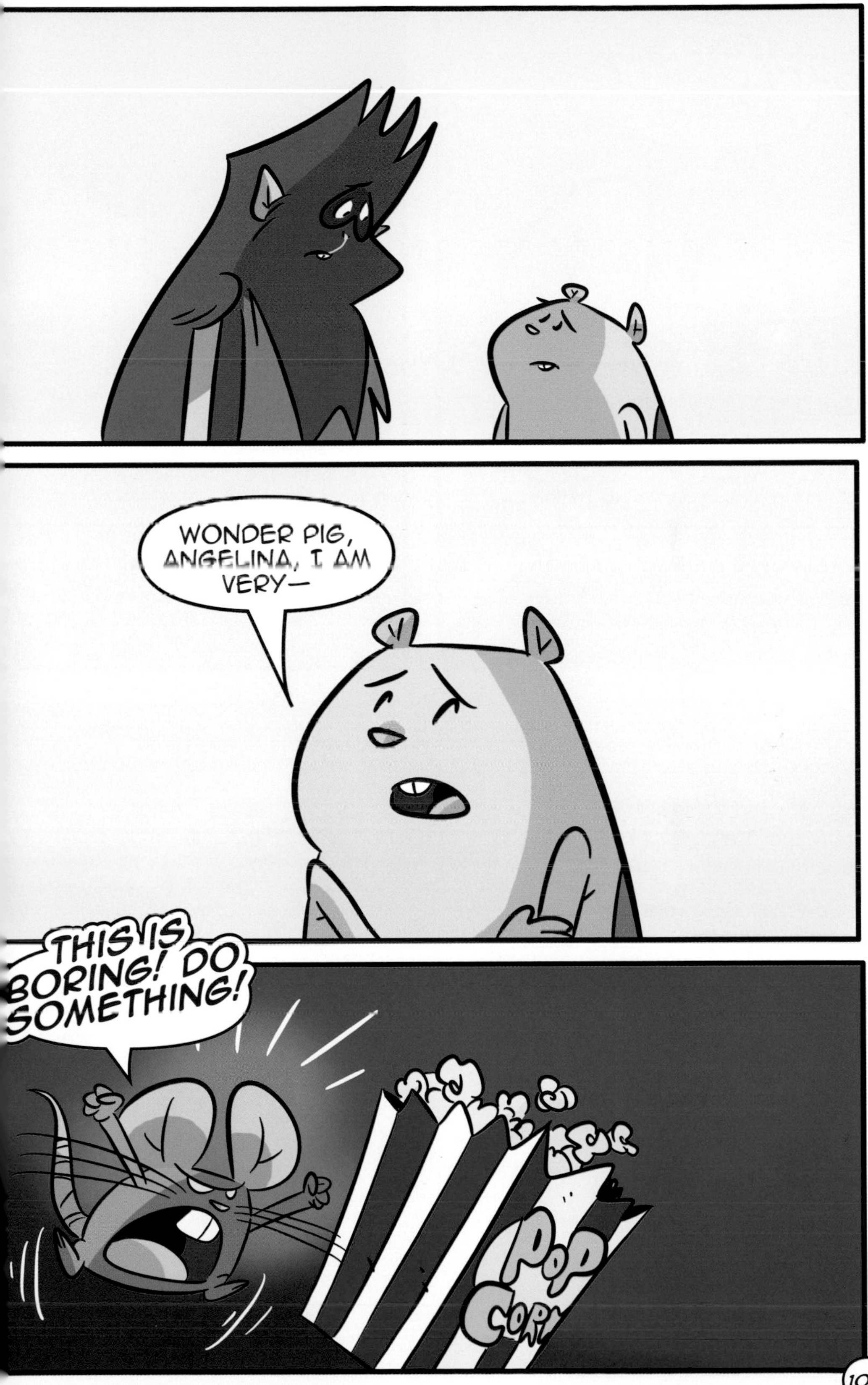
WONDER PIG, ANGELINA, I AM VERY—
THIS IS BORING! DO SOMETHING!
POP CORN

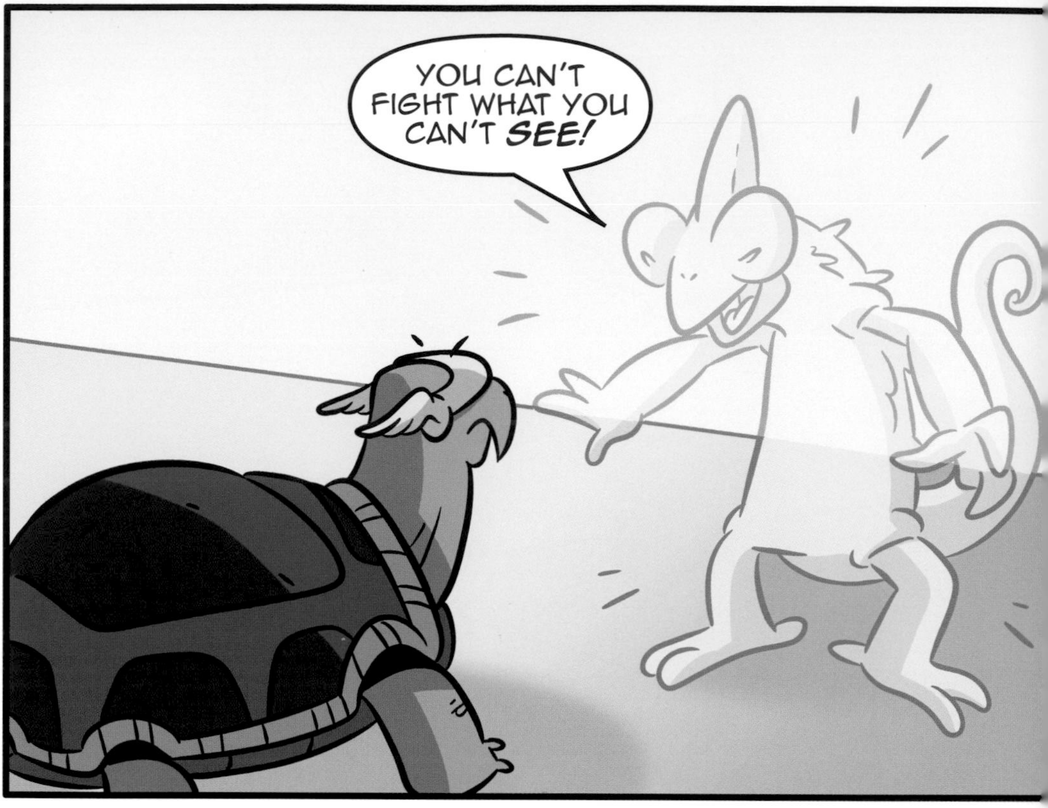
YOU CAN'T FIGHT WHAT YOU CAN'T *SEE!*

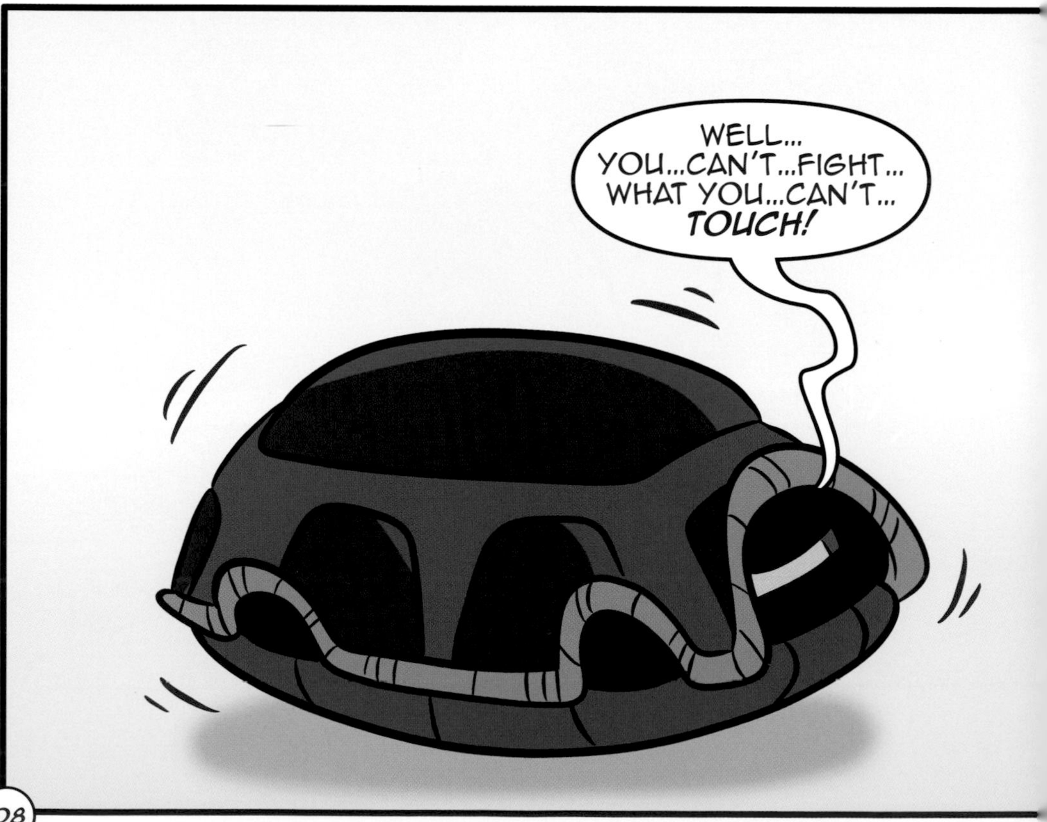
WELL... YOU...CAN'T...FIGHT... WHAT YOU...CAN'T... *TOUCH!*

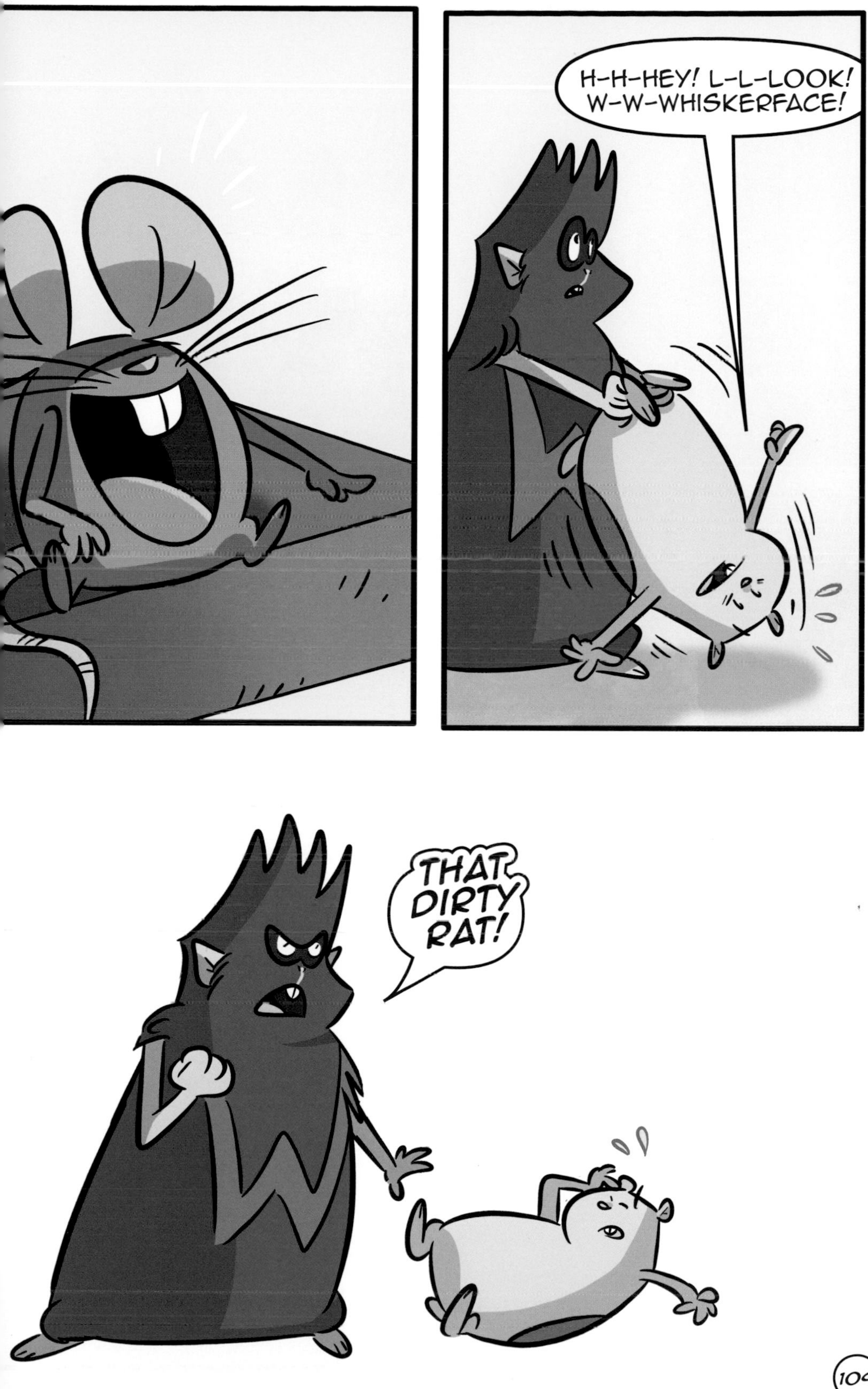
H-H-HEY! L-L-LOOK! W-W-WHISKERFACE!
THAT DIRTY RAT!

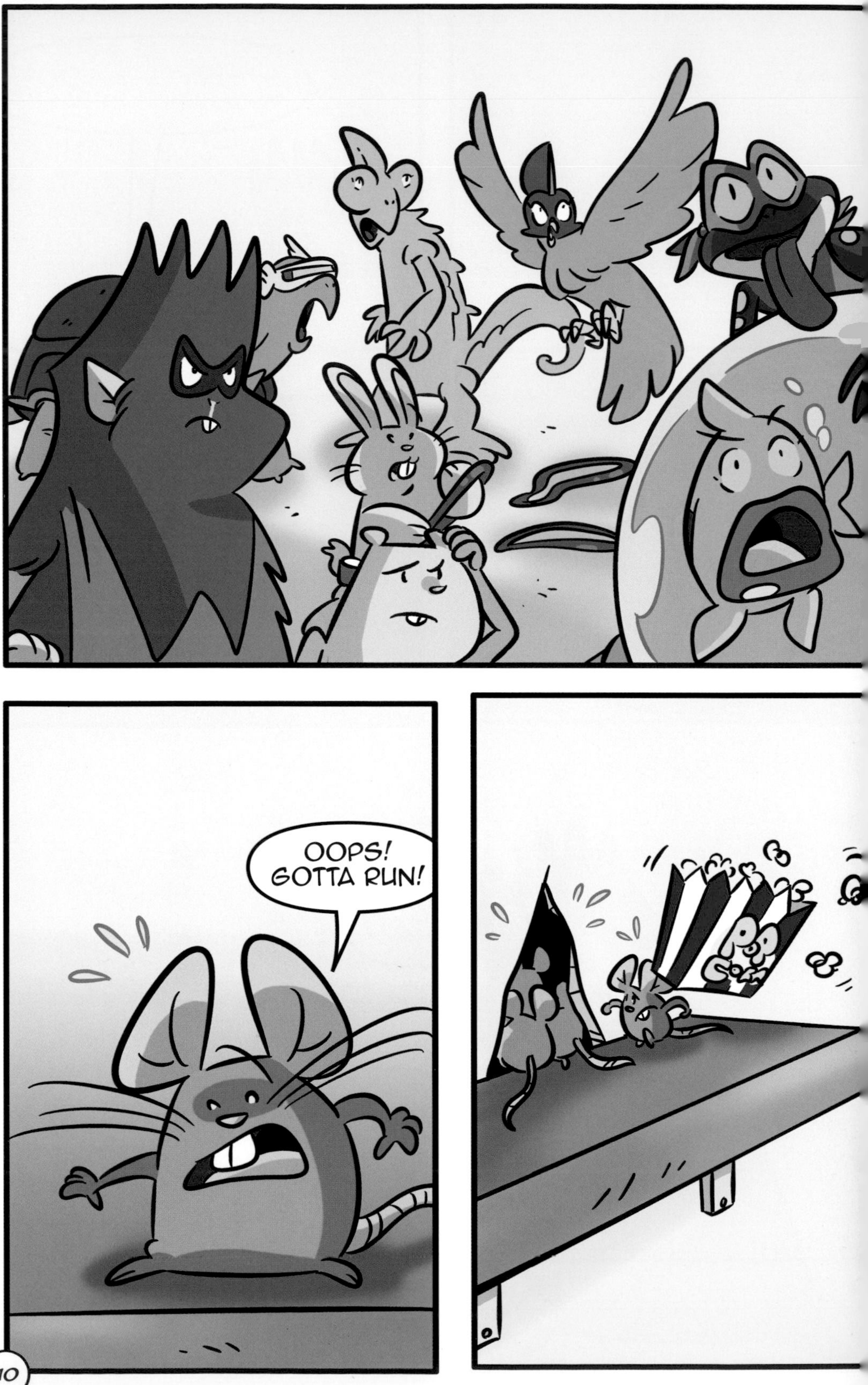
OOPS! GOTTA RUN!

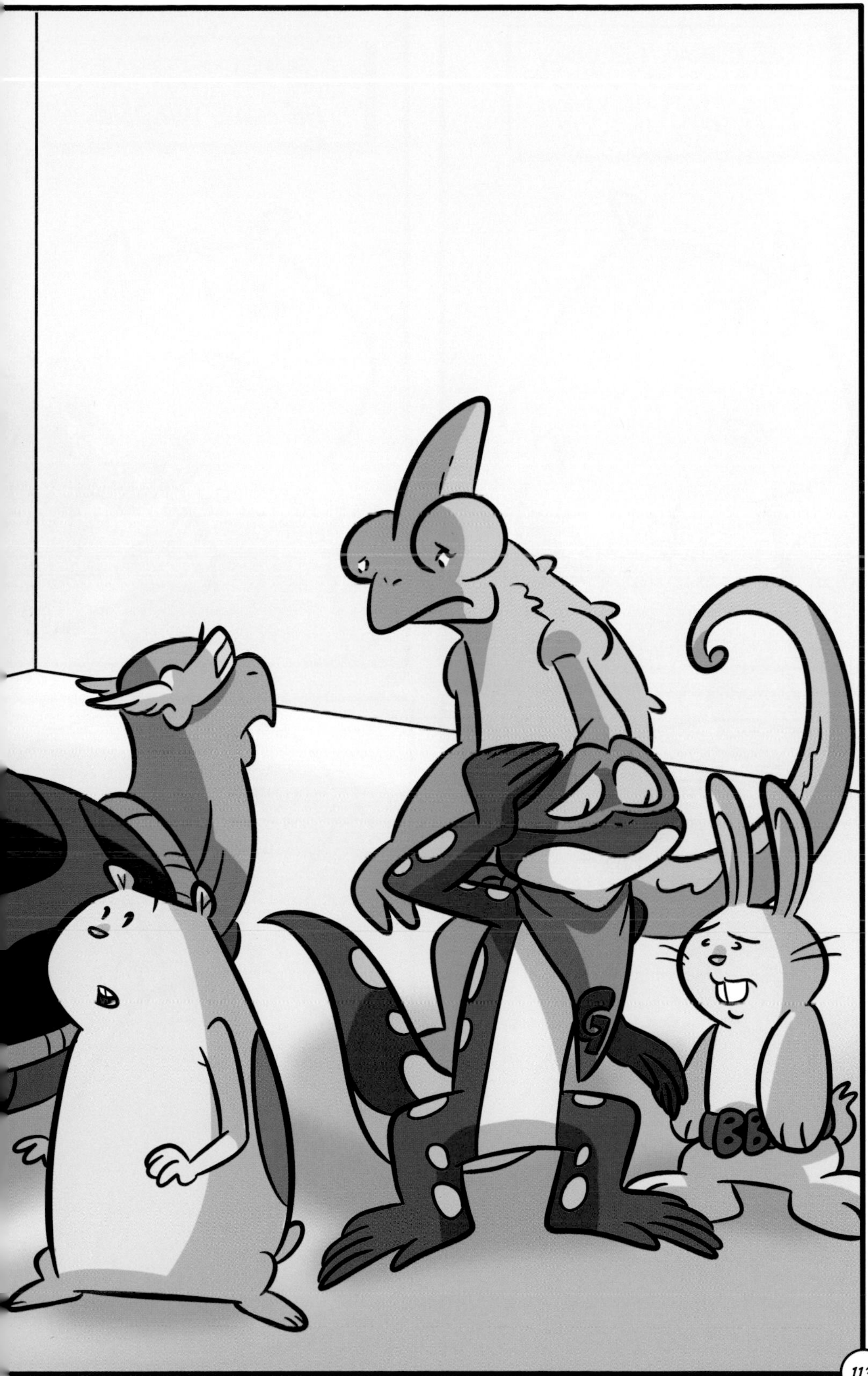

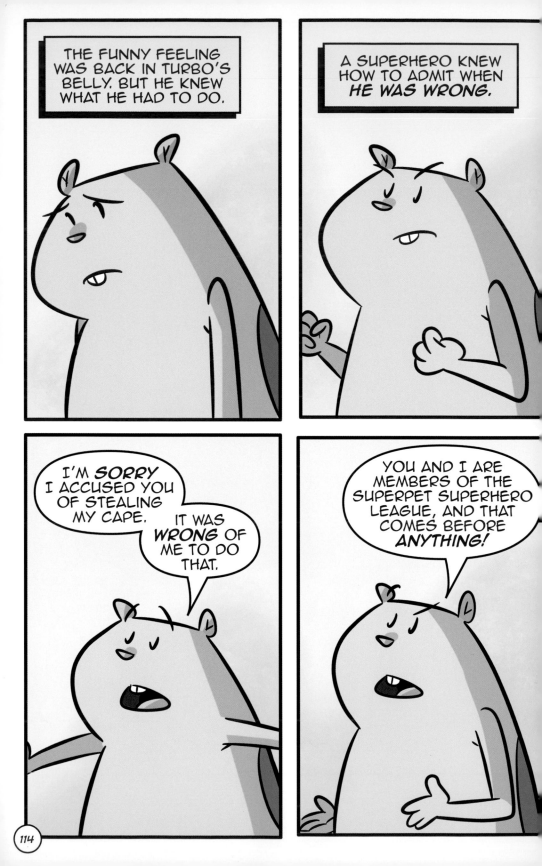

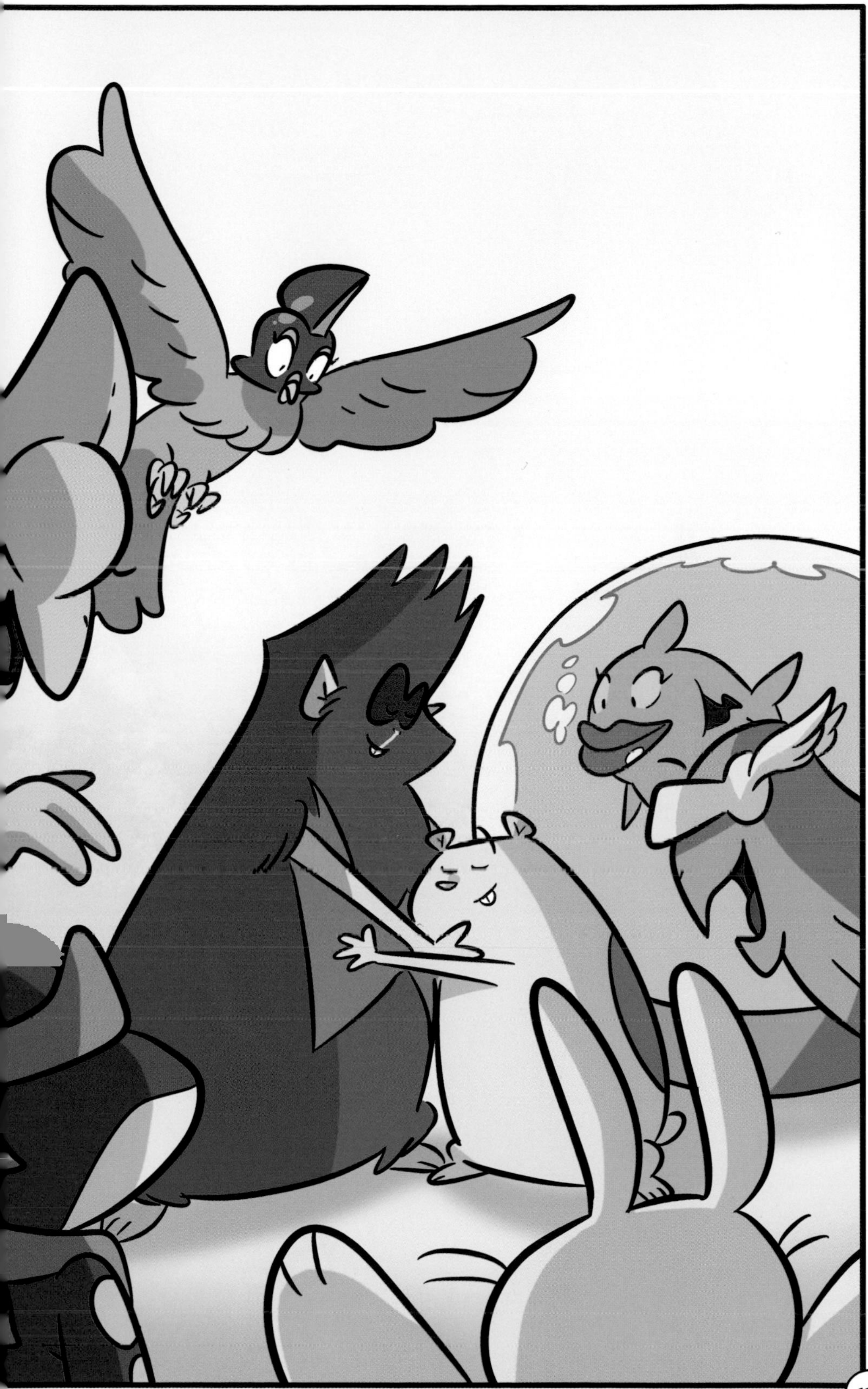

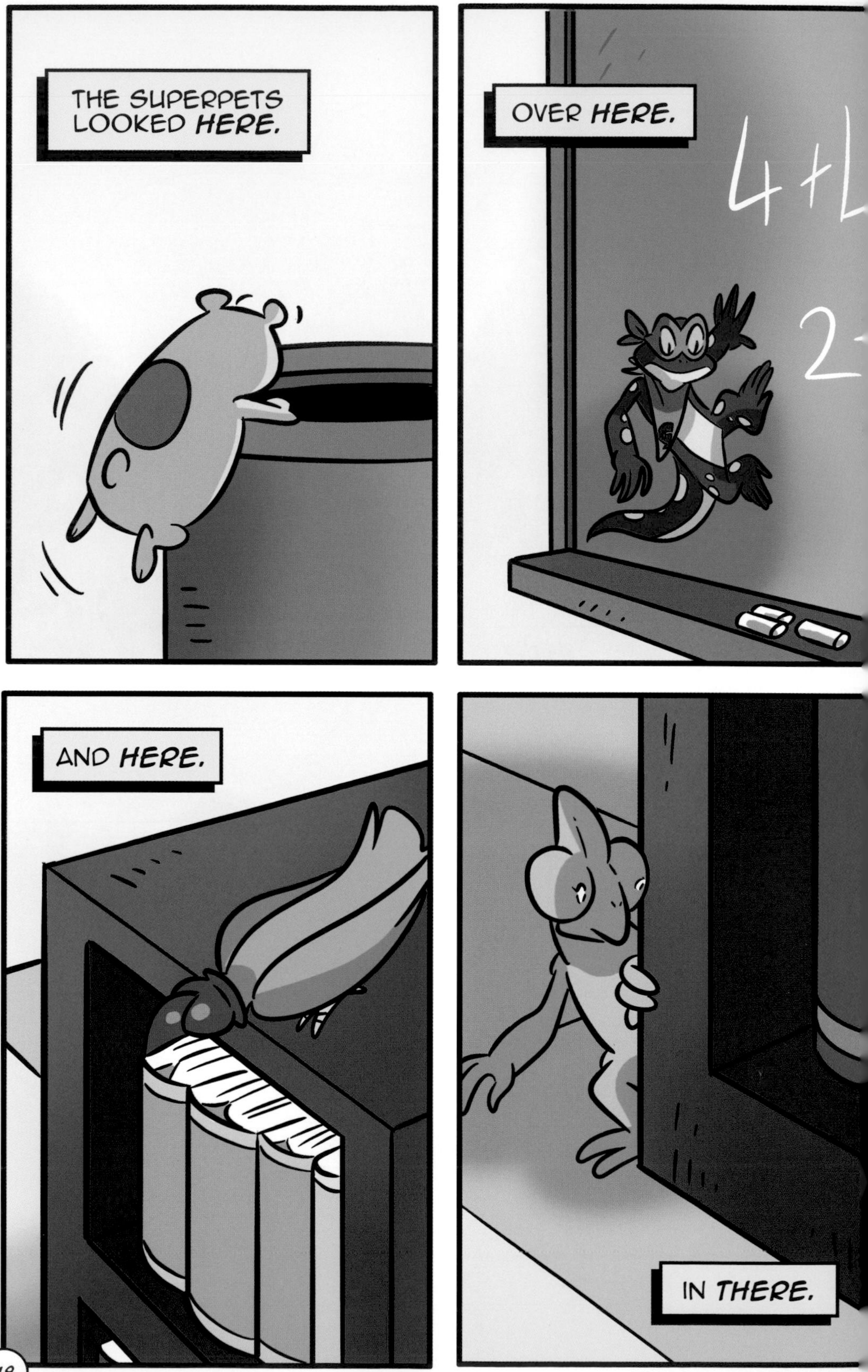
THE SUPERPETS LOOKED HERE.
OVER HERE.
4+4
2
AND HERE.
IN THERE.

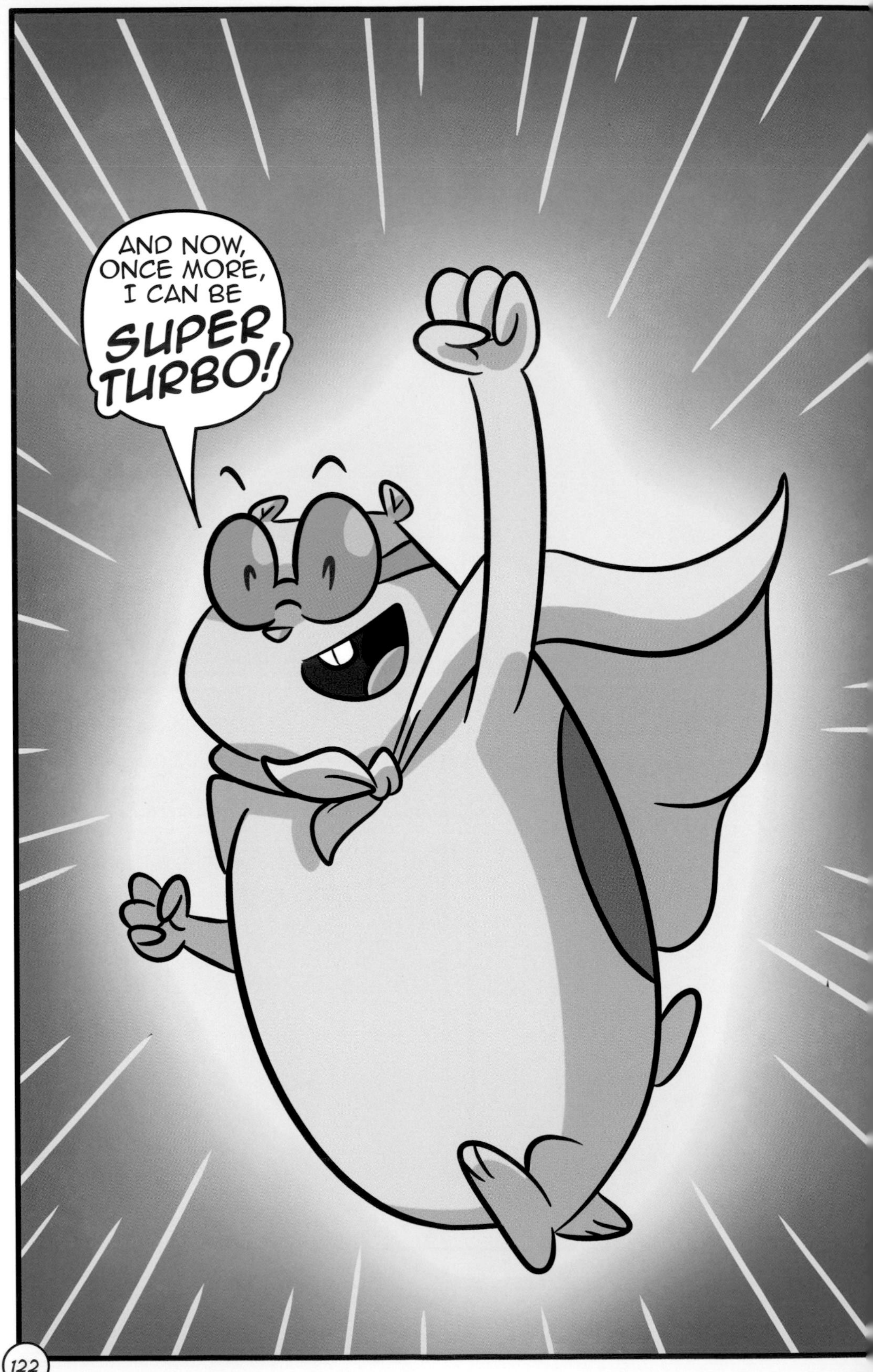
AND NOW, ONCE MORE, I CAN BE SUPER TURBO!

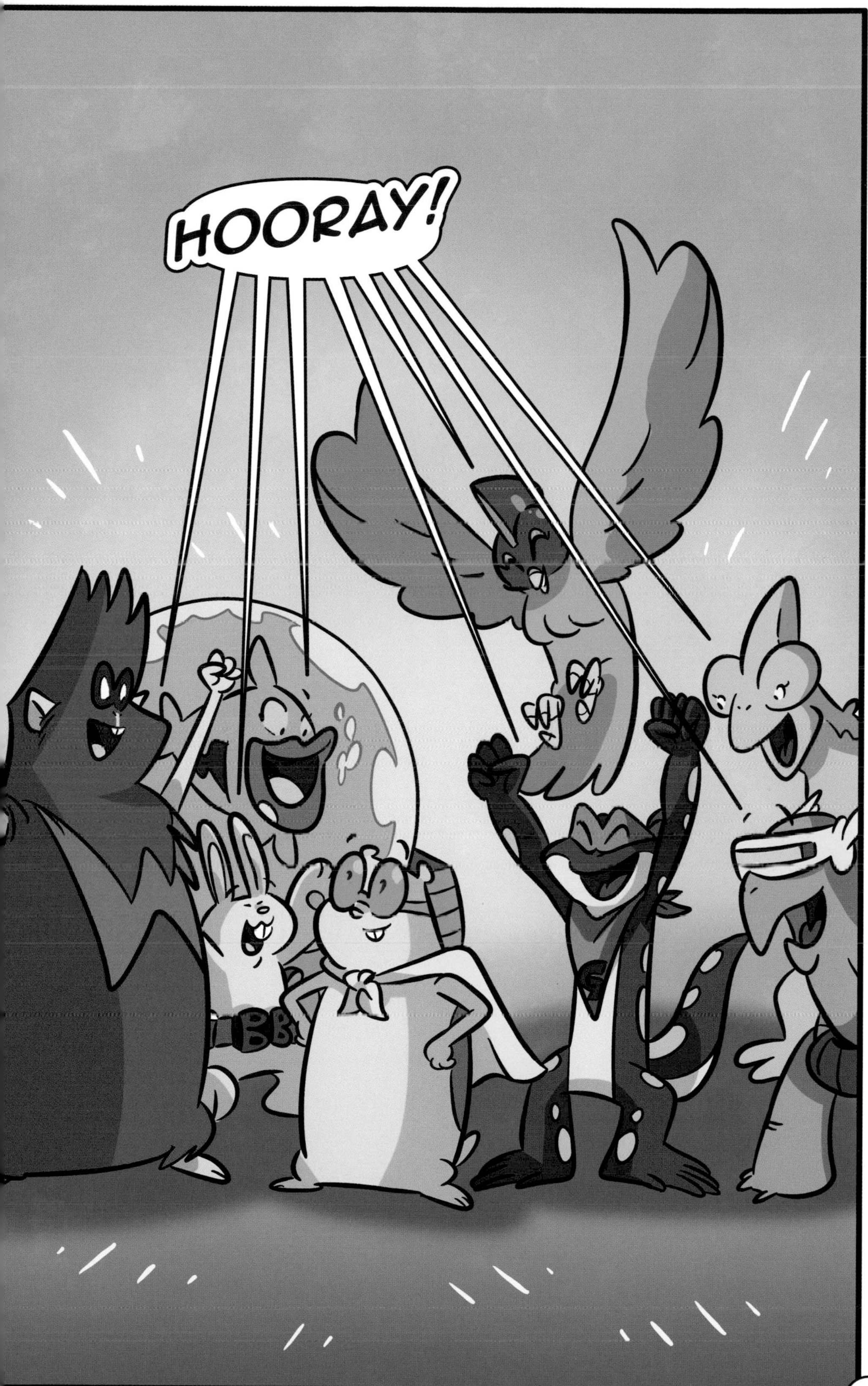
HOORAY!

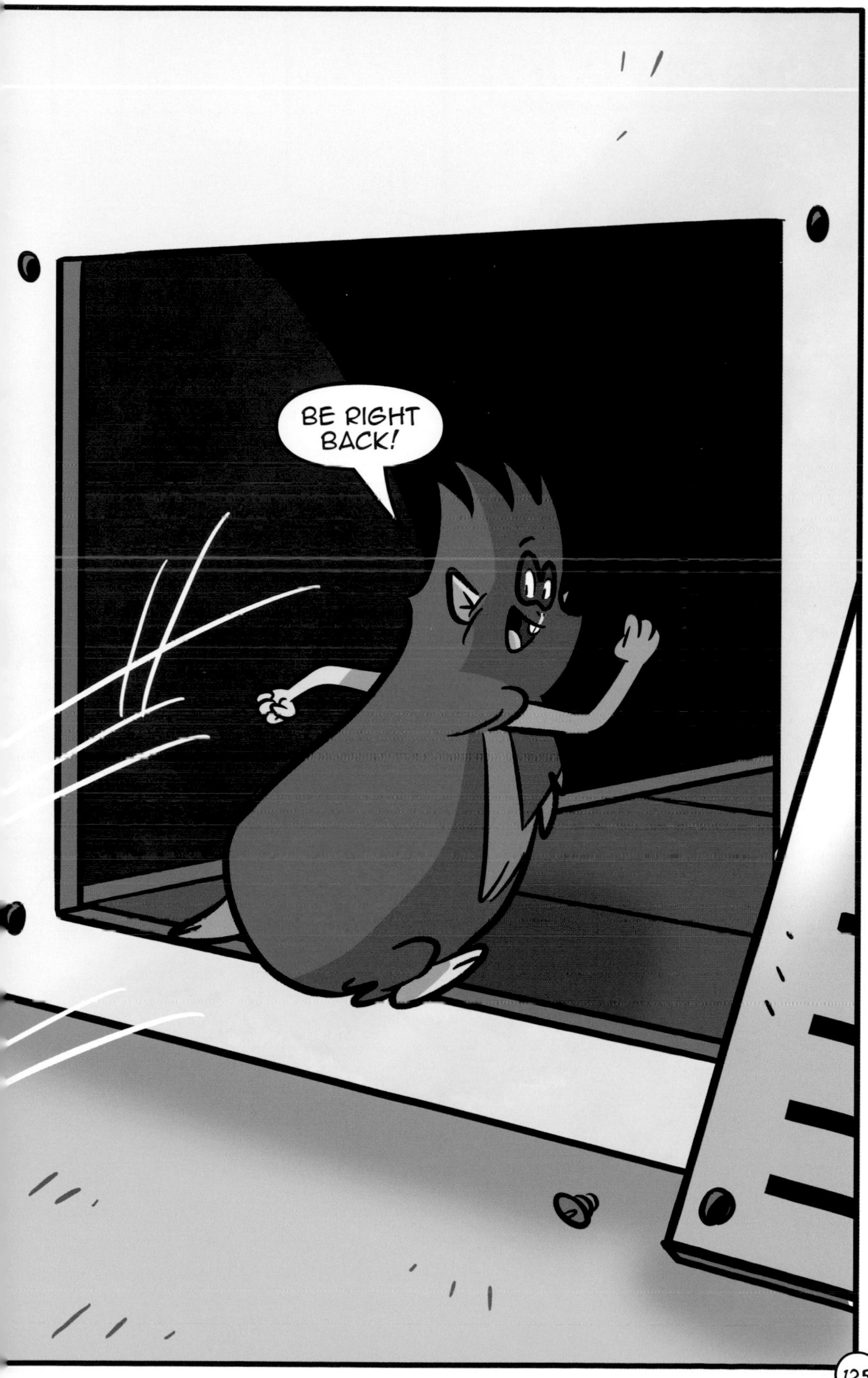
BE RIGHT BACK!

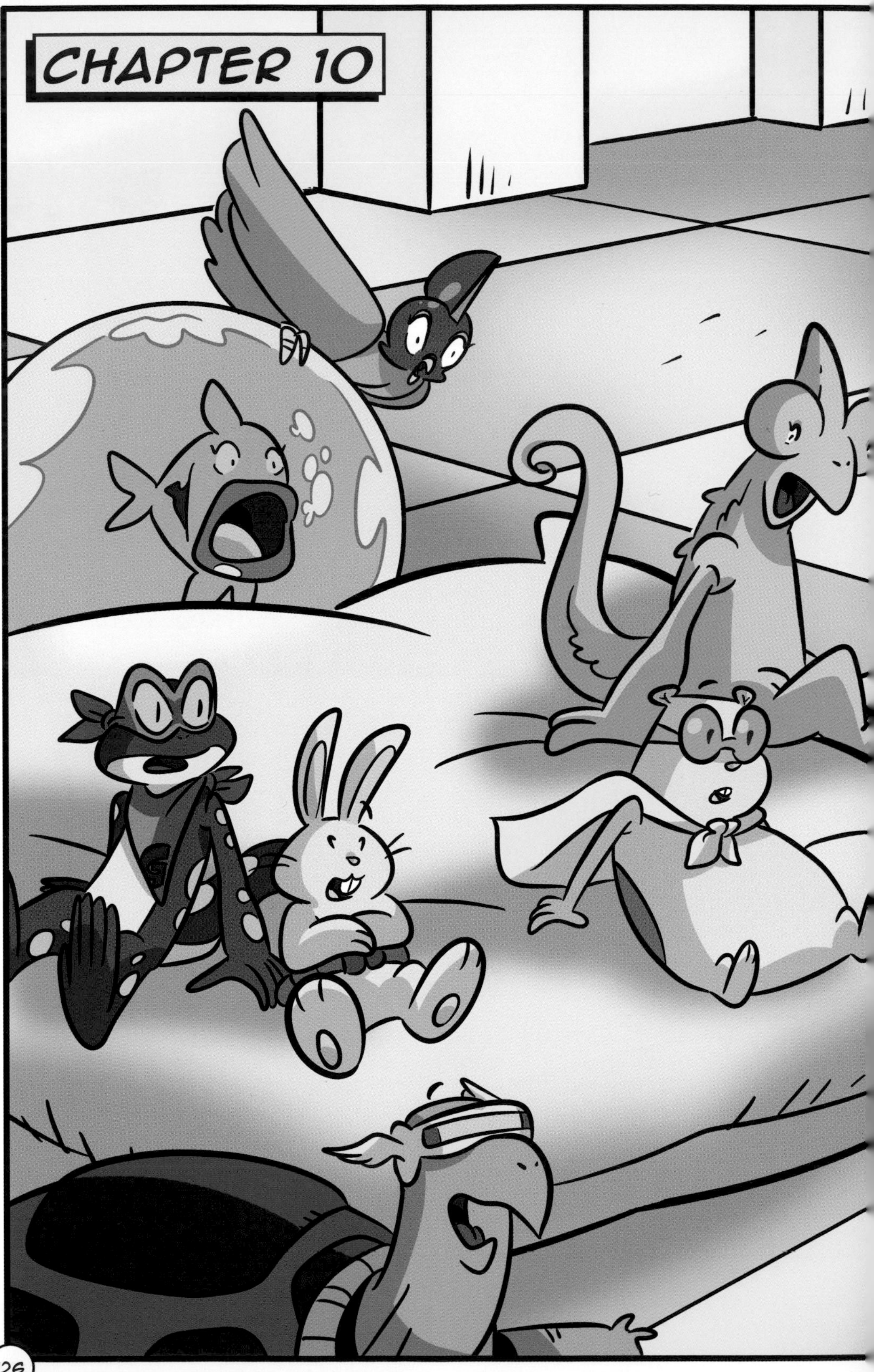
CHAPTER 10

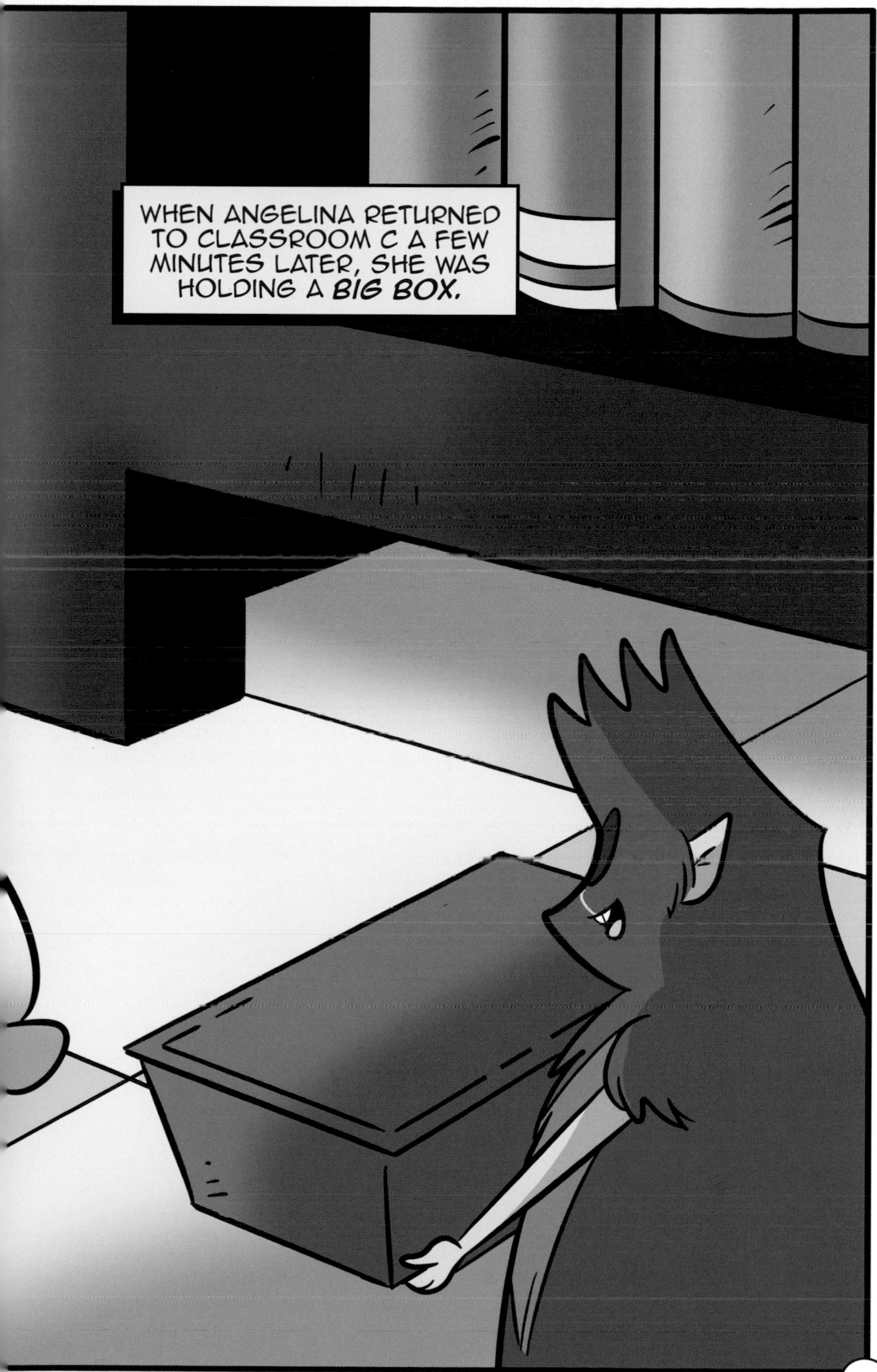
WHEN ANGELINA RETURNED TO CLASSROOM C A FEW MINUTES LATER, SHE WAS HOLDING A *BIG BOX.*

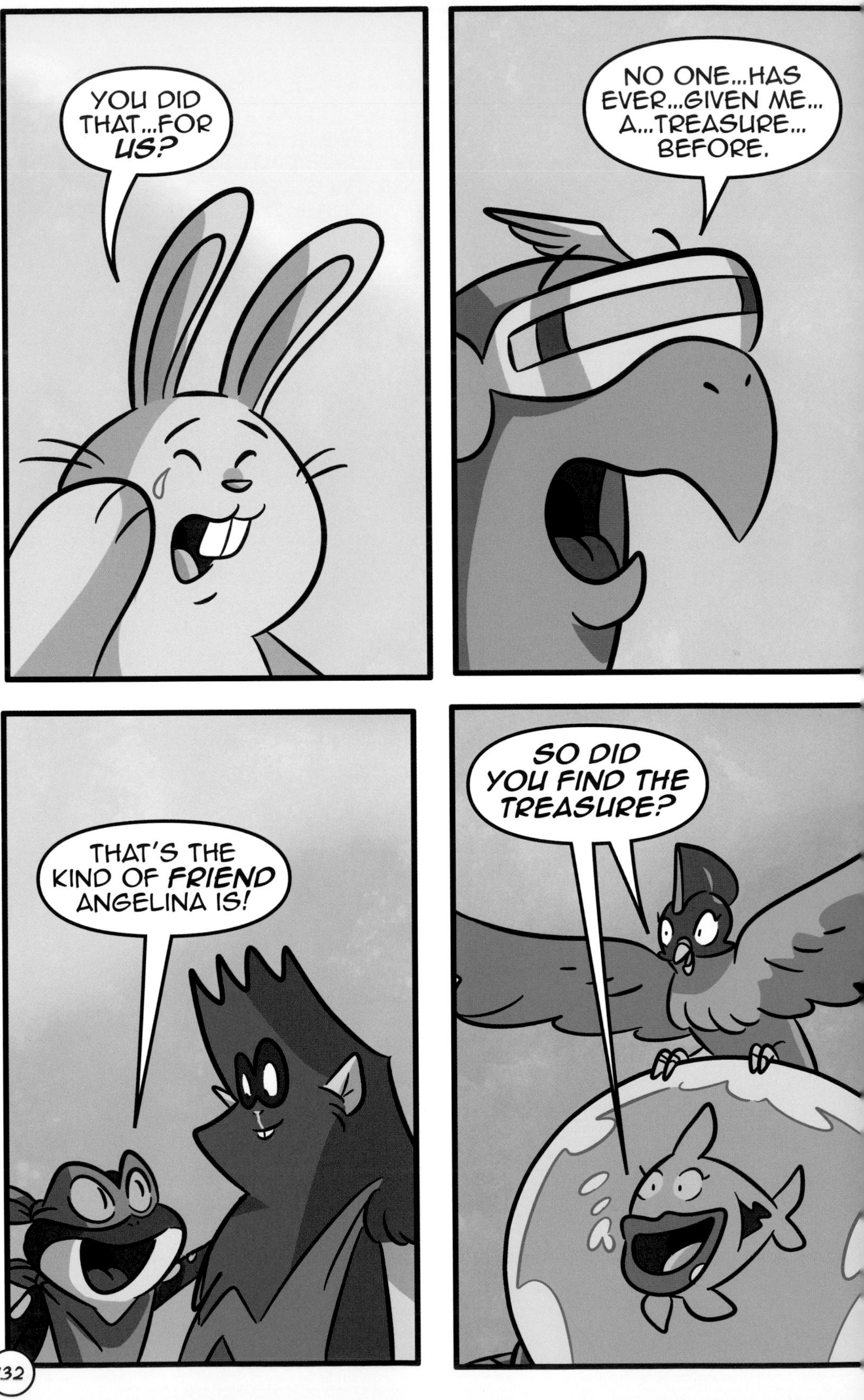
YOU DID THAT...FOR US?
NO ONE...HAS EVER...GIVEN ME... A...TREASURE... BEFORE.
THAT'S THE KIND OF FRIEND ANGELINA IS!
SO DID YOU FIND THE TREASURE?

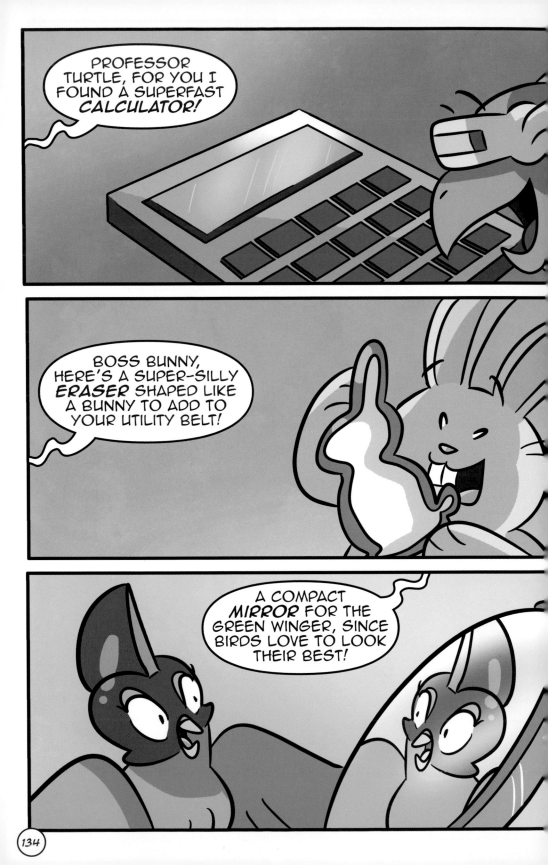

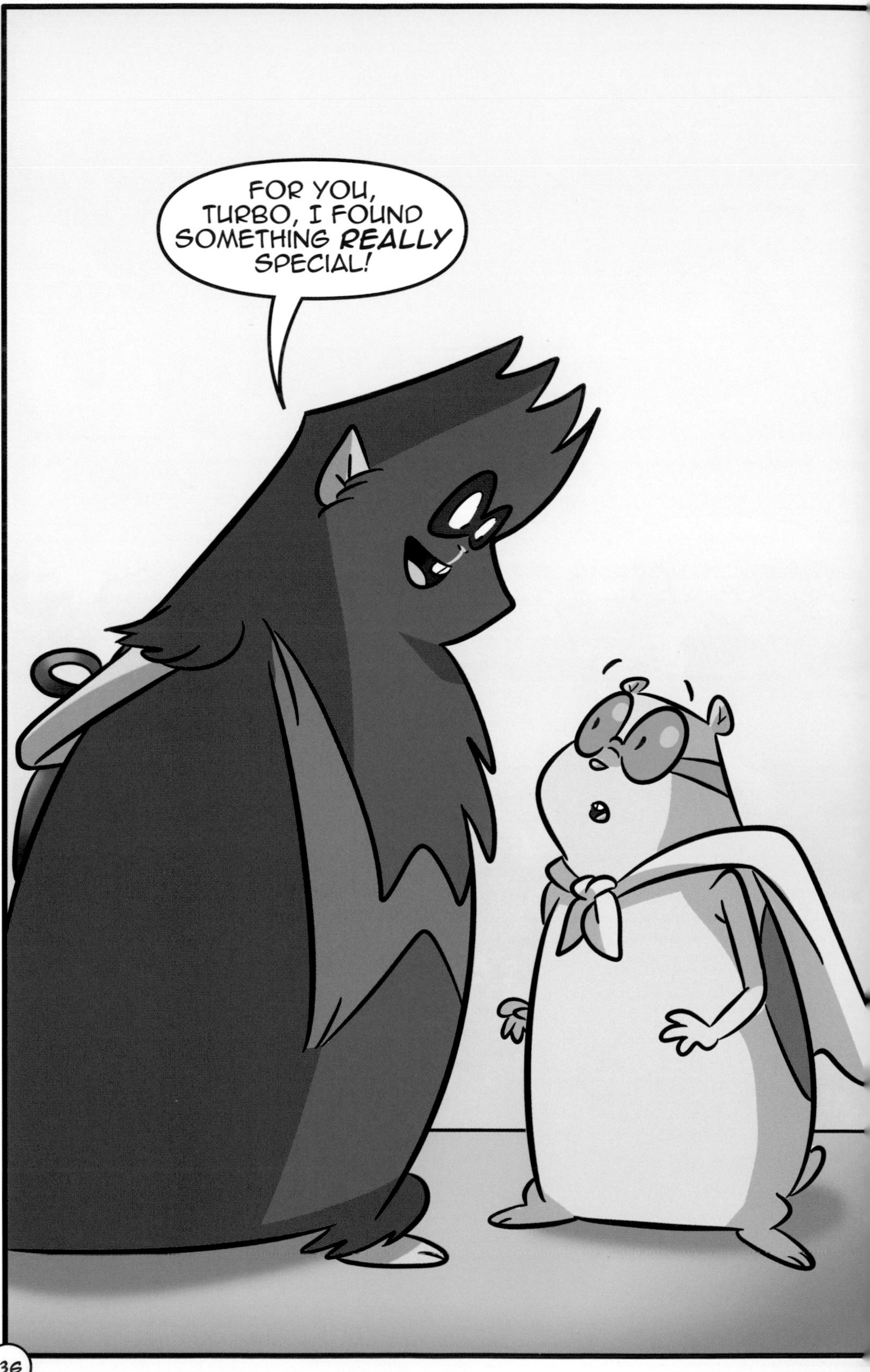
FOR YOU, TURBO, I FOUND SOMETHING REALLY SPECIAL!

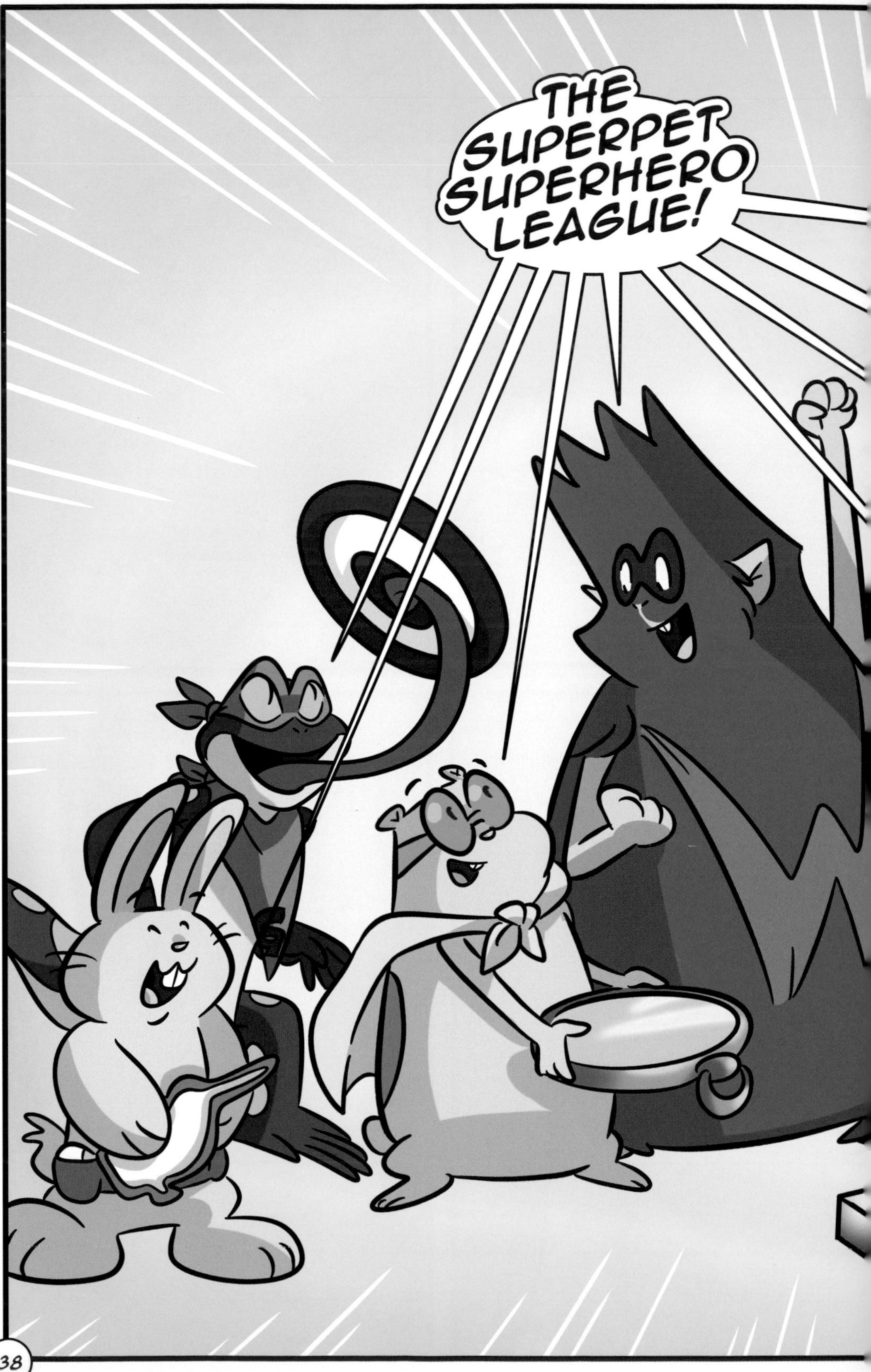
THE SUPERPET SUPERHERO LEAGUE!

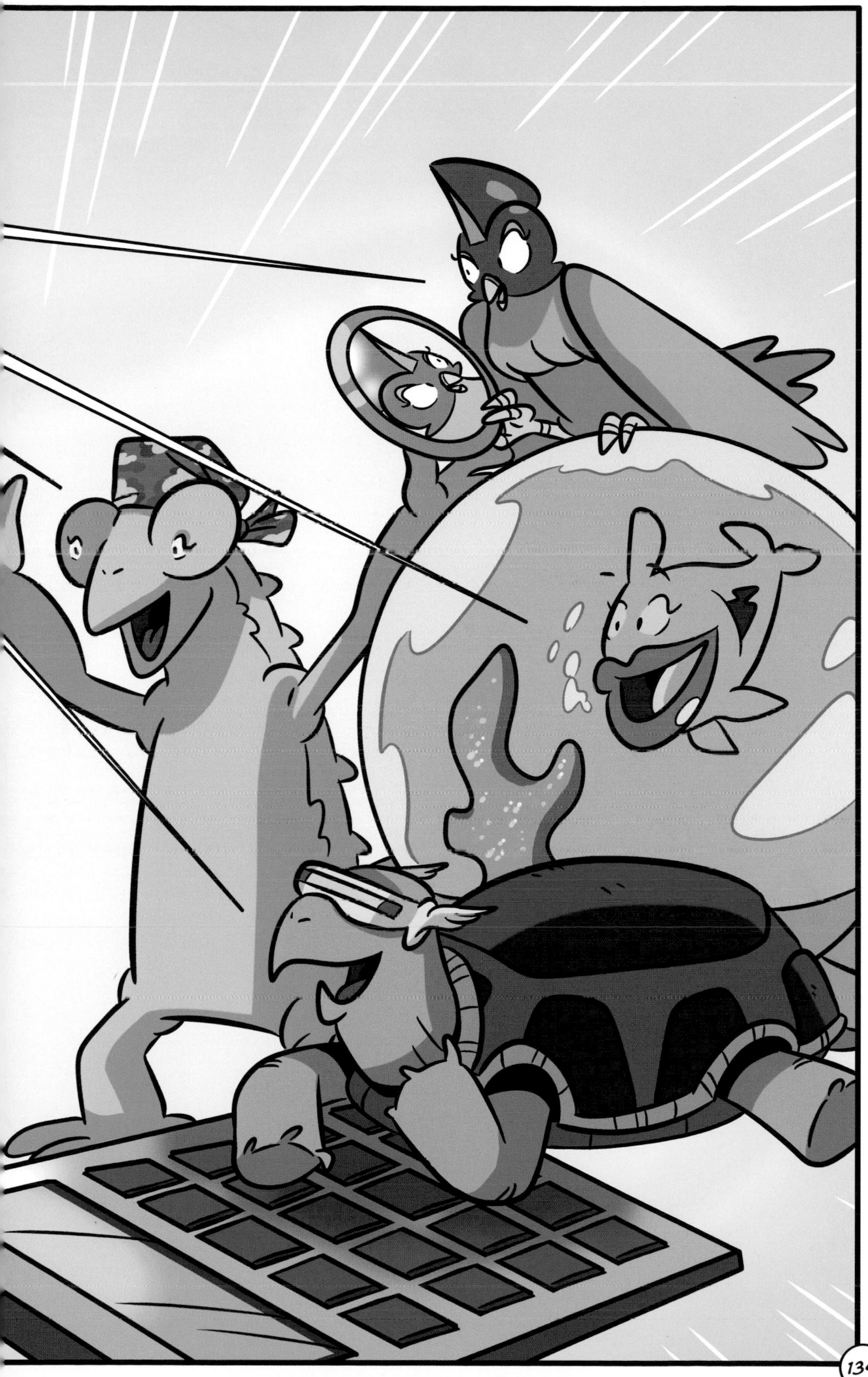

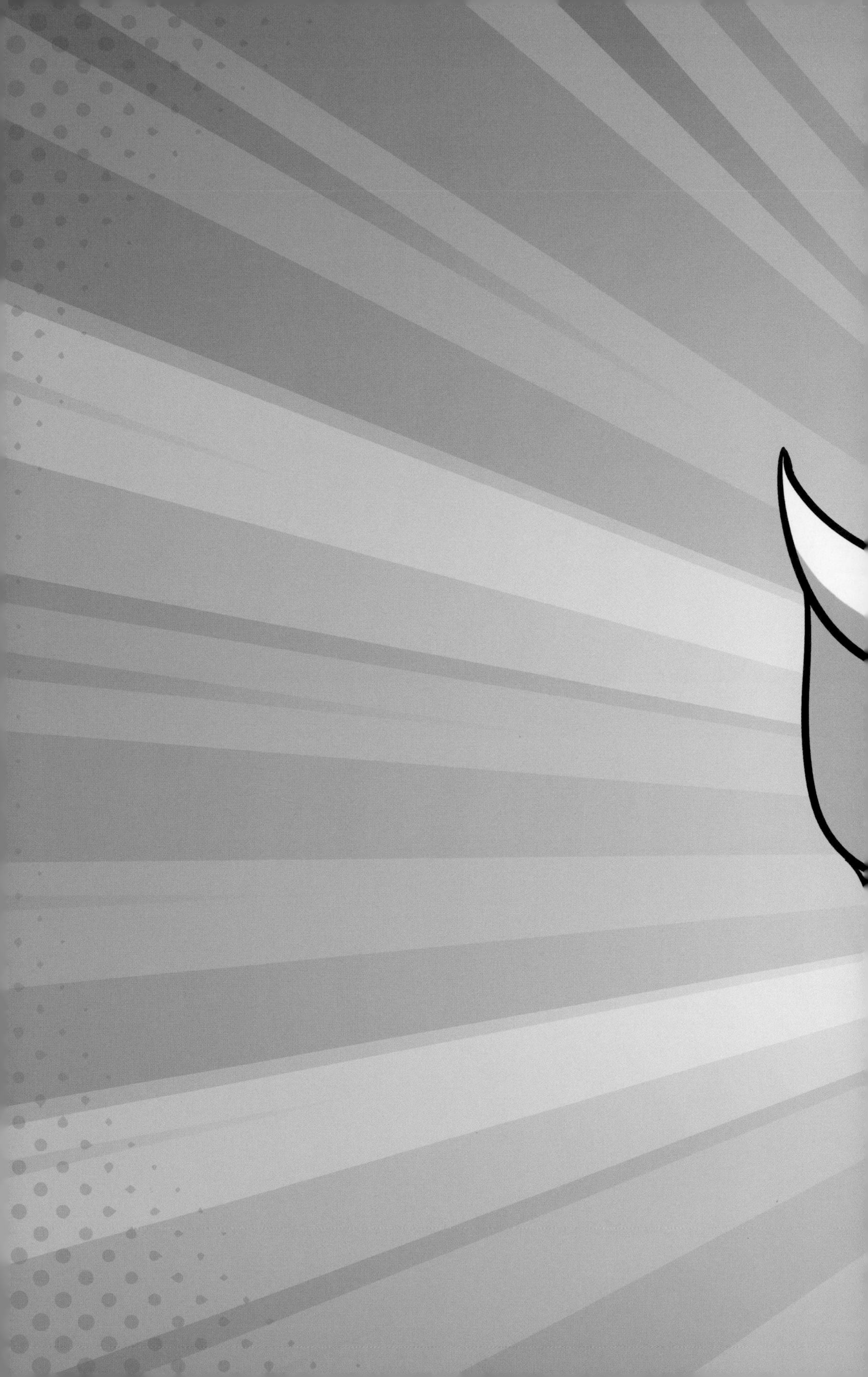

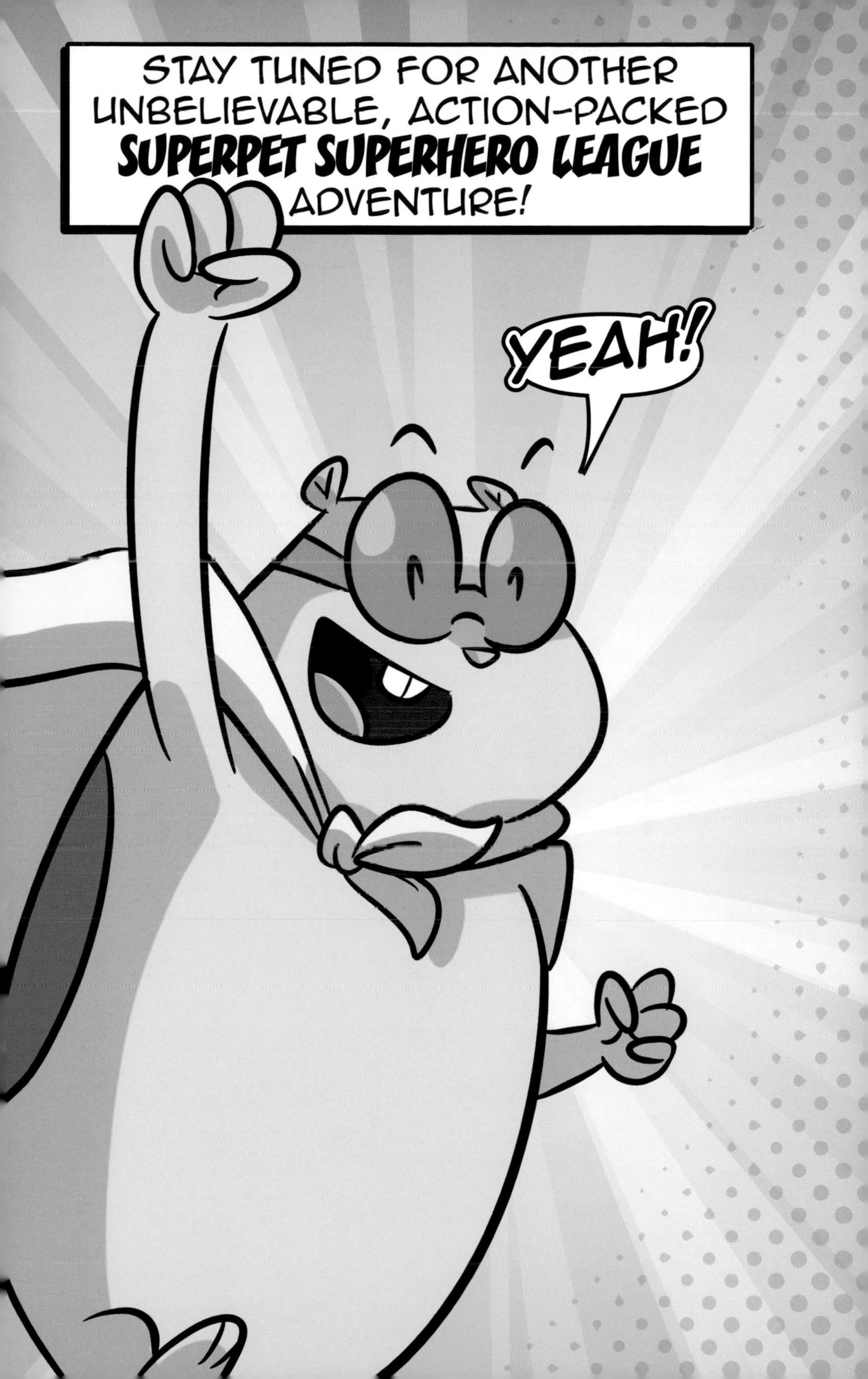
STAY TUNED FOR ANOTHER UNBELIEVABLE, ACTION-PACKED SUPERPET SUPERHERO LEAGUE ADVENTURE!
YEAH!

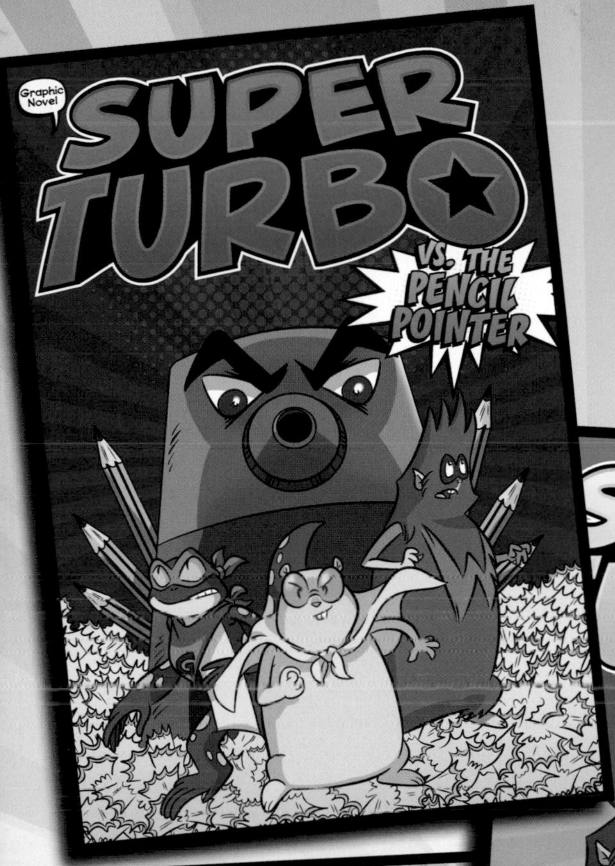
Graphic Novel
SUPER TURBO
VS. THE PENCIL POINTER

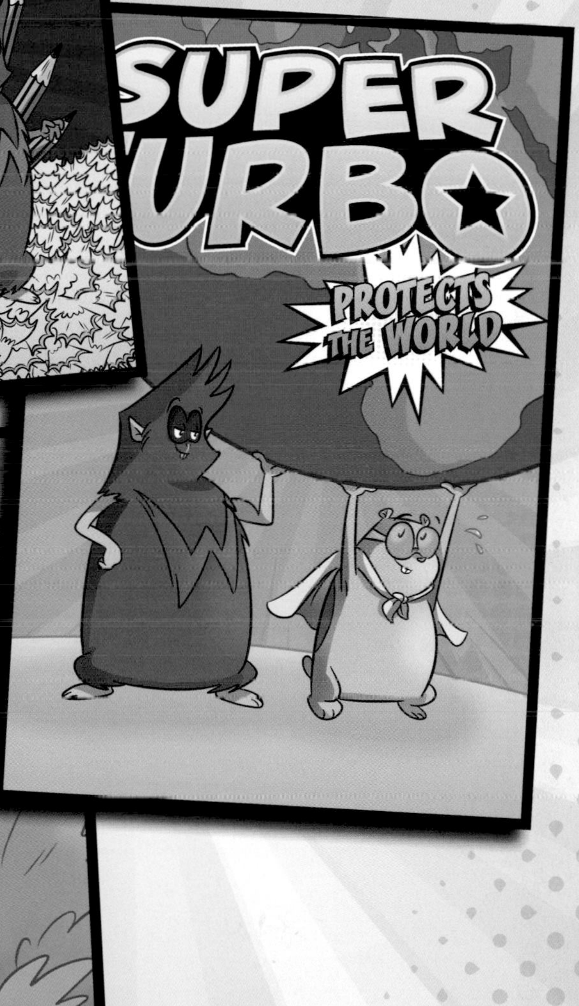
SUPER
PROTECTS THE WORLD

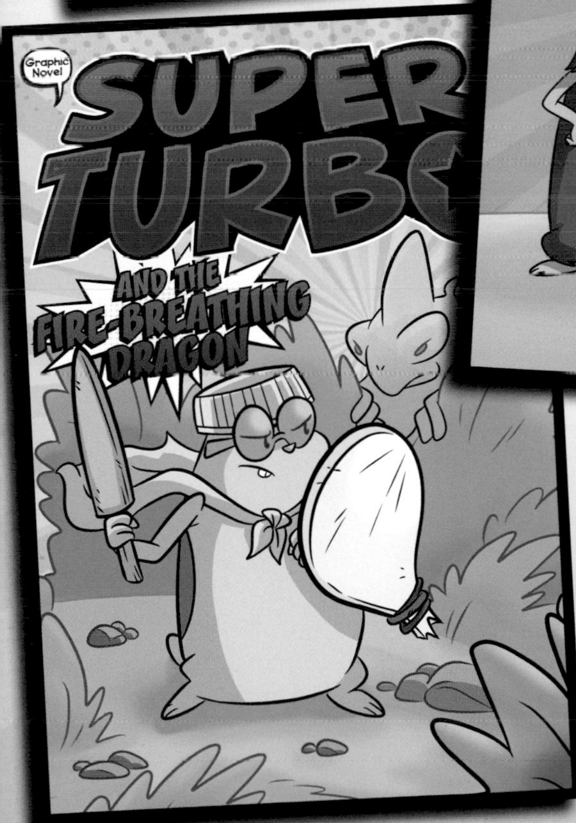
Graphic Novel
SUPER
AND THE FIRE-BREATHING DRAGON